# I, ROBOT

## The Illustrated Screenplay

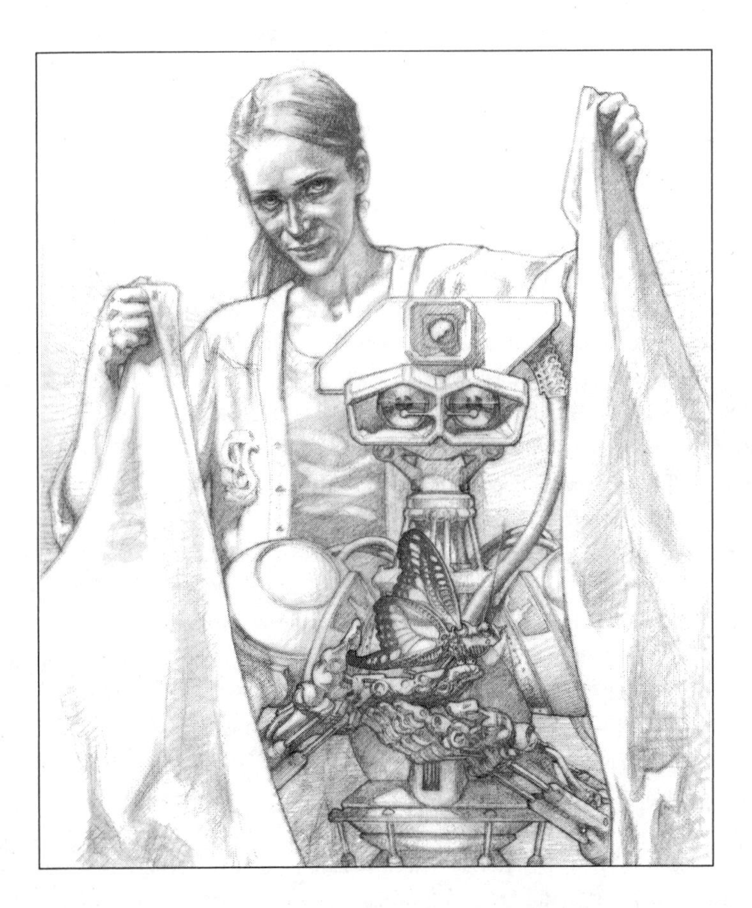

## BOOKS BY HARLAN ELLISON

**NOVELS:** WEB OF THE CITY [1958] THE SOUND OF A SCYTHE [1960] SPIDER KISS [1961] **SHORT NOVELS:** DOOMSMAN [1967] ALL THE LIES THAT ARE MY LIFE [1980] RUN FOR THE STARS [1991] MEFISTO IN ONYX [1993] **GRAPHIC NOVELS:** DEMON WITH A GLASS HAND (with Marshall Rogers) [1986] NIGHT AND THE ENEMY (with Ken Steacy) [1987] VIC AND BLOOD: The Chronicles of a Boy and His Dog (with Richard Corben) [1989] **SHORT STORY COLLECTIONS:** THE DEADLY STREETS [1958] SEX GANG (as Paul Merchant) [1959] A TOUCH OF INFINITY [1960] CHILDREN OF THE STREETS [1961] GENTLEMAN JUNKIE and other stories of the hung-up generation [1961] ELLISON WONDERLAND [1962] PAINGOD and other delusions [1965] I HAVE NO MOUTH & I MUST SCREAM [1967] FROM THE LAND OF FEAR [1967] LOVE AIN'T NOTHING BUT SEX MISSPELLED [1968] THE BEAST THAT SHOUTED LOVE AT THE HEART OF THE WORLD [1969] OVER THE EDGE [1970] DE HELDEN VAN DE HIGHWAY (Dutch publication only) [1973] ALL THE SOUNDS OF FEAR (British publication only) [1973] THE TIME OF THE EYE (British publication only) [1974] APPROACHING OBLIVION [1974] DEATHBIRD STORIES [1975] NO DOORS, NO WINDOWS [1975] OE KAN IK SCHREEUWEN ZONDER MOND (Dutch publication only) [1977] STRANGE WINE [1978] SHATTERDAY [1980] STALKING THE NIGHTMARE [1982] ANGRY CANDY [1988] ENSAMVÄRK (Swedish publication only) [1992] SLIPPAGE [1994] **COLLABORATIONS:** PARTNERS IN WONDER sf collaborations with 14 other wild talents (1971) THE STARLOST #1 Phoenix Without Ashes (with Edward Bryant) [1975] MIND FIELDS: 33 stories inspired by the art of Jacek Yerka [1994] **OMNIBUS VOLUMES:** THE FANTASIES OF HARLAN ELLISON [1979] DREAMS WITH SHARP TEETH [1991] **NON-FICTION & ESSAYS:** MEMOS FROM PURGATORY [1961] THE GLASS TEAT essays of opinion on television [1970] THE OTHER GLASS TEAT further essays of opinion on television [1975] THE BOOK OF ELLISON (Edited by Andrew Porter) [1978] SLEEPLESS NIGHTS IN THE PROCRUSTEAN BED: Essays (Edited by Marty Clark) [1984] AN EDGE IN MY VOICE [1985] HARLAN ELLISON'S WATCHING [1989] THE HARLAN ELLISON HORNBOOK [1990] **SCREENPLAYS; ETC.:** THE ILLUSTRATED HARLAN ELLISON (Edited by Byron Preiss) [1978] HARLAN ELLISON'S MOVIE [1990] I, ROBOT: THE ILLUSTRATED SCREENPLAY (based on Issac Asimov's story-cycle) [1994] THE CITY ON THE EDGE OF FOREVER [1995] **RETROSPECTIVES:** ALONE AGAINST TOMORROW A 10-Year Survey [1971] THE ESSENTIAL ELLISON A 35-Year Retrospective (Edited by Terry Dowling with Richard Delap & Gil Lamont) [1987] **AS EDITOR:** DANGEROUS VISIONS (Editor) [1967] NIGHTSHADE & DAMNATIONS: the finest stories of Gerald Kersh (Editor) [1968] AGAIN DANGEROUS VISIONS (Editor) [1972] MEDEA: HARLAN'S WORLD (Editor) [1985] **The Harlan Ellison Discovery Series:** STORMTRACK by James Sutherland [1975] AUTUMN ANGELS by Arthur Byron Cover [1975] THE LIGHT AT THE END OF THE UNIVERSE by Terry Carr [1976] ISLANDS by Marta Randall [1976] INVOLUTION OCEAN by Bruce Sterling [1978]

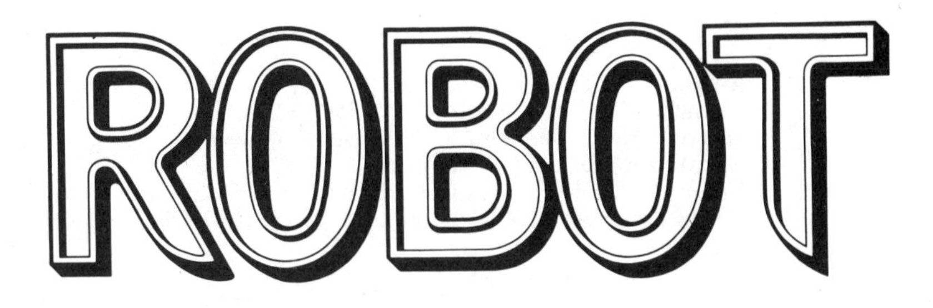

# I, ROBOT

## The Illustrated Screenplay


HARLAN ELLISON

Isaac Asimov

*Illustrated by Mark Zug*



A BYRON PREISS VISUAL PUBLICATIONS, INC. BOOK

ASPECT

WARNER BOOKS

A Time Warner Company

A WARNER ASPECT book published by arrangement with the Author.


Project coordinated by Byron Preiss Visual Publications, Inc.
Edited by Howard Zimmerman
Cover and interior art by Mark Zug


Warner Books, Inc., 1271 Avenue of the Americas, New York, NY 10020

A Time Warner Company

Printed in the United States of America

ISBN 0-446-67062-6

## EDITOR'S NOTE

Harlan Ellison completed his screenplay adaptation of Isaac Asimov's collected robot series, *I, Robot,* in 1978. Almost a decade later, with the screenplay still unfilmed, Ellison and Asimov agreed to serialize it in the pages of *Isaac Asimov's Science Fiction Magazine.* It ran in three issues in late 1987. Asimov wrote a foreword that accompanied the first part of the serialization. It is reprinted here, along with a new introduction from Ellison, to give readers an historical context for the screenplay, and an insight into its creation.


## ACKNOWLEDGMENTS

The Author wishes to thank that one-ninth of the total iceberg mass above the waterline, the most visible of the many hands who helped bring this particular dream to fruition. The vastly talented, surprise-out-of-nowhere Mark Zug, master imagist, interpreter of scenario instructions, eye of wonder, nominee to wear the mantle of Maxfield Parrish and N.C. Wyeth. The Universe loves us because it sent Mark to this project. Kristin Kest, for a butterfly and for good sense and for being an artist-amanuensis. Betsy Mitchell of Warner Aspect. Both here, and elsewhere, she had the vision and the tenacity and the smarts to get it done. Lucy Fisher of Warner Bros. In Hollywood, a champion of this screenplay and this project since 1977. Janet and Isaac, well, you have to know this wouldn't have happened without them. My wonderful wife, Susan, who cried because I was so confused when this material had to be faxed off before we hopped a plane to Chicago, that I forgot to add her to this list. I am not a spousal abuser. And finally, to Howard Zimmerman and Byron Preiss, who suffered along with us, who took the abuse and the frustration and the screwups and still stood the gaff. Both Isaac and I bless you.

Harlan Ellison, June 1994

TO ISAAC

my buddy

who, simply put,

made this a better world

## Harlan Ellison's I, Robot
### *by Isaac Asimov*

I have never had a novel or story converted into a motion picture or television play. Some people think that the motion picture *Fantastic Voyage* is mine, but that's wrong. The motion picture script existed, and was written by Jerome Bixby and others, and I was asked to make a novel out of it. I finally agreed and, because I work quickly and movie people work slowly, the derived novel came out six months before the movie. That made it seem as though the novel was original and the movie an adaptation, but the reverse was the fact.

My non-appearance on the screen has not bothered me. I am strictly a print-person. I write material that is intended to appear on a printed page, and not on a screen, either large or small. I have been invited on numerous occasions to write a screenplay for motion picture or television, either original, or as an adaptation of my own story or someone else's, and I have refused every time. Whatever talents I may have, writing for the eye is not one of them, and I am lucky enough to know what I can't do.

On the other hand, if someone else—someone who has the particular talent of writing for the eye that I do not have—were to adapt one of my stories for the screen, I would not expect that the screen version be "faithful" to the print version.

Why should it be? The mere fact that I am completely at home in print and completely helpless in the visual convinces me that two widely separate interpretations are involved.

The medium of print uses the word. Images may be evoked by the word, but this is a subsidiary side effect. It is the sound of words tiptoeing their way through the mind that is primary.

The medium of the screen uses the image. Dialogue is almost always involved, but this is a subsidiary side effect. It is the patterned light of colored images flashing their way past the retina that is primary.

In telling a particular story, the medium is the message (as it was once a short-lived fad to say). In using words, certain things are stressed; in using images, other things are stressed, even if the same events are described in both cases.

A mediocre book can be translated into a good movie and a good book can be translated into a mediocre movie. The point is, though, that if a good book is translated into a good movie (or, less frequently, vice versa) this is not because there was a literal conversion of one into another, scene by scene. There would have to be differences, even radical ones, if both are to be good.

This is especially true if the book is written by one person and the movie adaptation written by another, each person being equally imaginative and creative. Notice that "equally" does *not* mean "identically." If the adapter follows slavishly the model with which he is presented, as I did in the case of *Fantastic Voyage,* he is denying himself. That is why I was never satisfied with *Fantastic Voyage* even though it did very well in hardcover and superlatively well in paperback. In fact, that is why I finally wrote *Fantastic Voyage II*—published in September 1987—which is, in a way, a similar story, but written as I would write it so that it is totally different from the movie, and from the earlier novel.

This brings me to the occasion on which I *nearly* had a book translated to the screen. Twenty years ago, a producer, John Mantley, grew interested in *I, Robot* and, after considerable dickering, an option was agreed to. I have frequently had stories and novels optioned for the movies and it represents a moderate source of income but nothing ever seems to come of it.

For a while, nothing seemed to come of *I, Robot,* either. For years, in fact. The option was renewed, and renewed, and renewed. Finally, after a dozen years it was actually bought and the creaking machinery of Hollywood was set in motion. They asked me to do the screen adaptation and, of course, I refused. So they did an extraordinarily intelligent thing. They got Harlan Ellison to do it.

Harlan and I are close friends. He knows my work and likes it. I know his work and like it. Though he and I are alike in many ways—extroverted, loud-mouthed, charismatic individuals—our writing couldn't be more different. Mine is almost entirely cerebral, his almost entirely emotional. And that's good. Seeing my stuff through Harlan's eyes is bound to add another, and very intriguing, dimension.

So Harlan wrote the screenplay, some years ago, and sent me a copy and I loved it. Susan Calvin was in it, so were Gregory Powell and Michael Donovan, so were some of my robots. The plot that Harlan built up out of the materials I had provided in the book was viewed through a distorting glass that brought out new and startling facets. His screenplay would have made a *marvelous* movie, in my opinion.

But note the conditional. It *would* have made one. The fact is it didn't.

There were several reasons for this. One was that Harlan's imagination took no account of the economic facts of life. The picture would have cost some thirty million dollars to make, and the movie people were not sure they could get their millions back. I really can't fault them for being concerned about that.

Secondly, Harlan's screenplay came after the motion picture *Star Wars* had appeared, and Hollywood people are not exactly known for their ability to break out of a money-making mold. Since *Star Wars* had coined millions, Harlan was asked to make the robots "cute," like R2-D2, and they also wanted him to make Susan Calvin young and pretty like Princess Leia.

Thirdly, Harlan is not known for his equanimity and pliability. When he is asked to do something stupid, he is quite likely to say, "This is stupid," with some ornamental additions of his own. And Hollywood executives are likely to take this amiss.

So the picture was never made, and for additional years remained in limbo. Then, finally, Harlan regained control of the screenplay and, unwilling to see it gather dust, decided to try to publish it in the magazine that bears my name. The editor of that magazine, Gardner Dozios, read the screenplay and thought it might make a unique item for the magazine. He consulted me and I agreed. I agreed all the more readily because it is *not* a slavish adaptation, so it can't be considered a matter of self-aggrandizement on my part. The screenplay is as much Harlan Ellison as the book is Isaac Asimov, and even if you've read the book, you'll find the space allotted to the screenplay is anything but wasted.

And you'll be sorry, as I am, that Hollywood didn't make the movie.

## ME 'N' ISAAC AT THE MOVIES
### A Brief Memoir of Citizen Calvin
### *by Harlan Ellison*

My heart bleeds like a rock when I have the dream. I always cry; or if I'm in public, I pretend it's an allergy that's making me get all choked up. This dream . . . I never have it at night, asleep. It *always* comes to me when I'm off-guard, when I'm awake but my mind is elsewhere. A daydream, a looking-off-through-the-air . . . unmanned, disarmed, fit to be bushwhacked.

In the daydream, the daymare, Isaac and I are in a movie theater. We're sitting side-by-side, watching this movie. *This* movie, this screenplay you have in front of you, the one it took a year of my creative life to write, this movie that Isaac liked so much. Isaac and I, we're sitting there watching *I, Robot.*

It's a *terrible* daydream, and I come out of it shaking my head trying to get the pictures out of the darkness where I play them over and over in the Cinerama dome of my memory. Isaac really liked this screenplay a lot, and Warner Bros. studios never made the motion picture, and now Isaac is dead and will never see it, and I keep having this awful, damned daydream in which we sit together enjoying what might have been. And it doesn't matter if I have the daydream a hundred times, I cannot keep myself from crying when I wrench out of that theater of memory. Like Isaac's dear Janet, and Robyn, and Stan, and all the rest of us who won't see him again, it is impossible for me to convey the pain that seems somehow to never go away completely, a pain that we willingly endure because it serves to bring him back at memory's behest; in my case, there in the movie theater.

After several rewrites of the first draft, I sent the final to Isaac early in August of 1978. He wrote me on the 18th, "I picked up the completed manuscript a little after 10 P.M. last night just to glance through it and see what changes you had made. I began reading word for word and, with bedtime at 11, I was done at 12:30 A.M. with Janet reasoning with me that I need my sleep.

"It's terrific, Harlan. I asked you in my letter of 9 March to make it 'the first really adult, complex, worthwhile science fiction movie ever made' and you've done it. You've put your own frame around four of my stories, kept the stories mine in essence and in much detail, made the frame your very own (with a skill and imagination I could never even dream of matching) and yet kept it in the spirit of *I, Robot* also. In particular, you kept Susan Calvin *my* Susan Calvin and that is wonderful."

I quote from that letter—a letter that went on much longer and enthused even more than what I've set down here—even the parts that are embarrassingly self-serving, because it is imperative to me that anyone who picks up this book understands that this is not one of those work-for-hire afterthought books that capitalizes on Isaac's name, or the work he did that made his reputation. This is no succubus expansion of a short story, or twiddle that springboards from a "treatment" Isaac may have sold to some merchandiser. It is a novel-for-the-screen that was written by me, with Isaac's seed-quartet of stories and the living shadow of Susan Calvin as sun and rain that brought forth an entirely different creative work. I quote Isaac's affection for that new work, because he gave me what I needed to do the job, and he loved me enough to trust me and let me go my way, and I gave him something he admired in return for that love and trust. And I need the reader to know this is truly the end-result of a friendship that lasted more than forty years.

Isaac left at 2:30 A.M. New York time on Monday, April 6th, 1992. I'd been working on this book, with Mark Zug and Byron Preiss and my editor Howard Zimmerman, for almost a year at that time. And though Isaac had seen the screenplay's initial publication in the monthly magazine that bears his name—and had beamed like a proud poppa when he was told that not only had the screenplay won "by popular acclaim" a 1987 Reader's Award from *Asimov's Science Fiction Magazine,* but that it was a finalist on the ballot for the 1988 Hugo Award—he never got to admire the work of young Mark Zug, never got to see how Mark has given eyes to my scenarist's artifice, never got to see this film-novel. (Wryly, teeth grinding with the desire to insert a railroad spike at least an inch deep into the left eyeball of such critic-*manqué* as the woefully bitter, jealous, and untalented Gregory Feeley or Sheldon Teitelbaum who regularly *kvetch* that I am no-price because I don't write novels, I gleefully point out that I have written at least *twenty* novels: in the form of motion pictures. *I, Robot* is a 90,000 word novel, but the members of the Baby Weasel Brigade, who create and alter the rules to fit their mendacious purposes, cannot countenance such a concept. One can only despair at how they would discount Laurence Sterne's TRISTRAM SHANDY or William Burrough's THE TICKET THAT EXPLODED for daring to present themselves in any experimental garb other than the usual straitjacket of "the Novel.")

Yet I can say that I spent an entire year at the movies with Isaac Asimov (and never once did I have to share the popcorn).

It broke both our hearts that the film never got made, but that was neither Isaac's nor my fault; it was the fault of the monumentally inept and wasteful System that obtains in Hollywood. (I've been here since 1962, and I've written about the System at length elsewhere, as have thousands of other bludgeoned writers.) It was the fault of a jerk named Bob Shapiro, who was Head of Production at Warner Bros. at the time, who ain't there no more, and good riddance to him. You may find this interesting:

From December 1977 through December 1978 I wrote nothing very much . . . apart from two hundred and thirty-five single-spaced pages of intricate screenplay. How it happened was this:

Legendary writer-producers (*The Rogues, Mannix, ad seriatim*) Ben Roberts and Ivan Goff were the start of it. In 1964, when I was working on the original *Burke's Law* at Four Star Studios, Ben and Ivan were across the hall crafting urbane *Rogues* scripts for David Niven, Charles Boyer, Gig Young, Robert Coote and Gladys Cooper. (This has nothing to do with anything, but it was there, at what has become CBS Studio Center, that I met Dick Powell and June Allyson, and learned that it had been Powell who had changed Ronald Reagan from a Democrat to a Republican. Sigh.)

Ben, who passed away in 1984, was a remarkable man. Not only an excellent novelist and scenarist, top-line tv producer, nifty gin rummy player and raconteur, but he was a celebrated painter. His oils were much prized, and sold in the galleries for considerable sums. I, of course, lusted after one of those ebullient primitives. But couldn't afford one. Nonetheless, every time I ran into Ben in the commissary or at a screening, I would whimper and look woebegone. Finally, about 1972, when Ben and Ivan were at Paramount and so was I, Ben took pity on me and sold me a small oil for a nominal price. But he did it with the proviso that, "Some day you'll owe me a favor." I agreed.

It wasn't till February of 1977 that Ben called in the favor—during one of those recurrent periods when I'm a "hot" writer.

He and Ivan were producing *Logan's Run,* the tv series, over at MGM. The scripts stunk, even before debut, and the network had told Ben and Ivan to go out and get some "name writers." Ben called me and said, "I need that favor."

I went over to see Ben and Ivan on February 25th, and they screened the pilot and a couple of rough-cut episodes for me. They said they needed something outstanding, with my name on it, for the upcoming ratings crunch. So I plotted out a segment titled "Crypt" and I handed in the treatment on April Fool's Day. After consultations with Ben, and changes required by cast alterations, I handed in the revised treatment on April 13th. On that day I visited the set and met with the stars of the series. Afterward, Ben and I went to the MGM restaurant, the Lion's Den (with adjacent snack bar called The Cub Room), for lunch. As we sat there eating and chatting, John Mantley came over to the table.

John had been the long-time producer of *Gunsmoke* and was working on a new James Arness series at Metro. I hadn't seen him in years. We greeted each other warmly—Mantley is one of the industry's true *mensches* and has a reputation for taste and ethical behavior that remains unsullied after fifty years in film and television—and John asked if, after lunch, I had a spare moment, would I stop by his table to discuss an idea he had? I said I'd be pleased to do that thing.

Ben finally went back to work, I sashayed over to John Mantley's booth, and he got right to it: "Do you know the Isaac Asimov *I, Robot* stories?"

"Absolutely. Isaac's an old friend."

"Did you know that for the past twenty years I've held the film option on those stories?"

"No, I'd never heard that."

"Well, I do. And for twenty years I've kept renewing those options, trying to get a film off the ground. And for twenty years no one has been able to beat the script."

"I'll bet they always want to do it as an omnibus film, right? Like *Dead of Night* or *Quartet?*"

John smiled and nodded. "I gather you think that's a wrong way to go."

So I told him how it should be done.

John seemed pleased not only that I was thoroughly familiar with the canon, but that I had definite ideas why the project hadn't succeeded in two decades . . . and what it took to pull a screenplay together. He told me that Warner Bros. had made a deal with him to film the Asimov robot stories, and that the producer who had taken it to Warners was Edward Lewis. I knew Edward Lewis's name: his credits include such films as *Spartacus* and *Missing*. (I'd heard conflicting stories about Lewis. On the one hand, industry rumor suggested he was ruthless and not unfamiliar with the concept of tossing an associate to the wolves when the best-laid plans went astray. But on the other hand, he was the man who had broken the detestable Hollywood blacklist by not only hiring Dalton Trumbo to script *Spartacus,* but by insisting that Trumbo be given full credit sans pseudonyms.)

I went to meet Lewis. We hit it off. He hired me to write *I, Robot.* And from December 1977 through December 1978, I worked on virtually nothing else. I was consumed by the project. Eddie Lewis encouraged me and I slaved over the script night and day. It was my life's work. And when it was done, and it went through two rewrites to factor in Isaac's one scientific correction (something built into one of his stories, that later satellite information proved erroneous) and Eddie Lewis's suggestions, it was mimeographed in just ten copies by a Hollywood script service, it was bound in metallic covers, and it was sent to Bob Shapiro at Warners Bros. for his attention.

We all thought it was a shoo-in.

But don't forget two things. First, this was post-*Star Wars* and its accompanying breakthroughs in special effects: it *could* be done, the technology existed, at a level previously unthinkable in terms of production costs. But . . .

> "Writing is an occupation in which you have to keep proving your talent to people who have none."
> *Jules Renard* (1864- 1910)

When this jerk who was the head of the studio received the manuscript, and we waited and waited for his "input," and weeks went by and we heard nothing, I finally asked to have a meeting with him, to find out what was happening. And in the course of that meeting, during which he mumbled nebulosities without specificities, it became clear that *he had never even read the script*! (This cannot be, I thought, with genuine horror. Can you understand what was happening? Here was a man, head of production for one of the greatest film factories in the world, talking about spending between seventeen and twenty *million* dollars on an international project that would tie up Warner Bros. for at least two years, employ thousands and thousands of people, and not only bring to life a work on which I'd spent a full year of my life and talent but at last—after twenty years of unsuccessful attempts—send Isaac's wonderful positronic cycle to hungry audiences throughout the world . . . who was making imbecile suggestions based wholly on *précis* of the complex and far-flung story by anonymous readers from his staff. This cannot be, I thought; I'm having a nightmare. So I set out to verify my suspicion. I began asking him specific questions on pivotal points in the plot. His responses were vague, general, disingenuous. I was certain I'd found him out, but just to make absolutely certain, I asked him how he liked such-and-such . . . a "major" scene . . . that did not occur in the screenplay at all. He admired that part, he said. He thought that part worked very well indeed, he said.)

At that point I knew he was simply shuckin' & jivin', and I pulled his covers. "You haven't read this script!" I said.

"What do you mean?"

"Just what I said. You haven't read a word of this material. I spent a year on it, you're planning to commit to the biggest project the studio has ever attempted, and you haven't even had the sense of responsibility to look at the work personally. Not only are you creatively irresponsible, but fiscally you're just dancing on thin ice! You've got the intellectual capacity of an artichoke!"

Well, we exchanged words. You see, *no*body speaks to the Great and Wonderful Wizard like that, not nobody, no time, nohow! And then I laid hands on him. I advised him that he had just twenty-four hours to read that script, to make notes *in his own hand* so we'd know he hadn't shunted the job to some flunky, and to get those suggestions back to me and Edward Lewis. Then I left the studio and went home, quivering with rage.

By the time I got home, and called Eddie to apprise him of the debacle, the spud from the studio had already phoned. With trepidation I asked Eddie what he'd said. Eddie was thrilled at the call: the man I'd just threatened and insulted had told him how impressed he was with my sincerity, my commitment to the work, and my desire to work closely with the studio. He said it had been a "fruitful meeting" and that he had had no trouble communicating with me. I sat down. Had I been at some *other* meeting, with some other studio exec?

Well, needless to say, we never got that list of suggestions. Not in his hand, or anyone else's. That meeting took place on October 25, 1978. On October 31 I began revising the script based on the non-suggestions we had earlier received. By January of 1979 I'd been dropped from the project.

Warner Bros. then spent almost two years having other screenwriters do at least three subsequent versions of my script. One of the writers had major credits. All three of the follow-up scripts were shopped around Hollywood, in search of a major director who would take the assignment. I was kept up-to-date on the machinations. Apparently, the scripts were insufficiently loveable (according to my informants) and none of the top directors who saw them cared to accept the job. The spud from the studio, when approached by *Variety* to explain why I had been dropped when my screenplay was so universally admired, said—in print, for attribution—"I'll close the studio before I rehire Ellison! No one tells me I have the intellectual capacity of an artichoke!"

(It was my feeling that only an intellect on the level of a foodstuff would *admit* to having had such a thing said about him, when he could have kept it to himself. Thus validating my perception of the guy.)

But by June of 1980, Warners had approached Irvin Kershner (who had just completed directing *The Empire Strikes Back,* which had opened to rave reviews for his work); he had been aware of the *I, Robot* project for some time, and he said he was interested. But when they sent him the most recent of the follow-up scripts, he rejected the assignment. He didn't like the dream they'd offered him. But he asked them, "Wasn't there a script by Harlan Ellison on this?"

They fumfuh'd and hemmed, also hawed.

"Well, was there or wasn't there?"

They admitted there was such a creature extant.

"Let me see Ellison's version," Kersh said.

So they sent it to him. "This script I'll direct," he said. "But only if Ellison does the rewrite."

Bob Shapiro ground his teeth. He thought of railroad spikes and eyeballs. He was trapped. So he agreed to let Kersh rehire me if Irvin would sign a contract to direct *I, Robot.* It looked like a go.

Kersh came to see me in London, where I was working on a book, and we discussed how the screenplay should be redone. His suggestions were excellent. They cut the budget but did not impair the story or the subtext. It looked like a go.

That was in June of 1980. Kersh signed. Then the studio vegetable told him to go find a new writer. "But the deal was contingent on Ellison coming back aboard," he said. No way, said the honorable exec. "I'll close down this studio before I rehire Ellison. *No* one tells me I have the intellectual capacity of an artichoke!"

Kersh called me. He was locked into the deal, and they had double-crossed both of us. I wasn't surprised. I revised my estimation of the studio guy. A lima bean.

Well . . . it never happened. Kersh managed to get out of the deal; then Warner Bros. hired a Russian director who had had some critical success with a small film; and he met some guy at Columbia University with whom he worked on yet *another* version of my script; and that incarnation was represented to me by a top production executive as "the single worst script I've ever read in my life, made no damned sense at all." And *I, Robot* went into limbo, dumped on a shelf with the hundreds of thousands of other screenplays that had been written in this town over the decades, that had fallen between the cracks for reasons beyond the artistic or filmic value of the work itself. Eddie Lewis left the project, Warners had hundreds of thousands of dollars tied up in the project, the underlying rights to Isaac's stories (without which the film could not be produced) were lost by the Studio, litigation among the original participants followed, and there it remains—in limbo—to this day.

In 1985, the producer of *Star Wars* and *The Dark Crystal,* Gary Kurtz, approached Warners about taking over the project. He came to see me several times, and again it looked as if we might have a go. But the vast expenses already attached to the script, and the ongoing legal hassles, put the kibosh on Gary's desire to make this movie.

It remains, sadly, an unproduced epic.

It broke our hearts.

Because this screenplay is the story of Susan Calvin, I wrote it with Joanne Woodward in mind as Susan. George C. Scott as Rev. Soldash; Keenan Wynn and Ernie Borgnine as Donovan and Powell; Martin Sheen as Robert Bratenahl. You can picture them as you read. (Or substitute your 1990's star alternatives, but if you suggest Madonna or Garth Brooks, I will have to hurt you.)

We suffer, these days, in Hollywood, from a great many writers whose background is not in literature, but in television upbringing. They were raised on *I Love Lucy.* When some of these people go into theatrical features, they use as templates the shallow devices of the sitcom. Spielberg and Lucas make films that are hommage to Saturday morning serials, pop goods that are amusing for children but certainly cannot be considered great art. When I set out to interpret Isaac's stories, when I sat down to beat this problem of integrating only-vaguely-linked stories written over a long period, I knew that the key was not the robot . . . it was the human story of Susan Calvin. And for my model I decided to go to High Art. *I, Robot* is framed as an hommage to *Citizen Kane,* arguably the finest motion picture ever made. It was my hope that by treating Isaac's work in the most serious way from the start, I would produce not only an adult film that would make my liaison with Isaac something that would live forever, but would satisfy the disparate needs of the studio, the producers, my own creative desires, and Isaac's primacy of interest in the material. And would respond not to the *reality* of those fifty-year-old stories, but to the loving recollections of readers.

There remains one slim hope to get this motion picture made. That hope is you. You bought the book . . . now save the movie!

After the magazine publication of this screenplay, and the attendant accolades, I was content to let the work remain an unproduced but published chunk of my *oeuvre,* a stretch of good work that allowed me to pleasure myself in the linkage with my pal, Isaac. It had been ten years since I'd finished the script, and there had been dozens of crummy sf movies that had spent far more than had been contemplated as the budget for *I, Robot.* It was feasible to do the film, but the attendant problems seemed insurmountable:

Bob Shapiro is gone. Like most talentless people with a low animal cunning that informs their manipulation of inept systems, the artichoke-that-walks-like-a-man has been gifted with the title Independent Producer. (His big credit, more appropriate than even *I* could have parodied his career, is as the intellect behind *Pee-wee's Big Adventure,* a film that gave us director Tim Burton, but in and of itself isn't really what one would call an earth-shattering Work of Eternal Art. His current project—precisely at his level of artistic insight—is the film version of the old Richard Boone tv series, *Have Gun, Will Travel.* Yessir, just what we need in these artistically-rich days of widescreen versions of *Maverick* and *Dennis the Menace* and *The Beverly Hillbillies* and *The Flintstones* and . . . oh, gee, ain't we glad Bob is out of the loop that must be necessarily thrown around *I, Robot* to get it made!)

But the woman who was the great champion of this screenplay, the studio executive who saw what this film could do and told Shapiro he should put it on the production schedule, that woman is now an influential production head at Warner Bros. Her name is Lucy Fisher, and it is she who made it possible to publish this book, who gave me the authorization to go to press.

The lawsuit is over. On Wednesday, July 3rd, 1991, a three-judge panel of the California State Court of Appeal upheld a 1989 verdict reached by a Los Angeles Superior Court jury against Warner Bros., in favor of John Mantley, in the amount of $1.46 million, plus interest, as damages for squeezing John out of the *I, Robot* project.

The problem is . . . that money is now part of the "above the line" cost of making the movie. Warners lost the underlying rights to the Asimov stories; though they own the screenplay; and unless there is a groundswell of enthusiasm for the making of this motion picture . . .

It will remain on the shelf.

So write to Lucy Fisher. Just address it to her at Warner Bros. studios, in Burbank, California. Tell her you've read this book. (That's why we've done it, you see. To get the film made. And to showcase the enormous talent of Mark Zug. Both of these are honorable tasks.)

I won't even say please. As you read the screenplay, let the theater of your imagination throw the film on a screen behind your eyes. And then think what a cinematic experience it would be. With or without popcorn.

This is the movie Isaac loved. I'll never really sit beside him to see it, except in that troubling daydream; but if it gets made, well, then a piece of Isaac will live on. The piece he created called Susan Calvin.

The life of Citizen Calvin. The record of a wonderful year of hard work I spent at the movies with my friend Isaac Asimov, who first dreamed of metal men and a remarkable woman.

This one's for you, pal.

# I, ROBOT

**FADE IN:**

**1 BLACK FRAME**

The SOUND of an insistent high-pitched BEEP-BEEP is heard. It is not strident enough to make one wince, but it is very clearly intended to get and hold one's attention. The SOUND CONTINUES for several seconds, then in the center of the frame a line of copy prints itself in one of the machine languages (ALGOL, FORTRAN, COBOL or, more likely, BASIC).

**ALL OPERATORS HOLD INPUTS**

It begins to STROBE in FLUORESCENT GREEN in letters large enough to be easily read. The strobing is in sequence with the beeping. Then, below that line (still strobing), a second line prints out and we realize we are looking at a COMPUTER TERMINAL READOUT PANEL

**PRIORITY ONE INFORMATION<br>IN TRANSMISSION**

The second line begins to STROBE in GREEN in alternate sequence with the first line. Then both vanish to be replaced by

**THE THREE LAWS OF ROBOTICS**

The line holds for several beats as the beeping continues. Then the screen is cleared and the following appears:

**1—A ROBOT MAY NOT INJURE A HUMAN BEING, OR, THROUGH INACTION, ALLOW A HUMAN BEING TO COME TO HARM.**

This message HOLDS as we HEAR in b.g. the SOUND of WATER BUBBLING. The very faintest of luminescence begins to suffuse the frame, as though dawn were coming up far in the distance. We can still read the First Law clearly. Then it wipes and a second message prints itself:

**2—A ROBOT MUST OBEY THE ORDERS GIVEN IT BY HUMAN BEINGS EXCEPT WHERE SUCH ORDERS WOULD CONFLICT WITH THE FIRST LAW.**

This message HOLDS as the SOUND of BUBBLING WATER grows louder and the filtering of light in the frame grows more pronounced. Now we see gradations of brightness and darkness, and a vague upward movement of the b.g. as if we were reading the Three Laws through water. The Second Law wipes and a third message prints itself:

**3—A ROBOT MUST PROTECT ITS OWN EXISTENCE AS LONG AS SUCH PROTECTION DOES NOT CONFLICT WITH THE FIRST OR SECOND LAWS.**

This message HOLDS clearly and easily read in the glowing green computerese as the light fills the b.g. and we see bubbles of water rising in streams from the bottom of the frame. CAMERA BEGINS TO PULL BACK as the Third Law wipes and a final line of printout STROBES large and *RED*:

**THESE ARE THE THREE LAWS OF ROBOTICS. THEY CANNOT BE BROKEN.**

CAMERA BACK though we can read this last message clearly. As CAMERA PULLS BACK we realize we have been reading the printout in the ultramodern magnetic fluid tank of a very highly advanced "liquid memory system," one of the new "water computers" that use a magnetic fluid instead of printed circuits to store data. It is a huge unit, awesome in its complexity, backlit and seething with life as reflected in its terminals and control banks, but centered on that liquid intelligence in the great translucent pillar of bubbling fluid. CAMERA HOLDS on the fluid and its rising bubbles as we

**MATCH-DISSOLVE THRU:**

## 2 CHROMA/KEY SHOT — GRAVESITE ON ALDEBARAN-C XII MATCH WITH RAIN

The bubbles of the preceding SHOT MATCH with RAIN coming down in sheeting slanting grayness. We are clearly on another planet, in point of fact the twelfth planet out from the third sun of the triple-star Aldebaran. We are looking at a group of people, some human, some aliens, gathered around a peculiar gravesite. And we are seeing them in SOLARIZATION (bright, fluorescent color of choice). HOLD the shot in Chroma/Key solarization for several beats as we HEAR the VOICE of ROBERT BRATENAHL speaking o.s.

BRATENAHL (O.S.)
(hushed tones)
On this day of mourning, even the three suns of Aldebaran-C XII seem to have gone out.
(beat)
A sorrowful rain attends the funeral of Stephen Byerley, First President of the Galactic Federation.
(beat)
This is Robert Bratenahl, at graveside for *Cosmos* Magazine.

As the preceding DIALOGUE OVER progresses, CAMERA MOVES IN toward the gravesite and suddenly the CHROMA/KEY view of the scene moves aside so we can see it was an image in a VIEWSCREEN on a minicam sort of apparatus. Now we see the scene through our own eyes.

**3 GRAVESIDE SCENE — MED. LONG SHOT**

as we MOVE IN. The grave itself is a circular pit perhaps three feet in diameter. A shining metal pillar protrudes from the hole and embedded in the top is a wonderfully-shaped vacuum bottle in which a foglike mist floats, its substance sparkling with tiny scintillas of colored light. Through the slanting rain we can see a dozen forms, some of peculiar—but still humanoid—form, others clearly human. CAMERA MOVES IN STEADILY as we

**CUT TO:**

**4 ANOTHER ANGLE — INCLUDING BRATENAHL**

as he moves toward the group, yet is politely separated from them by protocol. Bratenahl is a tall, graceful man who seems

ROBERT BRATENAHL

to be in his mid-thirties, yet there is a fine, boyish quality about him, the young James Stewart perhaps. He wears a harness rig on which we see a modernistic piece of equipment that is obviously the camera and transmitting device through which we saw the solarized scene earlier. The screen has been swept back from in front of his face, but the minicam keeps filming as he walks through the rain.
We CONTINUE TO HEAR HIS VOICE OVER.

BRATENAHL (V.O.)
Earlier this morning, in a private pre-dawn ceremony, the body of President Byerley was atomized, by his specific request. The vacuum bottle you see on the burial pillar contains a token mist scintillated from the star chamber where the atomization occurred.

## 5 MED. LONG SHOT ON GRAVESIDE — MOVING IN

CAMERA MOVES IN STEADILY through the slanting rain as SHOT begins to FEATURE an old woman, huddled between two tall, heroically-proportioned young men. At first we cannot see her face because of the rain-hood. Each of the men holds a slim silver rod, as do several others of the mourners around the grave. The rods are held aloft, and though they are not attached to anything, the rain does not fall below the level of the rods. They are implements that create an invisible force-field, and though there are more important uses for them, in this case they are employed to keep the rain off the old woman. As CAMERA COMES IN we HEAR the VOICE of BRATENAHL OVER:

BRATENAHL (V.O.).
Clustered around the burial pillar are the living legends of our time, those select few Stephen Byerley called his closest friends. President Bramhall of the Orion Constellation; Dion Fabry of Perseus; Karl Hawkstein of the Triangulum . . .
(beat)
Well, I'll be damned . . .
(catches himself)
Central! Edit that out.

HAWKSTEIN

(beat)

Reference: punch me up a scan on C-for-cat Calvin. First name, Susan. Robopsychologist.

As the preceding VOICE OVER ends we have come up to a CLOSE SHOT on the old woman standing dry and huddled as the rain pours down around her force-field shield. For the first time we see the face of SUSAN CALVIN. She is eighty-two years old, but because of the anti-agapic injections looks a well-preserved and alert sixty. She is a small woman, but there is a towering strength in her face. Tensile strength, that speaks to endurance, to maintaining in the imperfect world. Her mouth is thin, and her face pale. Grace lives in her features, and intelligence; but she is not an attractive woman. She is not one of those women who in later years it can be said of them, "She must have been a beauty when she was younger." Susan Calvin was always plain. And clearly, always a powerful personality.

**CUT TO:**

## 6 MINICAM IMAGE — SUSAN CALVIN

It is the same face, but younger. See: she wasn't pretty, even then. But the potency is there. The image, broadcast from Central, light-years away in another star-system, fills the FRAME as we HEAR the VOICE of Bratenahl OVER:

BRATENAHL (V.O.)

(jubilant)

I was *right!* It's Calvin!

(beat)

Central! Give me everything readout you've got on Susan Calvin.

(beat)

Especially cross-reference materials with Calvin and Stephen Byerley together.

The image breaks up into scintillance, is replaced by green fluorescent words in lines that stream onto black field. (Full text to be provided for production.)

BRATENAHL (V.O.)
Born 1994, Old Earth Time. Father, Edward Winslow Calvin, middle-level executive, U.S. Robots Corp., died 2004. Mother, Stephanie Ordway Calvin, died at birth of daughter . . .

**CUT TO:**

## 7 GRAVESIDE — ON BRAMHALL

officiating at the ceremony. BRAMHALL is in his seventies, tall, distinguished, dressed in the severe togalike clothing of his galaxy's home world, his three sets of arms folded across his middle, twenty-four fingers clasped.

PRES. BRAMHALL
(gently)
I've heard it said: life is only a troubled sound between two silences.
(beat)
Stephen Byerley spent nearly half a century, forty years Old Earth Time, gentling that troubled sound, sweetening it for the thousand races of the million worlds.
(beat)
Goodbye, Stephen, old friend . . .

PRESIDENT BRAMHALL
OF THE ALPHA TRIANGULI CONCORD

**CUT BACK TO:**

## 8 SAME AS 6 — VIEWSCREEN OF MINICAM

as a series of READOUT SCENES (some in b&w, some in single-color overlay, some in full color, some in Graphiconversion pattern overlays flash on and off the minicam showing a variety of clips as the CENTRAL COMMUNICAST VOICE succinctly identifies each scene OVER:

SAME AS 48—ASSEMBLY ROOM, U.S. ROBOMEK: on the balcony running around the perimeter of the robot assembly complex. Susan (age 21) and ALFRED LANNING with HALF A DOZEN EXECUTIVES of U.S. Robots, smiling, shaking hands, pointing out across the buzzing conveyor line of robots assembling robots.

COMMUNICAST VOICE (FILTER)

At age twenty-one, Dr. Susan Calvin joins staff of U.S. Robots and Mechanical Men as first fully accredited robopsychologist; year, 2015. *(Year spoken as: twenty-fifteen)*

SAME AS 272 — INT. U.S. ROBOMEK TEST AREA NINE: four LNE model robots cutting diamonds in the b.g. as we see SUSAN CALVIN, ALFRED LANNING, NORMAN BOGERT and various REPS OF THE COMMUNICATIONS MEDIA being shown LENNY, one of the robots.

COMMUNICAST VOICE (FILTER)

Year 2032, Dr. Susan Calvin develops multi-purpose robot based on LNE model.

SAME AS 216 — INT. EARTHCENTRAL COMPUTER COMPLEX: down the shaft into high-ceilinged tunnel filled with complex, multifaced, flickering computer banks of incredibly advanced design, to the group of EARTHCENTRAL OFFICIALS, STEPHEN BYERLEY and a small group of others. FREEZE-FRAME and MOVE IN on the group of others till we get SUSAN CALVIN, hidden in that group, in CU. A red fluorescent circle appears around her face.

COMMUNICAST VOICE (FILTER)

Year 2036, rising political figure Stephen Byerley taken on tour of the underground EarthCentral computer complex.

(beat)

Total Central scan reveals this as first public appearance of Byerley and Calvin together. No mention made of this at the time.

**CUT TO:**

## 9 DESCENDING BOOM SHOT — ON GRAVESITE

as DION FABRY of Perseus steps forward. He wears an all-enshrouding blood-red cape that has a high-standing stiff collar. We can barely see his features. As he comes to the pillar, he sweeps back the cape to reveal long, thin insectlike arms ending in leafy pads. He places the fronds of his hands on the pillar and speaks. His voice is strange and deep, hardly what we would expect from a creature half-human, half-vegetable.

DION FABRY
(sadly)
He saved my world and my race. What can I say in love and loss to this container of his essence that was never said to him in life?
(beat)
God be between you and harm in all the empty places you walk, Stephen.

**CUT BACK TO:**

## 10 CLOSE ON BRATENAHL — SPEAKING INTO MINICAM

BRATENAHL
(urgently)
I don't care if he's on Withdrawn Status! Patch this through, Priority One! Yes, dammit, I'm still recording!

A face begins to assume shape in the lines on the minicam. It is the face of a bulldog-man, half-asleep, jowly, but with quickening alertness in the eyes. It is ROWE, the editor of *Cosmos* Magazine.

ROWE
(angrily)
What're you, a brain-damage case? You know what time it is here?
(blinks)
Who the hell is that . . . Bratenahl? What's the matter?

BRATENAHL
Susan Calvin is here at Byerley's funeral!

ROWE
(astounded)
Damn! Did you catch it for record?

BRATENAHL

Of course.

ROWE

(jubilant)

*Hot* damn! She finally turned up! And at Byerley's *funeral*! I always had a feeling that rumor about them being lovers was true.

(beat)

Go get her!

BRATENAHL

Hey, wait on there, Rowe! She hasn't even been *seen* for twenty years, much less given an interview. This is high level security out here. They could pull my matrix and ground me if I invade personal space.

ROWE

Bratenahl: you miss this and *I'll* pull your matrix. You'll be grounded so goddamned long they'll plant potatoes in you.

BRATENAHL

(worried)

Will *Cosmos* back me?

ROWE

All the way.

BRATENAHL

On the record?

ROWE

Yes.

(beat)

If you get busted I'll have to go to the publishing committee to bail you out . . . but I'll do it. You have my word.

BRATENAHL

Your word? Rowe, I don't think human speech is your natural tongue. You ought to rattle like a snake.

**CUT TO:**

## 11 ANOTHER ANGLE ON GRAVESIDE — MED. SHOT

as the pillar is lowered into the ground. Everyone stands with heads bowed. As the pillar descends, an attendant steps forward with a laser-sealer and melts the ground till it bubbles and glows yellow and turns to glass that seals the hole. All that remains is a smooth, circular reflective surface that hisses as raindrops spatter on it.

The crowd begins to move away, to disperse. As Susan Calvin and her two GUARDS walk TOWARD CAMERA, Bratenahl—still recording—moves into the FRAME and toward them, on a course that intersects them.

## 12 CLOSE ON SUSAN CALVIN

as her face comes up from its shadowed rain-hood hiding. She looks directly at us, and at Bratenahl o.s.

## 13 TWO-SHOT — BRATENAHL & CALVIN

as he comes up to the trio.

BRATENAHL

Dr. Calvin? I'm Robert Bratenahl from *Cosmos* Magazine. May I—

Her face is a mask of anguish. There are tears in her eyes. A lost expression overlying the power of her presence. CAMERA PULLS BACK SLIGHTLY to include the two Guards with her.

1st GUARD

Excuse us, please. It's raining.

2nd GUARD

Not now, sir, if you please.

BRATENAHL

But if you could spare me just a mo—

1st GUARD

(with an edged voice)

It's *raining*, sir. Dr. Calvin might catch cold.

BRATENAHL

(to Calvin)

There are tears in your eyes. Millions would have come to pay tribute, but only a dozen were allowed; only the few who were closest. And you have tears.

She stares at him more closely now. Her mouth tightens. Her eyes flash with anger.

CALVIN

(quietly)

Doesn't Central have a readout, Mr. Bratenahl? Isn't that the final responsibility of all cheap gossip?

She starts to move forward. The two Guards put themselves in Bratenahl's path, even as they continue to hold the force-field rods over her. She goes past, with 1st Guard protecting her, keeping her dry. The other speaks to Bratenahl:

2nd GUARD

This was very poor form, sir. It should be evident this is an inopportune moment for such things.

BRATENAHL

I suggest it's the first moment in twenty years, OE Time. I'm a communicaster, sir. It's my job.

2nd GUARD

And mine is guaranteeing her privacy. There are laws, sir. Let us go quietly.

And he moves away, hurrying to catch Calvin. Bratenahl watches.

## 14 LONG SHOT — PAST BRATENAHL

as Susan Calvin and her two Guards reach a low pyramidal structure sitting alone on the empty plain, nothing near it. It is perhaps eight feet in height, a squat pyramid of smooth metallic sides that seem to have peculiar chromatics rippling in the surfaces. As the three people approach, one of the faces of the pyramid pivots open, the wall disappearing into a slit in the adjoining wall. The1st Guard steps into the utter darkness within the pyramid as CAMERA ZOOMS IN on him.

His shape suddenly breaks up into a million light-motes, all scintillating and vibrating, shot through with gold and silver highlights, but retaining a human shape. Then the shape contracts to a mass of closely-packed atoms, and as we watch they seem to be fired off in a stream of light, like tracer bullets in the night. Then Susan Calvin steps in, and the same thing happens; then the 2nd Guard, and he is gone. CAMERA ZOOMS OUT FAST to HOLD Bratenahl in CU. With his back to us, we HEAR him say:

BRATENAHL
There are tears in your eyes, Dr. Calvin.

**DISSOLVE TO:**

## 15 BRIGHT LIGHT FILLS FRAME

as CAMERA PULLS BACK we see it is a point of light at the end of a light-fiber. CAMERA CONTINUES BACK and we see the light-fiber filament is being inserted into the womb of a pregnant woman in a cold-chill trough on an operating stage. Three medical technicians work around her. One of them is BERNICE JOLO, a surgeon specializing in the cellular science of amniocentesis: the withdrawing of amniotic fluid from the embryonic sac. The fiber is inserted, and hooked to a complex mechanism that is revealed to be a video-microscope.

BERNICE

Fine-tune it, Eunice.

The second technician fiddles with dials, and a picture of the sac and the embryonic child within appears on a TV relay screen.

BERNICE

You were right. The left arm is twisted under. Let's go in.

Incredibly tiny "waldos" (manipulable metal fingers on the end of slim armatures) are extruded from the complex mechanism, and inserted into the womb. The technicians bend over the woman. We watch the work on the screen.

## 16 ON BERNICE — CLOSE

as she works over the woman, keeping her eyes on the relay screen, manipulating the waldos to turn the fetus. CAMERA BACK to ENLARGE SCENE taking in the relay screen so we see what she is doing.

BERNICE

All right, now: turning.

CAMERA IN ON SCREEN as we see the fetus being rotated. We HOLD a BEAT then CAMERA RISES to show us the entire operating theater. Hanging above and to the side of the surgeons is a large transparent bubble where spectators can sit to watch the operation below. CAMERA UP TO BUBBLE LEVEL and PULLS BACK to include bubble large in f.g. Then CAMERA IN on bubble till we see one man inside, sitting watching two screens: the first is a replica of the relay screen below, with the fetus being turned, the other is a small screen on a wristwatch comm-unit.

## 17 INT. BUBBLE — PAST BRATENAHL

As the screen with the fetus glows in the b.g. we COME IN PAST BRATENAHL to the screen on his wrist. Rowe is on the screen.

ROWE

What the hell are you doing on Sigma Draconis 5?

BRATENAHL

I've got a friend here who might be able to give me a lead on Susan Calvin.

ROWE

You shouldn't have let her get away to begin with.

BRATENAHL

You saw the playback; what'd you expect me to do, fight off her side-boys and jump on her back?

ROWE

I've got faith in you, boy. You'll find her. . .

(beat)

And just to *prove* my faith, we did some digging, and Research came up with something that might help.

(beat)

So stop whining; this is the best story you'll ever luck onto. She helped change the face of the galaxy and then vanished; we know damned near nothing about her . . . or what she was to Byerley.

(beat)

This could win you the Prix Galactica.

BRATENAHL

It could win me a cell on Abraxis.

ROWE

Do you want what Research found, or don't you?

BRATENAHL

(resigned)

Sure. What is it?

ROWE

Segment of the personal memoirs of Alfred Lanning, first Director of U.S. Robots. Recorded in 2034, the year before he died. We had to call in some favors but the Lanning Archive coughed it up. I'll put it up on your screen. Just one thing, though . . .

BRATENAHL

What now?

ROWE

Just remember, kiddo: you win the Prix Galactica for this, and I want a chip off the statue.

BRATENAHL

How about the cell next to mine?

Rowe snorts, and his image vanishes. The screen scintillates and green read-out appears:

**STANDBY:**
**TRANSMISSION OF DATA**

But at that moment the relay screen from the operating stage below goes dark. Bratenahl looks down and sees Bernice Jolo leaving the theater, pulling off the skintight coverall and gloves—all one-piece disposable—as she goes out through the door that irises open to permit her exit. He speaks into the wrist mechanism:

BRATENAHL

Put the transmission on hold.

Then he gets up and leaves the bubble.

**CUT TO:**

## 18 INT. SEX-TANK — THROUGH MIST

A space without space. Pale milky mist floats everywhere. A naked man and woman, tastefully obscured by the mist, float around each other, kissing, touching, embracing. It is a no-gravity sleeping tank, in this case a rendezvous for Bratenahl and Bernice Jolo. CAMERA IN ON THEM.

BERNICE

Good to see you again.

BRATENAHL

Good to be back.

BERNICE

Any trouble with the teleport booth?

BRATENAHL

No, not this time. Not like a year ago.

BERNICE

(laughing lightly)

It was funny! They were reassembling your atoms all the way out to Ursa Major. Sure they didn't miss picking up something valuable?

BRATHENAHL

(ruefully)

Thing I like best about your sense of humor is that it's so black it slops over into the ultraviolet.

She rolls over him, they turn and turn in the weightless air.

BERNICE

Okay, now tell me what brought you back to me. I know it isn't sex.

BRATENAHL

A base canard. I came like a shooting star, bearing my heart before me, a slave to your wonderfulness, just to rifle your privates.

BERNICE

An A for performance, but you flunk for purple prose. Now, come *on,* Bob, what do you want from me?

BRATENAHL

An in to meet Susan Calvin.

Bernice shoves away from him. Because they are weightless and every action has an equal and opposite reaction, he sails across the tank and brings up short against the soft inner surface. He gives a squeal.

BERNICE

What a vermicious slug you are.

He swims back to her, pushing off from the wall.

BRATENAHL

Hold it a minute . . . listen to me . . .

BERNICE

(furious)

I can't believe you'd try to use me like that! It is absolutely loathsome that you remembered an idle remark I made two years ago and just *waited* to spring it on me.

BRATENAHL

I remember *everything,* dammit! I have an eidetic memory; is it my fault?

BERNICE

My *God,* what a shit! Listen, Bratenahl, you wretch, I saw Susan Calvin *once,* just once in my whole life, when my father went to Brazil, Old Earth and operated on her. She won't even remember who I *am*!

BRATENAHL,

She'll remember. She remembers everything.

BERNICE

How the hell do *you* know?

He is quiet. They float there close together. She looks at his face. There is something reflective and troubling in his expression. It softens her anger.

BRATENAHL

(quietly)

I met her. At Byerley's funeral.

She studies him.

BERNICE

My ego's bruised, but you'd better tell me about this.

CAMERA PULLS BACK as they roll slowly in the tank and we

**DISSOLVE THRU MIST TO:**

**19 INT. MAGNUM HOTEL ROOM — NIGHT**

Bratenahl sits in a formfit chair that seems to take his shape. He speaks into the wrist mechanism.

BRATENAHL

This is for Rowe, *Cosmos* Magazine.

(beat)

I've got someone who once met Susan Calvin, who might be able to get me an audience with her. But it'll take some time, and I'm going to teleport back to Old Earth in the morning to see if I can get to her on my own.

He punches some heat-sensitive plates in the table beside the chair, a slot opens and a drink in an ultramodern glass rises. He picks it up, the slot closes, and he sips.

BRATENAHL

Okay, run that tape for me now. Put it up on the big screen.

He turns in the chair and CAMERA SHOOTS PAST HIM to a large section of wall that suddenly rolls back to reveal a screen. The room dims. Light from the screen washes his features. A readout line in green appears:

STANDBY: TRANSMISSION OF DATA

CAMERA IN ON SCREEN as the line wipes and an ANNOUNCER'S VOICE speaks.

ANNOUNCER

Alfred Lanning, 1952 to 2035. First Director of U.S. Robot Corporation, renamed U.S. Robots and Mechanical Men. This is Volume 15 of the archive memoirs.

The screen flickers and we see a very old man, lying in a bed, speaking to the CAMERA. It is ALFRED LANNING. He is wasted, clearly not long for life, but furiously intent in saying everything he has to say before he dies.

LANNING

The first time I saw Susan Calvin, she was six years old. Her father was my second assistant manager for development. His first wife had died in childbirth, and he had remarried. We became fairly close, but I didn't meet the child till 2000, when Edward Winslow Calvin pulled one of our first nonvocal robots off the line to serve as a nursemaid for his daughter.

The VOICE of LANNING slowly goes to ECHO CHAMBER and CAMERA MOVES IN steadily on the flickering screen image, until it becomes a random series of phosphor-dots, multicolored. The VOICE CONTINUES as CAMERA goes into the flickering dots.

**CAMERA BACK:**

## 20 CAMERA OUT TO FULL SHOT — CALVIN HOME — DAY

A futuristic living room. EDWARD CALVIN paces around, clearly disturbed. He is a slight man with a kind face and a mustache. Short, but well-built. He resembles, perhaps, Brian Donlevy. Solid warm good looks.

As he paces, his wife BELINDA CALVIN works with a small robot mechanical, a robomek. It is scurrying around the floor, up the walls, cleaning, purring softly. She sits in a swivel chair of modern design directing it by voice command. She is clearly pissed off at Edward Calvin.

EDWARD

You've got to stop acting like the Wicked Witch of the West, Belinda! Susan is getting more withdrawn each day.

BELINDA

(to the robomek)

You missed a spot in the corner. Go back and do it again.

The robomek scurries over, dips its vacuum snout into the corner and, with its rear section waggling, purrs up the dust. It looks like a cross between a child being told to stand in a corner and a puppy snuffling after a bone.

EDWARD

Where is it written in stone that a stepmother has to hate her husband's child?

(beat)

Robbie loves Susan. And more important, *she* loves *him*.

(beat)

Accept it, Belinda; and stop this rancor.

BELINDA

(to robomek)

Get the picture window.

The robomek scurries up the wall, extrudes a long segmented arm with a squeegee on the end and begins swabbing the big window of the living room. Through the window we can see spacious front yard, old maple tree, and under the tree, a little girl. Standing with her face to the tree, hiding her eyes. There are large clumps of bushes everywhere.

EDWARD

I'm *talking* to you! Can't you stop working that robomek and answer me?

BELINDA

(to robomek)

You're smearing. Be more careful.

CAMERA MOVES SLOWLY TOWARD WINDOW as Edward and Belinda are phased out of FRAME but we HEAR their conversation even as the action with them slips from the side and we BEGIN TO FOCUS THRU WINDOW on the little girl, and we DIMLY HEAR UNDER the SOUND of her counting.

SUSAN

(very faintly, like a subliminal melody)

Sixty-six, sixty-seven, sixty-eight . . .

She continues *seriatum.* Edward goes to Belinda and kneels before her.

EDWARD

Honey . . . *please*! I'm trying to hold it together, and you're making it tougher for me . . .

She looks at him, and begins to cry. He takes her in his arms.

BELINDA

They look at me when I go shopping; they say things under their breath. They're afraid, and *I'm* afraid . . . I don't hate Susan . . . I'm just *afraid*!

EDWARD

There's nothing to be afraid of. Robbie has a positronic brain, he *can't* defy the Three Laws . . . they'll understand that one day . . . they *must*.

BELINDA

Please, Edward, please send it back to the company.

EDWARD

(bitterly)

It's that damned Church of the Moral Flesh! Those damned crazies!

BELINDA

They're not crazy, they're afraid of robots . . . Reverend Soldash said . . .

EDWARD

(vehemently)

Be *damned* to what Soldash said, that hysterical fundamentalist! He ought to be running the Scopes Monkey Trial!

CAMERA THRU WINDOW with VOICE OF SUSAN rising and VOICES of Edward and Belinda fading. CAMERA TOWARD SUSAN.

## 21 TRUCKING SHOT — SUSAN CALVIN — REVERSE DIRECTION OF SCENE 20 — EXTERIOR — DAY

CAMERA COMING IN on SUSAN CALVIN, six years old, small even for her age, but with a child's voice that has a ring of strength in it. As CAMERA IN, if we strain very hard, we can see, past Susan leaning against the tree with her hand over her eyes, the elegant and futuristic Calvin home sitting on a short rise across a spacious lawn, heavy stands of bushes all around. And through the enormous bubble window, two vague figures holding each other in the living room.

SUSAN

Ninety-eight, ninety-nine . . .
*one hundred*! Ready or not, here I come!

SUSAN CALVIN AGE 6

She turns away from the tree and looks DIRECTLY INTO CAMERA as we TRUCK IN AND STOP at CLOSEUP. Six-year-old lovely, but with the sharp eyes of a ferret. Susan Calvin, as a child; and we see the shadow of the woman-to-be. She looks around, seeking the one hiding, but nothing is in sight. She puts her fists on her hips with that special little-girl affrontedness.

SUSAN (CONT'D.)

(loud)

No fair! I told you *lotta* times, it's no fair goin' in the house!

She runs off as CAMERA REMAINS IN FIXED POSITION. She runs here, she runs there, runs toward the house, back into MEDIUM CLOSEUP. As she runs off to the left, we see movement from the middle of a huge clump of trees and bushes to the right. CAMERA COMES IN on the bushes just as ROBBIE emerges.

As he stalks out of the concealment of the bushes, we see why it was that Susan couldn't find him. He is close to seven feet tall, but his legs have the capacity to telescope themselves. He has extended himself to a height of ten or twelve feet, so the bulk of his body was hidden up high in the foliage of a small tree, while his legs were concealed behind the boles of the trees there in the thicket. Now as he emerges, at the greater height, he begins to retract his legs in their tubular sections, and as he comes across the lawn he gets shorter, till he is his "normal" height of almost seven feet.

## 22 ANOTHER ANGLE — MED. LONG — INCLUDING ROBBIE & SUSAN

As the robot comes on fast across the distance between the bushes and the counting tree. He moves with an awkward and faintly stiff—yet curiously graceful—lope.

## 23 CU — SUSAN

as she hears something. She whirls and her eyes widen.

SUSAN
(shrieking)
Wait, Robbie! No fair! You promised you wouldn't run till I found you!

## 24 SAME AS 22

As she rushes toward the robot. He is moving very fast, but then, within ten feet of the goal tree his pace slows to the merest step and Susan, with one last burst of speed, lurches past him to slap the tree. She turns, laughing.

SUSAN
*Ha* ha, *ha* ha: Robbie can't ru-un Robbie can't ru-un! I can beat him any day!

The robot cannot speak, but it pantomimes shame and chagrin, and begins edging away as Susan comes toward him, till they are in a chase, with the little girl running in circles trying to catch the huge metal man. She tries to grab him, but he manages to stay out of her reach till suddenly, in one swift movement, he spins on her, lifts her high over his metal head, and swings her around. She squeals with utter delight.

SUSAN (CONT'D.)

Gimme a ride! Robbie, gimme a good ride!

The robot swings her to his shoulders and, holding her very securely, begins loping up the slope toward the Calvin home as CAMERA GOES WITH. Susan begins playing space pirates. She aims her finger as if it were a gun, and makes firing sounds.

SUSAN (CONT'D.)

I'm a space pilot! There's the space pirates, Robbie . . . over there . . . ack-ack-ack!

As they whirl past the house, the front door irises open and Belinda stands there, misery and horror on her face. Edward Calvin is behind her, looking strained and troubled.

BELINDA

Susan!

The robot and the child whirl past and Belinda takes a step outside. She calls more frantically.

BELINDA (CONT'D.)

Susan! Susan! Robbie, *stop!* Come here at once, put her down!

The robot glides to a halt, turns and comes to the adults. He reaches up, swings the child down and stands silently waiting.

BELINDA (CONT'D.)

Why don't you come when I call?

SUSAN
(petulant)
Awwww! We were playin' space pirates.

BELINDA
(to Robbie)
You may go, Robbie.
(beat)
Susan doesn't need you now.
(beat)
And don't come back till I call you.

SUSAN
(loudly)
Awww, *please!* Let Robbie stay. He won't make a sound, he won't even move, will you, Robbie?

The robot nods his massive head up and down. There is a charming, somewhat winsome manner in the robot's gargantuan movements.

BELINDA
Susan, stop it at once! If you don't obey me you're not going to see Robbie for a week. Now come inside and have your lunch.

Susan looks imploringly at her father, who smiles a sad little smile; then she looks up at Robbie, hugs his long metal leg, and then, with her head down, slouches past into the house. Belinda looks once at the robot with undisguised loathing, then turns and follows Susan.

Edward Calvin looks at Robbie. They stand there a moment.

EDWARD
(chummily, but sadly)
Life isn't easy for a nursemaid, is it, old son? Can you feel pain in that wonderful platinum-iridium sponge you call a brain?

(beat)

Well, you're not alone, Robbie. There are worse things than getting rusty.

He turns and goes into the house. The robot—whose head movements in response to Edward Calvin's words have been mutely responsive—stands there staring at the house like a faithful dog left out in the cold. He stands there, then his head slowly turns and we see, through a bubble window, little Susan Calvin, her nose pressed to the lucite, staring out miserably. They stare at each other longingly, with devotion, as we:

**DISSOLVE TO:**

## 25 INT. CHURCH OF THE MORTAL FLESH — NIGHT

CLOSE ON THE SYMBOL OF THE CHURCH. It is a metal and acrylic sculpture. Ominous yet evocative. A mound of gears and girders and rusted bits of metal as a base, with a muscular human arm emerging from the pile, its length extended toward the heavens, fingers spread, reaching. CAMERA PULLS BACK after a long study of this symbol, as we HEAR OVER the VOICE of Rev. Malachi Soldash:

SOLDASH

(charismatic; messianic)

They *tell* us these creatures cannot do harm. They *tell* us the thundering metal thinks. They *tell* us it obeys three vague commandments. But I tell *you* God made *Man* in his image, not thundering metal!

(beat)

I tell *you* that God never created the opposable thumb and raised Man from all fours to set his hand at the making of metal creatures without souls!

(beat)

"Thou shalt not make unto thee any graven image, or any likeness of any thing that is in heaven above, or that is in the earth beneath." The Lord Thy God gave *that* as the second of His Commandments to Moses atop Mt. Sinai . . . and there's nothing vague *about* it! It says *lay off!* It says don't do it! It says those who *don't* lay off are damned!

As the preceding speech REVERBERATES OVER the CAMERA PULLS BACK from the symbol as FRAME EXPANDS and we see the interior of the Church of the Mortal Flesh. It is an enormous cocoonlike cavern, without sharp angles or corners. Made of spun plastic like the inside of an irregularly-shaped egg, its walls are flesh-pink and the apse arches up into darkness, where the symbol shines against the shadows. CAMERA COMES DOWN through that darkness to show us REVEREND MALACHI SOLDASH apparently suspended in midair on an anti-gravity disc with slim lucite railings to keep him from falling off. He stands there, in midair, delivering his sermon as CAMERA BACK AND DOWN revealing the enormity of the Church. A group of six men and women sits in a semicircle on a high podium to one side of the nave. It is an incredibly dramatic setting. The nave and atrium are filled with the CONGREGATION who see Soldash not only in the flesh, suspended above and in front of them, high up where the altar would usually be in a basilica, but they also see him on individual video screens set into the backs of the pews, one for each parishioner. And Soldash's image is enhanced by closeups, key-shots of emotionally slanted stock footage, and shots of each of the six men and women on the high podium when he mentions them. CAMERA BACK AND BACK to show us this is a gigantic church.

## 26 thru 37 SERIES OF KEYNOTE SHOTS — INDICATED SUBJECTS IN CU

Soldash in CU. Handsome in a craggy way. He is a very contemporaneous figure, yet charismatic in a hellfire and brimstone idiom. Hip, but frightening. Powerful. (The memory conjures up George C. Scott in *The Hanging Tree,* 1958.) His clothing is not fabric, but a multicolored aura of fog and lights that swirl around him, limning his body yet concealing it. Flickers of gold and crimson and cerulean blue that shoot through as though seen under oil.

SOLDASH
(exhorting)
But *you* say to me . . . "These *things,* these unliving constructs, they can clean my house, they can watch my children, they can work in the big factories, so I can take it easy, so I can be a lazy smoothyguts and take the dippership

for a weekend in Bora Bora." And *I* say to *you,* forget God! Forget God's clear injunction! Look at the truth, that metal monsters will take your jobs, take your money, take the food from your children's mouths! Listen to what the Unions say. Here is Sister Madelaine Groth, President of the International Allied Trade Labor Guild . . .

REV SOLDASH

And he points toward the podium with the six men and women sitting in holy splendor. Light seems to flow off his fingertip and bathe one of the women. MADELAINE GROTH stands.

CAMERA GOES WITH THE LIGHT BEAM to CU on GROTH. She is a sturdy-looking woman in her early thirties, rugged jaw, no-nonsense manner. Not masculine, but tough-looking.

GROTH

Brothers and sisters, my statisticians have shown by *irrefutable* numbers that the introduction of robots into the work force will rob 35,000 people a month of their livelihood.

MATCH ON GROTH'S FACE, as seen in one of the video screens in the pews. CAMERA PULLS BACK from the screen to show us Belinda Calvin, wearing a hooded dress that half-obscures her face, sitting in the pew, listening. She is clearly frightened. At the message. And at the knowledge that *she* is one of the people under attack here . . . and she doesn't want to be. She wants to believe in the Church.

As Groth's VOICE is HEARD OVER in both FILTER from the video screen and in actuality there in the basilica, producing a strange reverberatory effect, the SCREEN shows men and women in breadlines, selling apples on street corners, rooting in garbage pails, begging . . . STOCK FOOTAGE of the Depression.

INTERCUT AMONG GROTH SPEAKING, VIDEO IMAGE OF GROTH SPEAKING. STOCK DEPRESSION FOOTAGE, BELINDA CALVIN & SOLDASH as we *begin to accelerate the intercuts . . .*

CU — SOLDASH

SOLDASH

Brother Karl Bunchi, the American Morality Congress . . .

He points; CAMERA GOES WITH the beam of light to illuminate another of the six in the podium setting, KARL BUNCHI, a thin, cadaverous, Ichabod Crane-like man. He is bathed in Soldash's light and stands, speaks:

BUNCHI

The blurring of the sexes . . .
the decay and rot of moral fiber . . .
our young people giving free rein to
lechery, lasciviousness, arrogance
and disrespect . . .

KARL BUNCHI
OF THE "AMERICAN
MORALITY CONGRESS"

Repeat of previous sequence with Groth, this time with Bunchi on the screen, Belinda watching, getting more distraught, more horrified. Stock footage of kids having wild parties, nude bathing, wild abandon, etc.

INTERCUT AMONG BUNCHI SPEAKING, VIDEO IMAGE OF BUNCHI SPEAKING, STOCK LECHERY FOOTAGE, BELINDA, GROTH, SOLDASH as the *intercuts accelerate faster and faster* . . .

CU — SOLDASH

SOLDASH

General Lester Joe McCaffrey of the Fighting 65th . . .

He points. Light beam. CAMERA WITH. Huge, rugged, bearded man in his fifties, wearing full-dress uniform, stands, begins exhorting.

McCAFFREY

War among metal men . . . unnatural slaughter . . . merciless armies of robots . . . rape and pillage . . . the new apocalypse . . . scorched earth . . .

Repeat of previous sequences with Groth and Bunchi, this time with McCAFFREY on the screen, Belinda watching, almost in tears, trembling, trying to keep herself concealed. Stock footage of explosions, buildings crumbling, robot soldiers moving in ranks, muzzles of flame rifles exploding, the classic shot of the crying child sitting in rubble, etc.

INTERCUT AMONG McCAFFREY SPEAKING, McCAFFREY ON SCREEN, GROTH SPEAKING, EXHORTING, BUNCHI DECLAIMING, WAR FOOTAGE, BELINDA WILD-EYED & SOLDASH, SOLDASH, SOLDASH as the *intercuts whirl faster and faster and faster . . .*

INTERCUT CU SOLDASH POINTING, LIGHT STREAMING.

INTERCUT ANOTHER OF SIX STANDING, ARMS RAISED.

INTERCUT THE SYMBOL BLAZING IN DARKNESS.

INTERCUT BELINDA ALMOST HYSTERICAL NOW.

INTERCUT BUNCHI. INTERCUT LANNING AS DEVIL.

INTERCUT GROTH. INTERCUT EDWARD CALVIN AS DEVIL.

INTERCUT CONGREGATION GOING WILD. INTERCUT BELINDA AGOG.

**SMASH-CUT TO:**

**38 INT. CALVIN BEDROOM — NIGHT**

Edward Calvin sitting up in bed, wearing pajamas. Belinda rushing about fully clothed, as we saw her in the basilica, but now the hood has been thrown back, as if she has just come in from outdoors.

BELINDA

(hysterical)

I don't care! I can't stand it anymore! I'm not going to be a guinea pig for U.S. Robots! That soulless *thing* has to go!

EDWARD

(stunned)

Belinda!

BELINDA

I want it out, today, this morning; or I'm filing for dissolution of this marriage! Do you understand me?

He flings back the covers, gets out of bed barefoot. He goes to her.

EDWARD

Belinda, *stop this!* Those crazy fanatics have you terrified. It's all lies . . . the positronic brain of the robots *can't* . . .

BELINDA

(flailing, screams)

No! It's against God and Man!

EDWARD

Stop this! Stop it, you'll wake Susan . . .

He tries to grab her, to quiet her, but suddenly she is wild with hysteria, flailing at him, spiraling higher and higher into a self-induced madness. They struggle, she has uncommon strength, slaps him, again and again, he tries to hold her, they fall, roll on the floor, her voice rises, inarticulate: CAMERA IN ON THEM IN CU.

Edward manages to pin her, and now, helpless, she dissolves in wretched tears, terrified, chagrined, a wreck. He holds her, there on the floor, begins rocking her gently.

EDWARD (CONT'D.)
(soothing)
Okay. Okay. It's okay, honey. Shhh. Take it easy. Don't cry, don't cry, shhhh, Robbie goes back today . . . I'll talk to Alfred Lanning . . . it'll be all right . . .

CAMERA PULLS BACK AND UP as SCENE SHOT THRU FILTER to produce gradually more misty look and CAMERA KEEPS GOING UP AND UP AND BACK looking down on them smaller and smaller there on the floor, rocking back and forth, more and more pitiful as the distance increases.

**DISSOLVE TO:**

## 39 INT. CALVIN LIVING ROOM — EVENING

as we HEAR VOICE OF SUSAN OVER:

SUSAN (V.O.)
Robbie? Robbie? C'mon, where you hidin'? Don't be mean, Robbie!

Through an archway we can see Belinda setting a formal dinner in the dining room. The huge wall-screen video is on and a NEWSCASTER is speaking as we see newsreel footage of a mob destroying a shop that sells robot home implements. Through this scene we HEAR the NEWSCAST UNDER.

NEWSCASTER
Another wave of vandalism against U.S. Robots Corporation shops broke out in Detroit today as mobs swept over three retail outlets, destroying property valued at close to one million dollars . . .

Susan comes into scene, looking in closets that open as she approaches them and claps her hands. She is looking for Robbie. She seems terribly upset that she cannot find her playmate.

SUSAN
Robbie? I'm gonna *spank* you if you don't come out right *now*!

Edward Calvin comes in, sees her and his face tightens.

EDWARD

Honey, come here a minute.

She comes to him. He sits down in a formfit chair and pulls her onto his lap. In b.g. we see Belinda lighting candles on the table, setting up crystal goblets, all the business of a formal dinner, but playing strictly in b.g. as she keeps an eye on her husband talking to the child.

## 40 TWO-SHOT— SUSAN & EDWARD CALVIN

She sits on his lap, looking worried. Calvin is torn by emotions.

SUSAN

Daddy, where's Robbie?

EDWARD

Robbie went away, honey.

SUSAN

Went away where?

EDWARD

He . . . he just walked away.

SUSAN

(innocent)

He did that?

EDWARD

Sometimes Robbies do that, baby.

SUSAN

(certain)

He wouldn't do that.

Calvin hugs her, presses her close to him.

SUSAN (CONT'D.)

I know he wouldn't. He din't say a thing 'bout it. He'd've *told* me, Daddy.

EDWARD

I bought you a present, baby.

SUSAN

Maybe he's sick, huh? Maybe he's feelin' bad somewhere, Daddy.

(brighter)

We gotta *fine* him, Daddy! We gotta go look for Robbie, he must be *some*where, feelin' bad.

She starts to struggle off his lap. Calvin holds her.

EDWARD

(intensely)

*Listen* to me, Susan! Now Robbie is gone, do you hear? He's gone off to work somewhere else, and I brought you a present, a new friend.

In the b.g. Belinda busies, and the newscast of the riot plays on. Susan gets tearful.

SUSAN

(crankily)

*No!* He wouldn't do that; he's my friend. *She* made him go 'way!

Belinda stiffens in b.g. Susan doesn't look at her, but tosses her head. Calvin gets tougher.

EDWARD

Stop it, Susan! Robbie is just a robot, just a tool, he's no more important than Mommy's robomek or the dish-washer . . .

SUSAN
(incensed)
No! He's a *person* like you 'n me!

Belinda suddenly comes in from the dining room, a tureen of something steaming in her hands. Her face is filled with horror.

BELINDA
Shut up! Don't ever say that. Don't let me *ever* hear you say that again, don't ever *say* that.

EDWARD
Belinda! For God's sake!

BELINDA
(distraught, catches herself, then murmurs)
Yes . . . for God's sake . . .

She turns and goes back into the dining room. Susan is now on the verge of hysterics herself.

SUSAN
(whispers)
Daddy, *please* . . . I want Robbie.

EDWARD
He's gone, Susan, and that's that. He's not coming back. Not now, not ever.

Susan starts to cry.

EDWARD (CONT'D.)
Look: a *new* friend . . .

He claps his hands and the front vestibule entrance irises, and in bounds a fuzzy little puppy, cute as a bug. It frolics around, leaping up on Susan. She starts to cry harder, and when the puppy pays more attention to her she screams.

## 41 REVERSE ANGLE — FROM DINING ROOM — WITH BELINDA

as she stops puttering with the now completely-set formal dinner table. She stumps in, grabs Susan off Calvin's lap, and swings her up.

BELINDA
That will do! You're going to your room.

EDWARD
Belinda! Let her get to know the dog at least!

BELINDA
Lanning and his wife will be here in a minute; I'm not having this evening ruined by a spoiled child!

She carries Susan, still howling, into another room and we see them rising to the second floor on an inclined slope that must be a conveyor belt for people. CAMERA STAYS WITH EDWARD CALVIN. He looks destroyed.

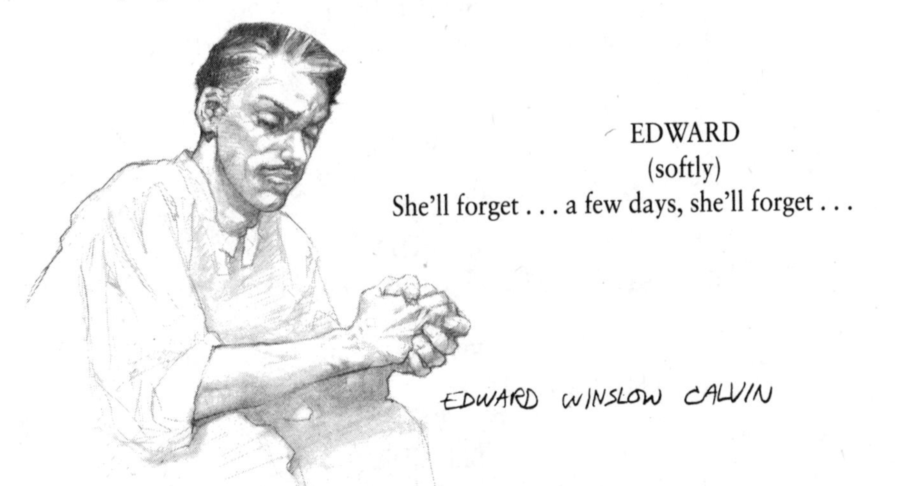


EDWARD
(softly)
She'll forget . . . a few days, she'll forget . . .

He is talking to the prancing puppy leaping at his knees. Silence in the living room, except for the ongoing newscast with newsreel footage of the riots, the start of the Robot Pogroms.

NEWSCASTER
Driven by hatred and fear of loss of jobs, this mob in Macon, Georgia put the torch to . . .

EDWARD
(very softly)
In the name of God, puppy, in the name of God . . .

**DISSOLVE THRU TO:**

## 42 SAME AS 21 — EXT. CALVIN HOME

Susan sits under the tree, plucking at the grass idly. She looks forlorn and miserable. The puppy capers nearby, unnoticed.

**DISSOLVE TO:**

## 43 INT. CALVIN HOME — PAST EDWARD & BELINDA

SHOT THROUGH FRONT WINDOW to Scene 42 setup of Susan under the tree. They stand with their backs to CAMERA, talking.

BELINDA
We could take the dippership to Jamaica; she'd love Disney Island.

EDWARD
Please.

BELINDA
I've tried everything; you've got to stop blaming me.

EDWARD
I don't blame you.

BELINDA
This thing can destroy us, Edward.

EDWARD
One more triumph for the Reverend Soldash.

BELINDA
Leave the Church out of this. It's the will of the people.

EDWARD

I suppose that was the justification for the Spanish Inquisition, too.

BELINDA

Is it bad at the company . . . ?

EDWARD

It's bad. Unless Robertson's pull in Congress works, unless they pass the bill, the Corporation may go under.

BELINDA

No one wants them, they're afraid of them . . .

EDWARD

(wearily)

I've heard all this, Belinda. I have to put up with it all day, spare me the party line when I'm at home.

Through the window we see Susan rise and walk desultorily across the grass toward the house. The puppy follows.

BELINDA

Is Lanning still angry with you?

EDWARD

He's not delighted. Returning Robbie was just another slap in the face. Everyone over there is jumpy.

BELINDA

What are you going to do?

EDWARD

Maybe now's a good time to go off on my own.

BELINDA

(nervously)

Stay with the Corporation. We need the security.

He turns to her, looks at her for the first time.

EDWARD
(ironically)
My God, dearest heart, you are an absolute *masterpiece* of contradictions. Stay with the Godless Corporation, they extend the hand with the paycheck.

BELINDA
When this is all over, U.S. Robot can convert to other products, good things that people need.

EDWARD
Let me guess: that's out of the mouth of labor messiah Madelaine Groth.
(beat)
What do you suggest U.S.R. produce? Paint-by-the-numbers portraits of Reverend Malachi Soldash? Cunning replicas of the Church symbol?

BELINDA
Here she comes.

EDWARD
(wearily)
Right. Here she comes, there we go.

**DISSOLVE THRU TO:**

## 44 INT. CALVIN LIVING ROOM

On Susan, sitting gloomily, not really watching a cartoon show on the wall-sized video screen.

**DISSOLVE TO:**

## 45 INT. AIRCAR — DAY

Susan in the back seat, looking out the window without interest. In the front seat Calvin and Belinda sit silently, as the automatic controls of the car blip this color and that color on the computer panel, projecting their course down the speedway. The countryside rushes past very fast. There is only the SOUND of air rushing past, otherwise it is silent. Maintain this silence for several beats, then:

BELINDA

I hope this works.

EDWARD

If you have a better suggestion . . .

BELINDA

I don't want to fight. I merely said I hope it works.

EDWARD

If she can stop thinking of him as a person it may bring her out of it.

BELINDA

I don't like going there.

EDWARD

You can always go to the Church and ask for expungement later.

She gives him a sharp, sudden look of revilement.

## 46 LONG SHOT — MOVING THROUGH

as the aircar speeds past us on the metal ribbon of road, without wheels. supported on a cushion of air, almost silently save for the passage of wind. It slips past and vanishes down the road.

**CUT TO:**

## 47 EXT. U.S. ROBOTS BUILDING — ESTABLISHING

Huge and modernistic. A large ultra-serif sign indicates this is the U.S. ROBOT CORPORATION HIGHLAND PARK DIVISION. The aircar pulls into the parking lot. The three riders emerge and walk toward the building.

## 48 INT. ASSEMBLY AREA — DAY

A smooth, sleek, anodized assembly line down there, stretching off into infinity. Huge machines, bubbling vats, computer consoles, and working on the line not humans, but robots. We are up on a walkway high above the assemblage. Calvin, Belinda and a GUIDE, a young woman in her twenties. Susan walks with them, not really paying any attention.

BELINDA
(to Susan)
You see, Susan, this is where they build the things.

EDWARD
Robots. Positronic robots, not things.

BELINDA
Whatever. Do you see, Susan?

The child doesn't respond.

GUIDE
This is the torso assemblage unit. The positronic brains are imprinted in subsections under this area and then come up through a feeder system for insertion . . .
(she looks embarrassed)
You know all this, Mr. Calvin. I feel like a fool conducting you the way I would some foreign businessman.

He smiles tightly. He is obviously nervous. He reassures her.

EDWARD
This is the first time for my wife and Susan. Don't worry about it.

BELINDA
(interested, despite herself)
Everything is moving so *fast.*

Overhead conveyors with assembled robot bodies zip along very speedily. The robots work at a blurred pace. (This is important!)

GUIDE

These drone robots are model 41s. Their reflexes are very good and, of course, this is fairly routine work.

EDWARD

It would take three hundred men and women a week to do what this cadre of robots does in eight hours.

They walk along the catwalk. There is a staircase that leads down onto the floor below. They pass it. Now they are right above a group of robots laser-welding torso shells together as the assembled bodies keep zipping past behind them.

BELINDA

There don't seem to be any safety precautions.

GUIDE

(proudly)

Few are needed. The drones are aware of the conveyor and stay out of the line of passage.

BELINDA

But what about human beings?

EDWARD

What humans?

GUIDE

This is fully automated. There are no people required.

Belinda's mouth tightens. It is as if she is hearing Labor leader Groth saying the robots will take human jobs. But we only see the tenseness for a moment, as Susan suddenly shrieks:

SUSAN

*Robbie!*

CAMERA WHIPS TO SUSAN and her face, suddenly lit with life and utter devotion. It is the happiest we've seen her in some time. CAMERA WHIPS

AROUND and ZOOMS DOWN to the floor of the assembly unit. All of the robots look alike but only one's head suddenly jerks up, looks around, and then fastens on the little girl. It is Robbie! We can tell!

### 49 CAMERA WITH SUSAN — ARRIFLEX

She is screaming Robbie's name over and over with undisguised joy. Suddenly she breaks away and rushes for the stairway down; to the assemblage floor.

EDWARD

Susan! No!

The child rushes down the stairs, almost falling, grabbing the rail, dashing down, jumping the last three steps to land on the floor. The conveyor keeps whipping past overhead, the incredibly heavy robot bodies hanging like slaughtered beef from the hooks. She starts running toward Robbie.

### 50 EXT. CU — ROBBIE

HOLDING his photoreflector eyes large. There is a light in them as he looks INTO CAMERA.

### 51 REVERSE ANGLE — PAST ROBBIE

as Susan dashes toward him.

### 52 SAME AS 50

On the eyes. Moving in to them in EXTREMELY TIGHT CU.

### 53 SPECIAL EFFECTS SHOT — THE SCENE

THROUGH ROBBIE'S EYES. Like the multifaceted eyes of a bee, we see a hundred octagonal pictures of Susan running toward CAMERA. The view shifts, and we see the conveyor belt of bodies very near the child . . . she is weaving right into the path. We HEAR the SOUND of relays clicking, though Robbie has no relays, only printed paths in the positronic brain.

### 54 WITH SUSAN

as she rushes with arms open at Robbie. And behind and above her, here comes one of the many-ton bodies of an assembled robot barreling down on her, clearly on a path to smash her. Very fast.

In an instant Robbie loses all his jerky movements and throws himself forward. In a few strides of his elongated, telescoping legs, he is on her. In one move he sweeps her up in his arms, holds her out of the way, and the conveyor carries the hurtling body directly into him as Robbie half-turns, braces himself, and gets smashed hard on the shoulder. One of his arms is ripped off as the torso goes whipping by. He is thrown off his feet, but even in falling holds the child out of danger. He skids to a halt on the floor, Susan still upheld and stunned but unhurt.

### 55 thru 59 SERIES OF INTERCUTS — REACTION SHOTS

EDWARD CALVIN screams Susan's name, breaks for the stairs.

BELINDA CALVIN struck dumb with horror, frozen in place.

ALFRED LANNING—a much younger version of the aged, dying man we saw in the memoir cassette Scene 19—as he comes through the portal at the end of the walkway and sees the whole thing: thunderstruck and shaken.

SUSAN stunned but hardly frightened, still with that awesome look of love at having found Robbie.

THROUGH ROBBIE'S EYES in that bee-faceted multivision of octagonal segmentation . . . looking across laterally from his supine position, at the child he loves . . . safe.

### 60 FULL SHOT — THE SCENE

as Lanning shouts into his wrist-communicator.

LANNING

Control! Shut down the torso assembly unit. Now! Right now! This is Alfred Lanning. I take full responsibility.

DR. ALFRED LANNING

And Edward Calvin practically swims down the stairs, the female Guide right behind him. Belinda still frozen on the walkway above them. The robots have stopped work. The conveyor slams to a halt, the torsos swaying like alien artifacts on a clothesline. CAMERA DOWN as Edward slides to his knees to grasp Susan. Robbie looks up to see it is safe to let go of the child. He nods in almost an old-man way as he sees it's Susan father. Susan isn't even ruffled. She grabs Calvin around the neck with joy, laughing and squealing.

SUSAN

Daddy! Daddy, it's Robbie! See?

EDWARD

(almost in tears)

Yes, honey . . . yes, yes, I *see*!

Then he looks up at the walkway, at Belinda. There are tears in his eyes and a new defiance.

EDWARD (CONT'D.)

*I* see! Do *you* see? Do you?

She nods slowly. She cannot argue now. And she stares down at the trio as Alfred Lanning comes up to her.

## 61 REVERSE PAST CALVIN — RISING BOOM SHOT

As CAMERA COMES IN on Lanning, we see him speaking to Belinda but HEAR his VOICE OVER, divorced from his image.

LANNING (V.O.)
(resonating echo)
That was the first time I ever saw Susan Calvin. I learned what had happened later, of course. He knew that robot had been put back on the line. But I never authorized that guided tour. The child might have been killed. It was just the kind of attachment between one of our units and a human that made for such public relations difficulties . . . and we were having serious problems in that area. It was the year 2000, the turn of the century . . . and the time of the Robot Pogroms.

CAMERA IN on Lanning's face as we

**SUPERIMPOSE PROCESS SHOT:**

## 62 SAME AS 19 — LANNING ON ARCHIVE CASSETTE

That flickering screen image of the dying Lanning, lying on his deathbed, relating his memoirs. TRIPLE EXPOSURE SUPERIMPOSITION of the multicolored phosphor-dot transmission. HOLD BOTH SHOTS for several beats as speech preceding OVER, then FADE 61 SLOWLY going to transmission SHOT FULL as this is said by Lanning:

LANNING (V.O.)
Matters with Calvin were strained, in any case. The unit she called Robbie was repaired. It didn't much matter. I think it was lost during one of the riots . . .

The phosphor-dot transmission congeals into BLACK & WHITE NEWSREEL FOOTAGE . . .

**SOFT-EDGE WIPE TO:**

## 63 NEWSREEL FOOTAGE — CITY STREET — DAY

A crowd of men and women has a robot that looks like Robbie backed against a brick wall. It has its hands up to protect itself, but one woman hurls a brick that hits the robot high on the chest, smearing its anodized surface. OVER we HEAR the VOICE of LANNING in DISTORTED ECHO:

LANNING (OVER)
(distorted)
"A robot may not injure a human being, or, through inaction, allow a human being to come to harm . . . A robot must protect its own existence as long as such protection does not conflict with the First or Second Laws . . ."

The Robbie robot tries to break out of the circle, but we now realize it has been trapped in an alley filled with refuse, with high walls. It tries to raise itself on its telescoping legs to get out of trouble, but a man with a laser welding torch rushes in and burns one of the joints in a leg. The robot is trapped at its usual height. A woman throws gasoline on it. The laser welder hits the gas with a burst of light and heat. The gas catches. The robot is washed by flame at its lowest level. In rushes a man with a ball-bat. He swings hard—he's a *big* man—swings like a man at a carnival trying to hit the gong on the strength tester. Another man with a huge spike-driving sledgehammer swings and crushes the chest cavity. A man with a pickax buries it in Robbie's thoracic region. Then the arms are broken . . . the head shattered . . . the robot goes down and the mob moves in through the flames to finish the job as we

**SUPERIMPOSE PROCESS SHOT:**

**64 SAME AS 19/62 — LANNING ON CASSETTE**

SPECIAL EFFECT of transmission phosphor-dot that HOLDS for several beats as the b & w newsreel footage of Robbie's destruction fades. The transmission effect fades and we are looking at old Alfred Lanning, lying on his deathbed, speaking to CAMERA.

LANNING
Old man Robertson, the founder, pulled every string he had in Congress. National Guard was called out. Saved the Corporation at the final hour. But they passed the Robot Restriction Laws; it was the only way to placate the Church and the Unions. No robots on Earth.

He begins to cough weakly. A white-sleeved arm reaches in to touch his shoulder and we HEAR the VOICE of a DOCTOR:

DOCTOR (O S.)
Mr. Lanning . . . that's enough for now . . .

LANNING
(cantankerously)
Loose ends! There are loose ends! I have to say this . . . get away from me with that stuff. . .

The hand vanishes. Lanning pulls himself together.

LANNING (CONT'D.)
What was I . . . oh, yes . . .
(beat)
Edward Winslow Calvin died four years later. A young man, really. Just forty. Always felt bad about that: can't recall just why, but I never was on very good terms with him after that business with Susan and her nursemaid.
(beat)
I didn't see Susan Calvin again till she was twenty-one. That was in 2015, when she came to work for me at U.S. Robots. Always felt a lot of loyalty from her . . . always thought she wanted to make good there because her father had failed.
(beat)
Thank God we had space travel. The Restriction Laws didn't stop us from using the units out there . . . saved the Corporation . . .

He begins coughing again. There is a flicker of movement on the tape, as if medical personnel were hurrying to take corrective steps, and then the screen goes to BLACK and a green readout line appears:

**END TRANSMISSION**

The screen is dark There is a click as it shuts itself off. CAMERA BACK OUT OF SCREEN.

## 65 ANOTHER ANGLE — FEATURING BRATENAHL — NIGHT

He still sits in the Magnum Hotel room where we left him in Scene 19. Still in the formfit chair, now staring at the darkened screen. It is dark in the room, we can barely see him. He stands. Walks to the huge bubble window in the room and passes his hand in front of the surface. It has been opaque. Now it clears and we SHOOT PAST HIM to a view of Sigma Draconis 5 at night. An alien view with three moons hanging in the night sky. He stands silently, staring out at the alien night. We HEAR a warm, masculine VOICE speak in the silence of the room. It seems to come from everywhere.

VOICE OF ROOM

Mr. Bratenahl? Excuse me, sir.

BRATENAHL

(distantly)

Yes?

VOICE OF ROOM

Just confirming the schedule of your teleportation transmission to Old Earth tomorrow, sir.

(beat)

Control would appreciate your being on the ready-line by 4100 hours.

BRATENAHL

No problem.

VOICE OF ROOM

That will be a relay transmission—three stages, sir. Via Rasket Beta 9, Mars Central, and then in to the Novo Brasilia booth on Old Earth.

BRATENAHL

I'd like to be left alone, please.

There is a moment's pause as the Room gauges the emotion in his voice.

VOICE OF ROOM
(soothing)
I perceive a touch of melancholy in your voice, sir. Is there anything the Magnum Hotel can do to make your night a little easier?

He turns to the Room. We see his face. It is strained.

BRATENAHL
Look, Room: it ain't melancholy, it's contemplation, reflective. I'm not a potential suicide. So stop hanging around like a doting parent. Go away.

VOICE OF ROOM
No offense intended, sir.

BRATENAHL
None taken. Go away.

VOICE OF ROOM
I am, after all, sir, just a congeries of mnemonic (*pronounced nee*-mon-*ic*) circuits. Occasionally I miss a nuance in the human voice—

BRATENAHL
(yells)
By damn, if you don't get the hell out of here—!

There is an audible sighing sound as the Room leaves him alone. Bratenahl turns back to the window; we HOLD on his back, as he stares out at the alien night.

BRATENAHL (CONT'D.)
(to the night)
I know you value your privacy, Dr. Susan Calvin; so do I.
(beat)

But I'm coming, anyhow.

(beat)

I need to know.

(beat)

I . . . just . . . need . . . to . . . know.

CAMERA HOLDS him staring into the distance as the three moons of Sigma Draconis 5 hurtle through the amethyst sky.

**SLOW DISSOLVE TO:**

### 66 NOVO BRASILIA TELEPORT RECEPTION AREA — DAY

ON THE BOOTH set in the center of a beautiful plaza, with the inlaid tile sidewalks the Brazilians favor. Bright sunlight, and the booth—as described in Scene 14—a dark and alien presence. We see the telltale scintillance deep in its interior that indicates someone's atoms are being hurled in a tracerlike line at us. And then in PROCESS we see Robert Bratenahl coalesce. And he's there. He steps out of the booth a little disoriented. He has, after all, been shot halfway across the galaxy.

### 67 LONG SHOT — THE PLAZA

Novo Brasilia, in all its splendor. Spread out, with the jungle in the near distance. The Xingú River, mightier than the Hudson and twice as long, snakes among the impenetrable stands of virgin timber, so clotted thick it seems to be a carpet. And down there, the plaza, the booth, and Robert Bratenahl. Tiny. Not as tiny as the mote that is Old Earth in the enormity of the cosmos, but tiny, very tiny for all that. We see a figure striding across the plaza toward Bratenahl. CAMERA COMES DOWN. We see them shake hands, then walk off together.

**DISSOLVE TO:**

### 68 ON THE XINGÚ RIVER — DAY

as a dugout canoe being paddled by two naked Indians passes through. Bratenahl sits high in the center of the canoe. Now he is dressed in safari gear. As the canoe passes us, we can see that the natives have ear-jacks insert-

ed, with cords running to small radios hung around their naked necks. And we HEAR very faintly the strains of a kind of futuristic rock music. The canoe goes through.

**DISSOLVE TO:**

## 69 ON THE FERRY ON THE RIO DAS MORTES

The entrance to the Mato Grosso jungle north from Xavantina. Bratenahl standing beside a stake-bed truck, staring across at the impenetrable wall of the jungle. Black cuckoo, kingfishers (called *martim pescador*), martins . . . all sit on the cable wire pulling the flat ferry across. On the far shore an emu, an ostrichlike bird, hustles away.

**DISSOLVE TO:**

## 70 DEEP JUNGLE

as Bratenahl and a half-breed driving the stake-bed truck bounce down a barely-traversable dirt road. Jungle on all sides. They climb a steep hill, overlooking a valley deep in the heart of the unexplored terrain. The truck stops. CAMERA HAS GONE WITH. Bratenahl and the half-breed step out. They go to the edge of the hill, looking down into the valley. The half-breed points. Bratenahl nods. He shakes the man's hand, and steps over the edge, toward the valley, on a barely-discernible path. He moves with skill. He doesn't look like a novice at this.

## 71 ON THE RIDGE

SHOOTING PAST BRATENAHL. CLOSE as he sweeps the area below. Heavy jungle, with the river serpentine through it. But down there, right in the middle, is something odd. As we stare past him we see a die-straight route has been clawed out of the wilderness. It is *incredibly* straight, as wide as an eight-lane superhighway. Because that's what it is. And at the terminus, we see a writhing, boiling mass of darkness that literally seems to be *eating* the jungle. The road extends itself a little farther. And we suddenly realize it is an army of deadly ecitons, the voracious midge ants of the central Mato Grosso, capable of devouring to the bare earth itself incalculable miles of living plants.

BRATENAHL
(idly)
Small snack for the *marabunta* . . .

He strikes off over the ridge, heading down toward the naked horror chewing the jungle below. CAMERA FIXED and he walks away from us.

**DISSOLVE TO:**

### 72 EXT. CU — BARROSSO

Uh, Barrosso is an ant. A large, brown-red eciton with a tough and surly demeanor. He is standing on a hand, and he is eating a leaf. We HEAR the VOICE of SIMON HASKELL.

SIMON (O.S.)
I'm not going to argue about it, you were supposed to be through that *caatinga* yesterday. You're dogging it, Barrosso!

The ant looks at him. We HEAR a high, whining, metallic sound that goes on for a moment. CAMERA PULLS BACK to show us Simon, a short barrel-chested man in his late forties; grizzled, tough, like something out of a Ring Lardner or Damon Runyon story, transplanted to the Amazon Basin. He is talking to the ant.

SIMON (CONT'D)
Don't give me that shit, Barroso! You made your deal with the project honchos, not with me. You've had all the sugar you're gonna get till you come up to schedule.

BRATENAHL (O.S.)
They tell me when you start talking to the ants it's time to go back to São Paulo.

### 73 TWO-SHOT — BRATENAHL & SIMON

The short man turns and sees Bratenahl coming through the camp toward him.

SIMON

Who the hell are you?

BRATENAHL

Bob Bratenahl. *Cosmos* Magazine. João from Cachimbo said he set it up with you to see me.

SIMON

Hah! João! That *caboclo!*

BRATENAHL

Speaks very highly of you.

SIMON

For two cruzeiros he'd speak highly of Plague Anna.

BRATENAHL

Don't know her.

SIMON

Killed off half the population of Xavantina with small-pox.

(beat)

She's a legendary figure.

BRATENAHL

So're you.

SIMON

So's João. And that leaves you.

BRATENAHL

Let's be friends.

SIMON

You wouldn't like me. I'm cranky.

BRATENAHL

And you talk to the ants.

SIMON

Only when they give me shit. Just the reverse when people talk to me.

There is a repeat of the high, whining sound. Simon looks down at his hand. Barrosso has finished the leaf.

SIMON (CONT'D.)

(to the ant)

So *take* it to the project honcho. No more sugar till we hit the *campo limpo.*

BRATENAHL

Can he be bribed?

SIMON

He's an eciton, ain't he?

BRATENAHL

I've got a jar of chocolate syrup coming up behind me with a native.

Simon stares at him curiously.

ROBERT BRATENAHL

SIMON

I don't know what you want, friend, but you must want it pretty bad.

BRATENAHL

I've got glass beads for the natives, too.

SIMON

Don't worry about them. They won't come within a hundred miles of the *marabunta.*

(to ant)

Listen, Barrosso: you get them dumb chewers back up to peak efficiency, I'll make sure you get drunk on syrup tonight.

The ant makes the sound.

SIMON (CONT'D.)

Okay. You got it.

He sets the ant down, watches it go. Then he turns to Bratenahl. He studies him a moment. Then jerks his head for the reporter to follow him.

## 74 ANGLE FROM SIMON & BRATENAHL — TO MICRO/TIGHT CU

as the CU MOVE INTO CAMERA and FRAME TO BLACK for an instant as they leave the scene. CAMERA HOLDS for a beat on the jungle and then ZOOMS DOWN AND IN on Barrosso. We HEAR the ridiculous high-pitched sound as if he is getting off one last insult at the human straw boss, then he scampers off into the jungle and we

**DISSOLVE TO:**

## 75 SIMON'S BASE CAMP — NIGHT

HIGH SHOT COMING DOWN THRU leaves of the trees. We HEAR MUSIC. The music we hear is old, old hotel ballroom music. (Specifically: "Does Your Heart Beat for Me" played by Russ Morgan and his Orchestra, recorded 4 January 1939; "Hot Lips" played by Henry Busse and his Orchestra, recorded 25 September 1934; "Nola" played by Vincent Lopez and his Suave Swing Orchestra, recorded 8 January 1940; and "Bubbles in the Wine" played by The Champagne Music Makers of Lawrence Welk, recorded 26 July 1938.) This music continues through the next scene. Down through the trees we can see a vague silvery scintillance. It is a force-field thrown up around the base camp to keep out the insects and animals. CAMERA DOWN to FEATURE the camp as SEEN THRU the SPECIAL EFFECT of the force-field.

## 76 CAMERA IN THRU FORCE-FIELD

SPECIAL EFFECT as if the camera were moving through a cloud of silver dust. MOVE IN on the scene, shot 77:

## 77 FULL SHOT — TRUCKING

There in the midst of the Amazon jungle, Simon Haskell has cobbled up for himself a replica of an Art Deco salon. The "walls" of the area are the silvery scintillance of the force-field, through which we can see the jungle as through a veil. But *inside,* in a large cleared space, we see a gorgeous Maples of London dining table and baronial chairs, a bird's-eye-maple sideboard and bar, exquisite deco lamps, and cobalt glass vases, mirrors, and a fabulous cobalt glass Spartan radio, circa 1937. It is from the radio that the period music emanates. Drinking from ruby-glass goblets and eating off Sèvres chinaware, as the Erté and Parrish and Chirico and Brangwyn and Poertzel etchings and blown-glass figures smile down on them, Simon and Bratenahl have their dinner. It looks like something out of a 1930s High Deco film from MGM. Bratenahl is clearly impressed, though bemused. He sips his wine from the ruby-glass goblet and looks around.

BRATENAHL

Nice place you've got here.

SIMON

(wryly)

It's not much, but I call it home.

(beat)

A little more of the Mouton Rothschild?

BRATENAHL

No thanks. I'm walking.

Simon pats at the corners of his mouth with a damask napkin. He sits back and stares at Bratenahl.

SIMON

I like you. You're obviously as bugfuck as I am.

BRATENAHL

Just a quiet country boy trying to make good in the news-cast biz.

SIMON

That chocolate syrup was a bold, brilliant stroke.

BRATENAHL

I heard you were cranky. Wanted to come prepared. You should see the crap I'm carrying, just in case.

SIMON

You wouldn't happen to have a Tsuba Samurai sword guard from the Gempei War, would you?

BRATENAHL

I could just kick myself silly for leaving it behind.

(beat)

How about volume one, number two of *Whiz Comics,* with the debut of the original Captain Marvel?

SIMON

What about volume one, number one?

BRATENAHL

There wasn't one.

SIMON

(pleased)

Yeah. You're bugfuck, too.

## 78 ANOTHER ANGLE

as something large and black throws itself against the force-field. It hits with a thump then runs away.

SIMON

Probably a harpy eagle. Don't worry about it. They can't get through the force-field.

BRATENAHL

(waves at the scene around them)

All this. You don't seem the sort of man who'd voluntarily live in the back on nowhere.

SIMON

(shrugs)

Many reasons; not the least of which is 5,000 credits a day.

BRATENAHL

Even so.

SIMON

Mmm. Well, I used to like to call myself a gadfly. Truth of it is that I'm a troublemaker. There are whole countries where I'm on the endangered species list.

BRATENAHL

And you talk to the ants.

SIMON

Low-level telepathy. Very dull conversationalists. You'd be shocked how little the ecitons know about galactic literature.

BRATENAHL

Which brings us to what you're going to do for me.

SIMON

You're sure I'll do it, whatever it is?

BRATENAHL

Sure.

(beat)

You like me.

SIMON

João said you were "like a man eaten by the sun." He

talks like that, bad poetry. But he's right. What's got you by the throat, Bratenahl?

BRATENAHL

Susan Calvin.

SIMON

Ohhhh, so *that's* it. You're after an interview.

BRATENAHL

(disturbed)

I suppose.

SIMON

Another one trying to find out if she was Byerley's mistress, eh?

BRATENAHL

I want to talk to her.

SIMON

Did you ever hear of Machu Picchu, the lost city of the Andes?

Bratenahl nods.

SIMON (CONT'D.)

(closes his eyes, recites)

"Then up the ladder of earth I climbed, through the barbed jungle's thickets . . . Mother of stone and sperm of condors . . . High reef of the human dawn . . ."

(beat)

For five hundred years the headwaters of the Xingú were an Indian fortress. Virtually impenetrable. Source of legend. Site of a great lost city. *Xingú Xavante.* Eldorado . . . Ankor Wat . . . Machu Picchu.

(beat)

Did you know Susan Calvin unearthed it?

BRATENAHL
(amazed)
There's never been a word on the news web.

SIMON
I've been gang-boss in the Mato Grosso for the past six years. That rabble of ants you saw has been eating the Trans-Amazon Highway out of the jungle for the last eight. They got pissed at the boss who had the job before me and cleaned him to the bones one day. Old Earth council has been trying to settle the basin for seventy years. It's a war with the jungle. Until they found a few of us could control the ecitons, it looked hopeless. So this was the most isolated, impenetrable place on the planet.
(beat)
She came here God knows how long ago, found that lost city, built—*or had built for her*—a home under the ruins, and no one goes in without permission.
(beat)
Now do you perceive dimly the enormity of what you're asking me to do?

BRATENAHL
I perceive clearly that you're telling me it can't be done . . . or at least that *you* ain't gonna do it.

## 79 CLOSE ON SIMON

as he rises, doing a little time-step to Henry Busse's "Hot Lips." He walks toward the force-field, looks out, hands clasped behind his back.

SIMON
You perceive incorrectly; it *can* be done; and I'll do it if I can figure a way.

Bratenahl gets up, pushes away from the table, and walks over beside Simon Haskell.

BRATENAHL

Not just because you like me.

**80 CU — SIMON'S FACE**

There is a tight, serious, strained expression there. He's looking at the past. When he speaks, it is low and slow.

SIMON

João said there's a bastard named Rowe who's squeezing you. I've been squeezed myself.

(beat)

There are better places to be than this fuckin' jungle . . . even for less than 5,000 credits a day.

(beat)

Better places. Cooler places.

(beat)

The enemy of my enemy is my friend . . .

**81 FULL SHOT**

as they stand there side by side, staring into the deadly jungle and we

**DISSOLVE TO:**

**82 LONG-RANGE TELESCOPIC SHOT — THE JUNGLE — DAY**

**FROM EXTREME CU — ZOOM OUT TO AERIAL VIEW**

(A breathtaking shot. At one with the memorable Victor Fleming trucking boom shot in *Gone With the Wind* that pulls back from an individual soldier to encompass two acres of wounded troops waiting for the train. This shot should just keep expanding and expanding till we are awestruck.)

CU on a blue-silver drop of rain, sliding down an incredibly green leaf. BEGIN ZOOM OUT to show the leaf on a vine. The vine on a piece of weathered stone. The stone one of many in a wall. The wall merely a facet of a ruined structure. The ruined structure a small building that is part of a much larger city now covered with vine and jungle, eaten alive by the hungry foliage. Back and back and back to show the lost city of *Xingú Xavante.* And the city almost lost to the naked eye in the midst of overflowing jungle. Back and back and back, and up till we see the entire basin, the city barely visible. Back and back to the ridge of the basin above.

SIMON (V.O.)
They flourished for a thousand years . . . then the fertile fields went fallow . . . or they lost a battle . . . or the earth trembled . . . and they stopped fighting the jungle, that green eating thing . . . and they died . . . and it was lost . . .

(beat)
Till she came and found it.

BRATENAHL (V.O.)
Dear God! It's incredible!

## 83 SHOT PAST SIMON & BRATENAHL

as they stand there looking down into the basin.

BRATENAHL
How the hell are you going to get me in there?

SIMON
(mock German)
Ve haff our vays, Herr Bratenahl . . .

CAMERA PAST THEM to the basin view as we

**DISSOLVE TO:**

## 84 DEEP JUNGLE — LATE DAY

CLOSE ON ANTS eating a patch of foliage. A huge, swarming mass of ants. And as they eat away the foliage we see something bright and metallic shining out.

## 85 SIMON & BRATENAHL

watching from a safe distance as the ecitons chew a patch in the side of the rise. Above the rise we can see the outermost walls of the lost city.

SIMON
Ventilation shaft, maybe. More likely a service tunnel opening.

BRATENAHL
The ants told you it was here?

SIMON
Barrosso. You have no idea what this will cost me, Bratenahl. Tonight, he'll get stinking gorged on sugar and turn maudlin, and I'll have to listen to endless saccharine sentimentality about the brutalized life of the intellectual.

BRATENAHL
I owe you.

SIMON
Pay the debt by not telling how you got in . . . when they catch you.

Simon steps up to the now completely revealed entrance hatch. He unships a small laser-pencil from his tool belt, and burns away the seal. The port swings open freely. Not a spot of rust on it, not a tendril of plant within. But dark.

## 86 BRATENAHL

as he watches. Simon finishes, steps back. He extends a hand, inviting Bratenahl to get down on all fours and go in. Bratenahl extends his hand. They shake.

SIMON
I like you, chum. You're bugfuck. But I'll likely never see you again.

Bratenahl summons up a dim smile, drops to all fours, and crawls into the aperture. Into the darkness. Simon closes the port and wedges it with some thick limbs. He stares at the closed port for a few moments, then turns to the rolling soup of ants waiting nearby.

SIMON (CONT'D.)

Come on, you guys. We've got a road to dig.

**SHARP CUT TO:**

### 87 thru 90 SERIES OF FOLLOWING SHOTS — LIMBO SET

behind Bratenahl as he crawls through the smooth, faintly reflective tunnels that bend and curve before him. Every once in a while he passes a dimly glowing plate in the wall of the tunnel, green, that casts a decayed pallor over his mildly trepidatious features. But he keeps crawling.

### 91 SHOT PAST BRATENAHL TO TUNNEL END

Beyond him, we can see the silvery scintillance of a force-field covering the circular mouth of the service tunnel. Bratenahl crawls to it. He stares at it. He puts his hand up to touch it, but pulls it back at the last moment. He looks down. There is a huge rhino beetle crawling across his hand. He doesn't recoil, merely reaches down, grasps it between thumb and forefinger, and lobs it at the force-field. It hits, there is a spark of power, and the beetle is vaporized. Bratenahl sighs deeply, beaten, and sits back against the tunnel wall, running his hands through his hair. To get this far . . . only to be stopped.

He sits for a few more moments, then crawls forward again, tries to see through the force-field. Dimly, he can see shapes, but it's a dense, powerful field, obviously meant to stop anything up to and including an anaconda that might, miraculously, like the rhino beetle that got in when he entered, slip into the tunnel. His face is as close to the field as possible without touching it . . . when it abruptly VANISHES. It is gone, and we are looking out past his head to:

## 92 BRATENAHL'S POV — WHAT HE SEES

An underground garden . . . heaven . . . low, futuristic buildings that are a cross between Peruvian and Oriental, if you can picture such a fabulous yet architecturally esthetic meld. Open atria filled with plants from all over the galaxy. High towers of glass and silver. A small citylike labyrinth, there under the lost city of the Amazon. Bratenahl gasps. And then, two pairs of arms reach down from above, into the FRAME, grab him by the shoulders, and yank him out. He looks down.

## 93 DOWN-ANGLE — PAST BRATENAHL'S FEET

He is dangling over an open abyss that plunges many hundreds of feet to the garden below.

## 94 THE SHOT— FEATURING BRATENAHL — REVERSE ANGLE

He is being held under the arms by two men who resemble the GUARDS we saw in Scene 13. The aperture is high up on a rock mountain wall carved out of the very earth. A ledge above supports the two men in their formal suits and blank expressions. Bratenahl dangling like something out of a Hitchcock film, terrified. They start to pull him up.

## 95 ON THE LEDGE

as they drag Bratenahl up. He is dropped to his knees on the ledge. Two flitterpaks (individual flying harnesses) lie on the ledge. He gasps for breath, starts to rise.

1st GUARD

Your persistence is illegal, Mr. Bratenahl.

He rises. The two Guards look at him wearily. He is a gnat.

BRATENAHL

I—

2nd GUARD

Invasion of personal space, sir.

He nods. Looks chagrined. Beaten. The Guards look at one another, nod, and shrug into their flitterpaks. Then they get him under the arms again, firmly, and with their free hands punch on the power. They rise from the ledge, sail out, and begin to descend.

## 96 SHOT FROM BELOW

On the trio as it slowly descends. Down they come, holding Bratenahl between them. They bump to a landing. CAMERA IN TO 3-SHOT.

1st GUARD

We'll have to detain you till we reach the authorities, sir.

2nd GUARD

Sorry to inconvenience you, sir.

Bratenahl looks beaten, downcast, embarrassed. He nods and they start to move off. Suddenly Bratenahl lurches into them, slamming one against the other. As they try to regain their footing he plunges off to one side, into the heavy garden foliage. In a moment he's gone from sight.

## 97 WITH BRATENAHL — ARRIFLEX

running, running, thrashing through the plants, crushing delicate blossoms underfoot, beating his way through the vines, running, running . . .

## 98 WITH THE GUARDS — ARRIFLEX

as they speak into wrist-communicators. We cannot hear what is said. Then they separate and go after him, running fast.

## 99 BRATENAHL — ARRIFLEX

running.

## 100 ON BANKS OF VIDEO SCREENS

in various colors, mostly pastel. Shot after shot of Robert Bratenahl running. Over some of them we get heartbeat readouts, metabolic functions codified. Running!

**101 thru 105 INTERCUTS**

BETWEEN BRATENAHL and the GUARDS in pursuit.

**106 PAST BRATENAHL**

as he plunges through a particularly dense stand of foliage, and sees a blue-glass pyramidal structure with terrazzo tiling in a plaza all around it. He smashes through the foliage and boils out onto the plaza. No one in sight. He looks this way and then that, trapped, but ratlike in his necessary panic. A way out! A way to Susan Calvin!

**107 ROBOT GUARD POV — WHAT IT SEES**

We are looking through the scanner eye of a robot. It has Bratenahl in its viewfinder. Targeted. Broken down into a dozen different images in all the primary colors. Moving in on him.

**108 CLOSE ON BRATENAHL**

Wild-eyed, as he turns and we see PAST HIM the robot guard rolling toward him. It is a smooth, low, boxlike affair with grasper arms on extensible limbs. It is coming fast, rolling toward him on trunnions.

**109 FULL SHOT**

as Bratenahl turns and rushes around the blue-glass pyramid structure. And there, in the near distance, is what must be the central house of the underground labyrinth. He rushes toward it, just as a Guard breaks out of the foliage beside him. Without hardly breaking step, Bratenahl swings and clubs the man in the throat. The Guard goes down, rolls back into the foliage. Now Bratenahl is running like an Olympic sprinter, gasping for breath, frantic, but determined.

**110 thru 114 SERIES OF SHOTS ON MUSEUM — BRATENAHL'S POV**

The large building, with a platform of steps, many steps, leading up to huge carved front doors as great as those on a cathedral. Each SHOT BRINGS

IT CLOSER, as though we are seeing it through Bratenahl's eyes, as he runs to it. We have the opportunity of scrutinizing its architecture. It is ornately carved and looks as though it is made of banyan wood. But as we get closer we perceive it is one huge molded form, perhaps some ultramodern acrylic. And the designs on it show Indian gods, ancient, ominous, but all-knowing.

### 115 REVERSE ANGLE

from the building, to Bratenahl, tiny before it, running to the structure and up the steps two at a time . . . falling . . . struggling up on hands and knees till he can rise . . . coming on once more . . . determined. In b.g., the Guards and robot.

### 116 ON THE DOORS

as Bratenahl rushes into the FRAME and throws himself at the doors. They have huge carved handles. He puts his shoulder to one of them, thinking it will be difficult to open, merely because of its size. But it pivots open on a central pin, with utter ease. He stumbles forward from his own momentum and goes crashing through to fall.

### 117 INT. MUSEUM — PAST BRATENAHL

He raises his head and CAMERA GOES UP AND UP past him to show us this is not a house, not a habitation, but a vast museum of artifacts from the lost city of *Xingú Xavante.* Fifty-foot high cyclopean statues of the long-gone Gods of a long-dead people. Terrifying yet somehow wise Gods who ruled over a race that had perished before Cabral discovered Brazil in 1500. Tapestries and stone paintings of a miraculous nature, codifying for even the dullest that the race that created them was wondrous in its intellect and imagination. Amphorae and casks; salvers and chests; vases and glass figurines; shields and weaponry; icons and armoires. Rank upon rank of the restored treasures of an unknown culture. But all dominated under that high, arching ceiling by the huge monolithic presences of the Gods, looking down from the dim, shadowed heights.

### 118 CU — BRATENAHL

stunned by all this. Awestruck and silent. Then he HEARS the sound of pursuit behind him and he rushes forward.

## 119 EXT. MUSEUM — SHOT UP STAIRS

as the two Guards and the robot reach the top. We see through the open door the dim exterior, and Bratenahl running back through the artifacts.

## 120 WITH BRATENAHL

as he pushes through a stand of small figures of naked Indian warriors hunting. And as he slides through the group of fifteen or twenty life-sized carvings, he suddenly finds himself staring at . . .

## 121 CU

Dr. Susan Calvin.

## 122 CU

Bratenahl, shocked into immobility.

## 123 TWO-SHOT

She is holding a splendidly glazed jar, set about with gold trim of anacondas writhing over the surface. She is dusting out dirt with an archeologist's sable-hair brush. She looks at him, and her eyes widen. Bratenahl is stopped.

BRATENAHL
(gasping)
Doctor Cal . . . vin . . . I—

She drops the vase. Bratenahl's eyes follow it down as we GO TO SLOW MOTION and the vase turns lazily in the air and RETURN TO NORMAL SPEED as it impacts and shatters into a billion flaming amber and gold pieces. It lies there between them, almost symbolically. He looks up and there is fear in her eyes. He stammers wordlessly, then, so ashamed he *cannot* speak, he drops to his knees and tries to gather up the pieces. He picks up several of the largest and rises. He holds them like a dead creature, and looks at her helplessly.

BRATENAHL (CONT'D.)
I never meant to—

Her hand comes to her mouth. There is such loss, such alienation in her face, that Bratenahl *cannot fail* to understand how he has shattered the moment. Nor can we fail to perceive it. A moment of tragedy.

## 124 CU — SUSAN CALVIN

as she stares at him and we

**FLASH-CUT TO:**

## 125 SUBLIMINAL INTERCUT — A MOMENT — SOLARIZED

Susan, as a child, as we saw her in Scene 40, sitting on the lap of Edward Calvin. He is holding her, and her head is against his chest.

EDWARD (V.O.)
(echo chamber)
Everyone has dreams, honey. The trouble is: most people aren't worthy of the dreams they dream . . .

**CUT BACK TO:**

## 126 THE SCENE IN THE MUSEUM

as Susan Calvin shakes her head, and we realize we have been inside her head, remembering what she was remembering. We don't know what it means, but it has a sense of loss that binds us to the shattered moment we are in now.

CALVIN
Why are you dogging me like this!?!

BRATENAHL
(imploring)
Dr. Calvin . . . I never meant . . . you're a legend . . .

CALVIN
(fiercely)
I'm an old woman and I've paid for the right to my solitude. Paid in the highest coin . . .

Behind them we HEAR the Guards coming. Bratenahl turns and looks over his shoulder.

## 127 BRATENAHL'S POV — WHAT HE SEES

The two Guards coming. The one he punched in the throat is dragging his left leg in a most peculiar fashion. The other one has a stun gun drawn. The robot slides along with them, its segmented arms waving.

2nd GUARD
(alarmed)
Dr. Calvin! Are you . . . ?

CALVIN (O.S.)
I'm all right. Don't hurt him.

## 128 WITH BRATENAHL

as he drops the pieces of shattered vase, looks once more at Susan Calvin.

BRATENAHL
Dr. Calvin, I'm no threat to you. I'm from *Cosmos* magazine. My God, *this is insane* that I should have to break into your home just to *speak* to you . . . !

CALVIN
Yes, sir, it is.
(beat, cold)
The laws of invasion of personal space were created specifically for people like you.

At that moment a heavy hand drops onto Bratenahl's shoulder. He is spun around. He shoves. The 2nd Guard goes back, falling into the life-size carvings of the hunters. The one dragging his leg comes forward. Bratenahl bolts in panic. CAMERA WITH HIM as he dashes into an alcove, finds himself blocked. He is at the feet of one of the great God statues. He cannot get out of the alcove. He starts to climb. CAMERA TRACKS UP WITH HIM as he climbs up the great statue.

### 129 WITH 2nd GUARD

as he raises the stun-gun, turns a dial on its side (and we are aware it is being adjusted), aims, and fires. A fanlike wave of amber light jumps from the weapon.

### 130 UP-ANGLE ON STATUE

as Bratenahl climbs across the folded arms of the animal-headed God statue. He rises, just as the bolt strikes him. He freezes, goes limp, totters a moment, then falls.

### 131 WIDER ANGLE

FEATURING BRATENAHL and the statue as he falls backward, limp as a fish. It is a great distance, perhaps forty feet. Bratenahl plunges toward the stone floor. The 2nd Guard has stepped closer. And as we watch he extends his arms straight out and *catches* Bratenahl. He is barely moved by the action. It is an impressive moment.

### 132 CLOSE ON BRATENAHL

lying unconscious, but clearly undamaged, in the Guard's arms. ANGLE WIDENS SLIGHTLY as the robot guard, the 1st Guard, and Susan Calvin come to them. She looks down at the unconscious reporter.

CALVIN

Leave me alone, sir. I beg you . . . leave me in peace.

And she turns and goes. The 2nd Guard turns INTO CAMERA and, carrying Bratenahl high, so his head and upper body dominate the FRAME, he MOVES INTO CAMERA as

**FRAME TO BLACK and**
**MATCH-CUT TO:**

### 133 CU — BRATENAHL

on his head and upper body. We think he is still being carried, but as the CAMERA ANGLE WIDENS we realize he is supine, flat on his back, on the ground. But he is moving. How can this be? CAMERA ANGLE WIDENS FARTHER and we see a silent Simon Haskell walking alongside a thick river of ants that disappear *under* Bratenahl. He is being carried through the jungle, back the way he came, on a tide of ecitons. HOLD THIS SCENE and

**SLOW DISSOLVE TO:**

### 134 INT. COSMOS CENTRAL

CLOSE ON BRATENAHL as in preceding scenes. He opens his eyes. He blinks. We HEAR the VOICE of ROWE OVER.

ROWE (O.S.)

Hell, I don't mind losing my job. I've only been here sixteen years O.E. time. I can always go back to pimping snake-women to the Kiwanis on Altair!

### 135 FULL SHOT — THE SCENE — DAY

Bratenahl is lying on a translucent-topped table, lying atop films sheets and photographs. This is the central coordinating room of *Cosmos* Magazine. People are bustling around at many kinds of recording and transcribing machines, all very modern and ultrafast. Rowe stands over him, looking down. The little bulldog editor is righteously pissed off.

ROWE

Get the fuck up off that comm-sink, you idiot.

Bratenahl tries to rise, cannot. He holds his head, then a hand over his heart.

BRATENAHL

(weakly)

Rowe . . . you got some . . . water . . .

ROWE

Water? You're lucky I don't *drown* your ass in the Silver Sea!

BRATENAHL

Gimme . . .

ROWE

Oh . . . shit!

He goes to a console on the wall, punches a button, and gets a bulb of water from the machine. He brings it over, but Bratenahl cannot squeeze it. Rowe lifts his head and squeezes water into his mouth. Now it's very public: a crowd watches.

BRATENAHL

On the eyes . . . put some on my . . . eyes . . .

Rowe rolls his eyes heavenward, but squeezes water out into Bratenahl's pained eyes. Then he helps him to a sitting position. More people join the clutch watching, listening.

ROWE

(exasperated)

How the hell did I inherit you? In what past life did I do such terrible things to rate getting mixed up with a frood like you?

BRATENAHL

I found her, Rowe.

ROWE

(mocking)

You *don't* say!

BRATENAHL

The location was right. She *is* in the Amazon basin, Old Earth . . .

He stops, looks around. Stunned.

BRATENAHL (CONT'D.)

How did I get *here*?

ROWE

Well, cuddles, the way I get it, they dumped your scaly hide into the jungle and a wandering band of gypsies found you and schlepped you back to the teleport booth and fired you back to me C.O.D.

(beat)

Fastest return in history.

(beat)

The only thing faster are the suits coming up for hearing against this humble periodical and your obedient servant. You really boiled it *this* time, Bratenahl!

BRATENAHL

She found a lost city . . . she lives under it . . . the place she lives in, it *had* to've been built with Federation money. Rowe, she *was* tied up with Byerley, she *must* have been!

ROWE

Forget it. You're off it.

BRATENAHL

I can't! I'm close, Rowe. Real close. I *saw* her down there!

ROWE

(screams)

You're *off* it, you stupid sonofabitch! Done! Finished!

**136 WITH BRATENAHL**

as Rowe stalks away from him, shouldering aside the staff and various onlookers. Bratenahl slides off the comm-sink, holds the edge of the table for a moment as if in extreme pain, then starts after him.

BRATENAHL

Rowe! Hold it! Just *listen* to me!

Rowe is walking toward a long, high, blank wall. He suddenly spins on Bratenahl, the crowd splitting like the Red Sea, as Bratenahl reaches him.

ROWE

(playing to the crowd)

I've listened to you enough. Now here's the word: you don't work here no more. And: the Jurisprudence League on Capella 8 pulled your matrix . . . don't try using a teleport booth. You're stuck on ground for the rest of your life, which oughtta be short, if there's any justice!

BRATENAHL

You sonofabitch! *You're* the one shoved me *into* this! You said you'd back me all the way if they slapped me with invasion of space!

ROWE

(dead calm)

You got proof of that, Bratenahl?

BRATENAHL

Damned right! Comm tape of our conversations.

Rowe smiles a nasty, dirty little smile. Bratenahl knows what's coming, but he can't believe it.

ROWE

(quietly)

I think if you run a scan you'll find nothing like that.

Bratenahl trembles. His jaw tightens. He looks this way and that, looking for another avenue of emotional release than the one he can feel opening before him. Rowe stands there smiling nastily. Bratenahl starts to turn away, then in one fluid, almost martial art manner, pivots on the ball of his foot and brings one up from the hip. His fist slams into Rowe's face, dead high alongside the nose, and Rowe is sent thumping into the blank wall. He slips, falls. Sits down hard, half-conscious.

## 137 FULL SHOT

as the now-overflowing crowd stares disbelievingly. Rowe is hurt. That was no love-tap. Bratenahl starts for him again, takes two steps and stops. He *wants* to get his anger under control. He stands over Rowe with fists balled as the editor groggily tries to stand up, slipping against the wall as an inept club-fighter dazed by repeated pummeling might try to stand up. It is pathetic to see. Finally, he gets up, hanging on the blank wall. He stares at Bratenahl, his face swollen, eye closing.

ROWE

Get outta here. You're dead in the water, son.

They stare at each other for a long moment, then Rowe wipes blood from the corner of his mouth, turns, and puts the bloody hand palm flat against the long, high, blank wall. The section of wall revolves, and there is an egg-like chair with electronic feeds like brain wave tendrils coming from it. He slumps in into the egg, it seems to fit close around him, as though he had sat in pudding, and almost instantly we HEAR in SOFT VOICES UNDER the sound of reporters all over the galaxy feeding in to his brain. This is the central core of *Cosmos,* the editor linked directly to his sources, pouring in pictures and data from the field. His eyes close as he begins to move his lips silently, as though talking in his sleep. Bratenahl stands and stares at him a beat, as the crowd watches; then he turns away helplessly as we:

**DISSOLVE TO:**

## 138 LONG SHOT — ESTABLISHING — THE ARCOLOGIES — NIGHT

The cityscape dreams of contemporary architect Paolo Soleri realized. Huge cities built as single buildings, octagonal-shaped, many-tiered, holding a quarter of a million people each, ten miles high, set out on empty and arid plains. MOVING IN on one of these "arcologies," as Soleri calls them. MOVING IN on one speck of light in the immense structure, one lighted window . . . save that the size of this city is so great, it is merely a speck of light, no more.

**MOVE IN AND DISSOLVE THRU TO:**

## 139 INT. WOODLANDS APARTMENT — NIGHT

STILL MOVING IN to maintain linkage of exterior/interior. This is Bratenahl's personal living space. It is, quite literally, an indoor woodlands construct, with a tiny brook pattering against grassy banks, trees of half a hundred different kinds, some of them even reminiscent of Old Earth. It is night in the woodland, but with a soft, fairy quality, like something from "A Midsummer's Night's Dream." CAMERA MOVES IN STEADILY on Bratenahl, sitting hunched over a desktop comm unit, and we see tapes, running in disordered sequence, across the face of the screen. He is plugged in with an ear-jack, so we cannot HEAR what he's listening to—all we HEAR is the SOUND of the woods at night—but we recognize some of the faces in those tapes: Edward Calvin, Susan Calvin, Stephen Byerley, Alfred Lanning, news cuts of the Robot Pogroms . . . in short, we perceive that he continues to be obsessed. He rubs his eyes wearily. He has apparently been at it for a long time. There is the SOUND of a gentle CHIME. He looks up, looks around as if just coming to awareness of his location, and speaks to the machine.

BRATENAHL

Kill it.

Screen goes to readout red.

BRATENAHL (CONT'D.)

Who's at the door?

Screen shows him Rowe standing at the guard entrance, the wall-mounted, swivel-based laser weapon aimed at him as is the custom in all security-protected arcologies housing so many thousands of people. Rowe has a plastic bandage covering his cheek and nose.

BRATENAHL (CONT'D.)

Let him hear me.

(beat; to screen)

What do you want, butcher? The slaughterhouses are on the third level.

ROWE

Open up, I want to talk to you.

BRATENAHL

Go to hell.

ROWE

*Open up, you dumb bastard! It's* not what it seems to be!

Bratenahl stares at the screen for a long moment. He walks around the room for a bit, then sighs, expelling breath in weary resignation.

BRATENAHL

Central . . . open the door.

He turns to the right and a light shines through the woods. It falls across the grass that is carpet, and strikes the simple, comfortable furniture carved from rosewood. Rowe comes through the trees, following the light-path, into Bratenahl's "living room." As they confront each other, the light vanishes, leaving them in dusky woodsiness.

They stand silently for a moment.

BRATENAHL (CONT'D.)

I'm locked in. The booths have been coded to reject my matrix. Just like a common criminal.

ROWE

I couldn't do anything about that.

(beat)

But I can circumvent it.

Rowe sits down, makes himself comfortable.

ROWE (CONT'D.)
Pay attention. I pushed you that hard back at the shop so the word would get out you were off the project.

Bratenahl is astounded.

BRATENAHL
That was all for *show?*

ROWE
Yeah. Otherwise I'd've broken your fucking back for hitting me like that.
(beat)
I want this story, and I'm stuck with you as the only one who can get it for me.

BRATENAHL
(yells)
Don't you know how to get anything out of people except by intimidation?

ROWE
No. I had an unhappy childhood.

BRATENAHL
So did your *momma!*

Rowe moves fast. Faster than such a fireplug should be able to move. In a bound he's out of the chair, over to the taller man, and he clips Bratenahl a short, hard one right under the heart. Bratenahl collapses, sits down fast and completely. Rowe goes back to the chair, sits down. He waits for the pain to clear out of Bratenahl's eyes somewhat, then he starts talking. Bratenahl cannot speak.

ROWE
Don't talk, kiddo. Just listen.
(beat)

You're doing okay so far. You found her. That's a big plus.

Bratenahl tries to get up, slips back onto one elbow.

ROWE (CONT'D.)

I've pulled a surrogate matrix for you. Don't ask how.

He reaches into his pouch, pulls out some papers, several slips of plastic, and lays them on the desk nearby.

ROWE (CONT'D.)

Booth coordinates. Names of two men who worked with Calvin. I'm told they can give you plenty of special information if you do it right.

(beat)

Take off as soon as you can.

He gets up, starts to go. Bratenahl is still on the floor. He stops, turns around, looks down at Bratenahl.

ROWE (CONT'D.)

You don't have to like me, kiddo. But play this one out with me and you'll be better than anyone's been at this game in a long time.

(beat)

I'm a shit, Bratenahl; but I go all the way. And you've got the stuff to be better than you think you are. Trust me, and you'll be talking about this the rest of your life.

He goes. Bratenahl still lies there on the floor as we:

**DISSOLVE TO:**

## 140 EXT. KITALPHA XVI — NIGHT

A BLAZING BALL OF SPIRAL LIGHTNING. FRAME ELECTRIC BLUE-WHITE as CAMERA DRAWS BACK and we see the sky of the 16th planet of the star Kitalpha in the constellation Equuleus. CAMERA BACK as we HEAR the incredible deafening crackle and whine of a billion bolts of lightning as they fill the night sky. Kitalpha XVI is a planet with an atmosphere heavy in ozone, producing eternal electrical storms. Nothing can live on the surface. It is pitted and cratered from forks of murderous lightning pounding the planet constantly. CAMERA BACK TO FULL SHOT of planet then DOWN AND IN on a teleport booth pyramid (see Scene 14 for description). We also see, not too far distant from the booth, a battered spaceship, rising into the sky. It is pocked and worn from much use, hardly a new model, and yet somehow valiant-looking. It is surrounded by a spidery webbing of metal lines and coils, a cat's cradle that serves as lightning rod to damp the ferocious assault of electricity from the sky. And as CAMERA COMES DOWN and IN on the pyramid, we see a figure emerge from the base of the spaceship and lope rapidly toward the pyramid.

CAMERA DOWN to CLOSE SHOT on teleport booth pyramid as the figure reaches it. We realize it is a robot. He is almost comical, he is so antiquated. Thin legs and arms, a rather amusing placement of the photoelectric eyes and other features. He is also rather rusty and tarnished. He wears a sort of wire crown that has coils jutting up. It is a smaller version of the lightning-rod arrangement that surrounds the ship and protects him from being blown in half by the storm. He carries a duplicate lightning-rod crown. His name is FRINKEL.

As he reaches the pyramid booth, one of the walls pivots open (same technique as in Scene 14), we see a stream of tracerlike lights coming out of the darkness toward the opening, and in an instant Robert Bratenahl materializes as his atoms gather together. As he steps forward, Frinkel reaches inside and places the crown on Bratenahl's head. A sudden blast of lightning nearby makes Bratenahl blink. He throws up his hands, steps back into the booth a pace.

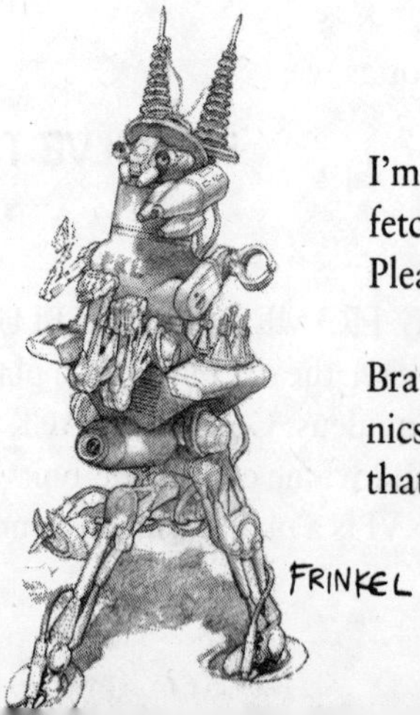

FRINKEL

(rusty voice)

I'm Frinkel, sir. Mr. Donovan and Mr. Powell sent me to fetch you. We just received coordinates for your arrival. Please wear the crown, sir. It's a lightning protector.

Bratenahl, blinking furiously from the aerial pyrotechnics, starting and jumping at every blast of lightning that hits in the vicinity, comes forward cautiously.

FRINKEL

PHILADELPHIA
SPICA
INSTELBOOTHS

FRINKEL (CONT'D.)
You'll get used to it, sir. It never stops. Atmosphere's heavy with ozone.
(beat)
But, uh, let's hurry to the ship, please. They're waiting for you.

Bratenahl, almost petrified by what he's walked into, nods. Frinkel turns and starts off at a slower lope than we know he's capable of maintaining. He's letting Bratenahl keep up with him. A nearby blast adds wings to Bratenahl's feet. They rush away FROM CAMERA toward the spaceship as the wall of the teleport booth slides back into place. CAMERA HOLDS them running across the blasted plain toward the ship as we

**DISSOLVE TO:**

**141 INT. SPACESHIP SALOON — FULL SHOT**

Frinkel stands against the wall, waiting quietly. It is a large cabin, circular, of course, with a panoramic windowscreen shield lowered to present a thin, semicircular backdrop of the exterior of the planet, washed and battered by a constant play of lightning bolts. But save for an occasional *thump!* as a bolt hits the earth close by, reverberating through the ship, or a crackling *sizzle!* that sends Saint Elmo's fire around the cabin as the lightning-rod superstructure outside soaks up the power, there is no noise in the cabin . . . except for music. It is the piano music of Robert Schumann (1810-1856), specifically the *Kreisleriana,* opus 16. (Recommended: the Alicia De Larrocha recording on London.)

Bratenahl sits in a swivel seat with the stuffing coming out at the arms. Across from him is MICHAEL DONOVAN, in his nineties, slim, brown as fried butter from exposure to a million suns. A weathered old spaceman wearing a torn tunic and cutoffs that expose his scrawny, blue-veined, knobbly-kneed legs. But he has an incredibly kind face. The eyes are deep-set and bright, in a face as old as an Egyptian glyph. For his age, he is in remarkable physical condition. But he is old, very old. And very thin.

Across the cabin, sitting at a chessboard on a low table, is Donovan's partner, GREGORY POWELL. Equally as old and as weatherbeaten. But a little bantam cock of a man. Just about 5'5", with a pugnacious face and thick white hair. He pays no attention to the conversation between Bratenahl and Donovan . . . keeps his eyes on the board. But we keep him in the shot and know he's listening. The interior of the cabin looks like bachelor digs. Not the shipshape image of a crack naval spaceship of the line we might have expected. It is messy, a bit raunchy, clearly the kind of place where two old men who have been living together for years have developed to accommodate each other's habits and foibles. Clothes lying on the consoles, shoes on the bar, notes pinned with stickum to the bulkheads. But as comfortable as a summer vacation cabin.

Bratenahl pulls a bottle of liquor out of his pouch. He hands it across to Donovan, who purses his lips in pleasure.

BRATENAHL

I brought it all the way from Central as kind of a bribe. It occurred to me it might've been a while since you'd had real bourbon out here.

DONOVAN

A bribe, Mr. Bratenahl. Hmmm, sounds weighty.

BRATENAHL

Well, I didn't think a jar of chocolate syrup would work.

DONOVAN

I beg your pardon?

BRATENAHL

Nothing; just something funny I was remembering. Forget it.

DONOVAN

What I don't understand is why you'd come all the way out here to Kitalpha just to ask us about Susan Calvin.

BRATENAHL

You worked with her; you knew her well.

DONOVAN

(muses)

Worked with her, yes, for many years. But "knew her *well*"? No, can't say that, can't say that at all. Hardly knew her at all, and *never* understood her.

Powell mumbles something from the chess table. Bratenahl looks over. Powell is still staring at the chess pieces.

BRATENAHL

Mr. Powell? Did you say something?

POWELL

(doesn't look up)

Said: meanest human being I ever met.

Donovan smiles slightly, makes a hand movement in Powell's direction that is intended for Bratenahl, intended to tell Bratenahl to take it with a grain of salt. Bratenahl grins and answers Donovan.

BRATENAHL

Well, I've met her twice now, in a manner of speaking. And I'd say she isn't all that fond of people.

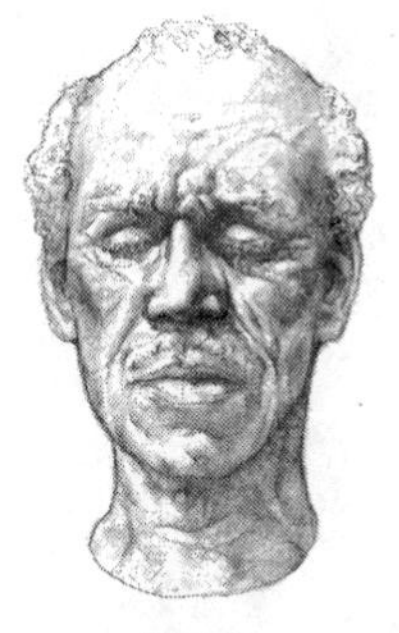

AGED POWELL

POWELL

She liked robots a damned sight better than people. And no "manner of speaking" about it.

DONOVAN

(ignores him)

Mr. Bratenahl, I'm not sure we can help you much. It's been a good many years since Greg and I have had any company . . . and well, would you excuse us for a few minutes?

Bratenahl nods. Donovan rises. He walks to Powell and puts a hand on his shoulder. Powell looks up, sighs wearily, and knocks over the white king. Then he stands and follows Donovan as they walk out of the saloon cabin and the port sighs shut behind them. Bratenahl looks at Frinkel.

FRINKEL

Can I get you some more coffee, sir?

BRATENAHL

No. Thank you.

(beat)

They seem very sad.

FRINKEL

You'd be sad, too, sir, if the only reason for living no longer existed.

BRATENAHL

I'm afraid I don't understand.

## 142 TWO-SHOT — FRINKEL & BRATENAHL

The rusty robot comes to him and without sitting speaks.

FRINKEL

They're the very last of their kind. The last of the space captains. The teleport booths put them out of business. With instant transportation from world-to-world, who needs something as slow as a faster-than-light spaceship?

BRATENAHL

I can see how they'd feel bitter.

FRINKEL

Can you, sir? I wonder.

Then he begins speaking in *POWELL'S VOICE*. Very clearly and without rustiness, imitating Powell exactly.

EKL

FINKEL (CONT'D.)

(in Powell's voice)

Time was . . . before the booths . . . even a sinkhole like this, way the hell and gone on the edge of the Coalsack, nothin' beyond but empty nothin' . . . time was you'd see a place like this *deep* with ships . . . the big ships . . . the inver-space ships, not a bucket like this one . . . the *big* ships, close together, hundreds of 'em like a stand of spears. Time was.

Bratenahl responds to the misery in the imitation.

BRATENAHL

Then what are they doing out here at the last stop of the booths, with a ship?

FRINKEL

There's still need of *one* ship, sir. This one.

(beat)

How do you think the teleport booths get to the next world when there isn't a terminus there already?

BRATENAHL

(softly)

My God. Every booth they plant means they've programmed themselves a little more into obsolescence. It's like self-exile.

FRINKEL

But they do it, sir. They keep right on doing it, because it's all they *can* do. And Central pays no attention to them, just sends through another batch of parts to construct the next booth farther out . . . and they go . . . and they wait for the next jump.

BRATENAHL

(somberly)

God, how useless they must feel.

FRINKEL

Not useless, sir. Not useless . . . just terminal.

The port opens and Donovan and Powell come back in. Powell looks at Frinkel and Bratenahl suspiciously, wondering what they've been talking about. Frinkel goes back to the wall. Donovan and Powell sit down across from Bratenahl.

DONOVAN

Where would you like to start?

BRATENAHL

What do you know about her relationship with Stephen Byerley?

DONOVAN

Not a thing. We were off-planet from 2020 on. Byerley came along maybe fifteen, twenty years later.

BRATENAHL

Well, maybe we should start with the first time you worked with her; if you can remember.

POWELL

We remember *every*thing, fellah. Old don't always mean feeble.

(beat)

2022. She was 28. The three of us, and an experimental robot named Speedy, we were the Second Mercury Mining Expedition.

DONOVAN

(puts in as explanation)

In 2018 a first mining expedition had gone to Mercury, built the station and then went bust for a lot of reasons.

**143 FULL SHOT — CAMERA COMING DOWN**

As the following DIALOGUE PROGRESSES the SCENE DARKENS as if night were descending in the cabin of the spaceship. We will HEAR the

VOICES of Donovan and Powell in VOICE OVER. This dialogue will not be filtered or echo-chambered, but straight, as if they are still sitting talking about the past. Except that we will be able to see the past as they describe it. CAMERA DOWN past the old men talking to one of the photoreceptor eyes of Frinkel, which glows red and alert. CAMERA INTO THE EYE as DIALOGUE CONTINUES and the scene dims into darkness around them.

POWELL (V.O.)
You know what it's like on Mercury, fellah?

BRATENAHL (V.O.)
Only vaguely. One side is always to the sun . . . hot . . . the other's always turned toward space and it's frigid. Airless.

POWELL (V.O.)
We're talkin' here blood-boilin' *hot*! Afternoon temperature 460° Kelvin . . . what they used to call 368° Fahrenheit. That's Lightside. And as soon as you cross to Darkside it drops to 90° Kelvin . . . that's 297° below zero Fahrenheit!
(beat)
Only thing kept that station from meltin' down was an electrostatic field powered by photocell banks that pulled in sunpower. Whole station was just one big energy converter.

SCENE FADES as we ENTER the robot photoreceptor eye of Frinkel . . . as we go INTO THE RED EYE and we HEAR their VOICES FADE but not entirely. And we

**DISSOLVE THRU RED TO:**

## 144 INT. MERCURY STATION — FULL SHOT

It is Spartan. A hemispherical metal and plastic dome that curves overhead perhaps ten feet above the heads of two young men whom we recognize as POWELL and DONOVAN in their late twenties or very early thirties. Donovan has just emerged from a porthole in the floor, having come up a ladder we can see through the porthole, from the sublevels below. Powell has apparently been searching for him, because he has just come through a sliding door in one bulkhead, looked around frenziedly, and then caught sight of Donovan coming up out of the deck. He rushes to him as Donovan climbs out. They react to one another vividly as each speaks in an animated fashion. *We do not hear them.* What we HEAR is the PRESENT-TIME VOICES of the group in the spaceship cabin, Scene 143.

MIKE DONOVAN

DONOVAN (V.O.)

We were sent to Mercury to *make* that failed mining operation work. Calvin came with us to oversee the new SPD 13 robot—what we called Speedy.

(beat)

We were there two days and the photocell banks started to fail. We'd broil alive in about 24 hours.

(beat)

What we needed to get them working again was a measly kilogram of selenium.

POWELL (V.O)

Seemed easy. There was pools of selenium all over Mercury's Sunside, nearest one only 17 miles away.

(beat)

So we sent out that robot, Speedy, to get what we needed. Seemed easy . . .

During all of the preceding DIALOGUE V.O. the young versions of Powell and Donovan have been arguing, then looking at a map of the surface of Mercury. And during their animated talk a 26-year-old SUSAN CALVIN has come through the sliding door in the bulkhead to join them. At first she has just stood listening to them argue, but now is pointing to the map and forcefully arguing with them. CAMERA has come in on them to show us their faces clearly, and now COMES DOWN on the map between them.

As CAMERA HOLDS on the map, with Powell's hand tracing a pattern, we see the station clearly marked, and the selenium pools around the area also clearly indicated. Circling the nearest selenium pool on the map is a series of dotted *bright red lines* . . . circling the pool four times.

Now we don't hear V.O. but the VOICES of the three people in the scene as CAMERA PULLS BACK AWAY from the map and we have segued into the action totally.

POWELL

I sent that damned robot out five hours ago. When he didn't come back I started tracking him by short wave.

(beat)

He's gone crazy!

DONOVAN

Looks like he's *circling* the selenium pool. Instead of going out and picking up what we need and coming right back he goes *close* to the pool, then turns around and starts back for the station . . .

POWELL

But he doesn't go very far. Just starts back for the pool and keeps repeating the runaround, round and round . . . and we're gonna fry!

CALVIN

You gave him direct orders?

POWELL

(looks at her with dislike)

Of course.

CALVIN

But the Three Laws . . . a robot can't defy the Three Laws.

POWELL

Yeah? Terrific. Meanwhile, we've got to go out on the surface and get Speedy back!

He starts for the porthole in the floor and they follow him.

**145 thru 151 SERIES OF MOVING SHOTS — WITH CALVIN & MEN**

Down through the port into the underground tunnels beneath the mining station. Through tunnels. Interlocking dogged ports. To a huge storage chamber where we see six enormous early-model robots, giant behemoths, sitting against a wall with their legs straight out before them.

POWELL

These're left over from the First Expedition. If we put on insulated suits we're safe outside for twenty minutes tops. Maybe we can get close enough in that time to call Speedy in.

DONOVAN

Why don't we just send a couple of them out to collect Speedy?

Even seated, the heads of the robots are seven feet in the air. They are surrounded by musty packing cases and the remains of the First Expedition's equipment. We see the three people considering the robots, and Susan Calvin opening the chest console of one of them. Using the leads from a small black service box she locates in the stack of equipment, she manages to insert the atomic pellet that brings the robot to life. It stands, towering high above her.

CALVIN

I'm afraid Powell's right. I know this model. An early service type. It has to have a human operator.

(beat)

We'll have to ride them.

And we see the three don the bulky, ugly insulated suits, and activate two other robots, who stand. There is some hurried preparation, then the robots make stirrups with their hands, and each of the three humans places a foot in the hands and swings upward. There is a seat built into the enormous shoulder of each robot, formed by a hump on the back and a shallow depression. The ears serve as handles. There they sit up there, and then the robots turn, as the three humans put on the helmets.

The three huge robots are maneuvered close together, as CAMERA COMES IN CLOSE on Powell, who is pointing to the terminus of a tunnel indicated on the map. It is near one of the indicated selenium pools . . . the one with the red dotted lines around it. WE HEAR HIS VOICE FILTER:

POWELL (FILTER)
The tunnel comes out on the surface three miles from the pool Speedy's circling.

They start off down through the chamber to a high doorway portal. It slides open as they approach. The robots go right through and the three people duck just in time to avoid getting their heads cracked open. CAMERA THRU the portal, which sighs shut behind them. Now we are in an underground tunnel lit only by the headlight eyes of the three giant robots. We move down the tunnel.

DONOVAN (FILTER)
I can't figure it out. Heat doesn't mean anything to him; he's built for the light gravity and the broken ground. He should be foolproof.

They come to the end of the tunnel. The robots stop. They are in a tiny substation: empty, airless, ruined. Donovan flashes a small light around, examining a huge rent in an upper wall. Then at a signal from Powell, the door in the substation wall slides up, and the room is flooded with sudden light. And we are looking at the surface of MERCURY.

A towering cliff of black, basaltic rock cuts off the most killing aspects of the sunlight, and the deep night shadow of an airless world surrounds them. Before them, the shadow reaches out and ends in knife-edge abruptness at an all-but-unbearable blaze of white light that glitters from myriad crystals along a cratered, rocky surface.

POWELL (FILTER)
It looks like snow!

As the substation door has slid up, they have flipped down a series of light filters over their helmets.

DONOVAN (FILTER)
The temperature is over 300° Fahrenheit.

Powell adjusts a binocular attachment to his helmet: it gives him the eye-stalked look of a snail.

**CUT TO:**

## 152 VIEW THROUGH POWELL'S VISIPLATE — HIS POV

It is a view TINGED WITH PINK and made viewable by filters. We see a dark spot on the horizon, about three miles away, that is the selenium pool.

POWELL (FILTER)
There's a dark spot on the horizon. Could be the selenium pool. But I don't see Speedy.

Then, we see something moving from the horizon line toward us. It catches the sunlight and throws a spark of bright reflection. The overlay imprint in the binocular attachment suddenly throws a green target across the scene, and zeroes in on the moving speck.

POWELL (FILTER) (CONT'D.)
I think . . . I think . . . yes! Damn him, there he is! Coming this way fast!

**CUT TO:**

## 153 FULL SHOT — THE TRIO

standing in the shadow of the cliff, three human beings in bulky white insulation suits and weird helmets, one of them eyestalked like a snail, high up like humps on the backs of giant, rudimentary-looking robots who stand with legs spread for balance. Now Donovan points in the direction of the moving dot.

DONOVAN (FILTER)

I see him! Let's move it!

He thumps his heels spur-fashion and yells in his helmet.

DONOVAN (FILTER) (CONT'D.)

Giddy-ap!

CAMERA FOLLOWS AND STAYS WITH THEM as the robots move off at a steady pace.

DONOVAN (FILTER) (CONT'D.)

Faster!

POWELL (FILTER)

No use! These junk heaps are only geared to one speed.

Suddenly they burst out of the shadow and the sunlight comes down in a white-hot lava flow around them. All this time Susan Calvin has been silent. By her very silence she has become a strange sort of focus for our attention. She rides her robot with grace, but silently.

## 154 ZOOM SHOT — TOWARD HORIZON — ON SPEEDY

As CAMERA ZOOMS IN on him, we see the SPD-13 robot loping toward us easily, as though happily at home in the burning hell of Mercury's wasteland. WE MUST *FEEL* WHAT 400° F. FEELS LIKE!! He is sleek, futuristic, graceful, an earlier ancestor of Frinkel but as advanced over the robots the humans are riding as a Maserati or Porsche is advanced over a Stanley Steamer. He's coming fast, throwing off a whole shower of sunlight sunbursts from his reflective skin.

### 155 REVERSE ANGLE — FROM DONOVAN'S PERCH

high on his robot. Now Speedy can be seen clearly with the naked eye. Coming on toward them fast, fast, fast! Donovan waves wildly.

DONOVAN (FILTER)

Hey, Speedy! Hey, baby!

POWELL (FILTER)

That's it, Speedy honey . . . come on you little devil! Move-a you ass!

DR. SUSAN CALVIN, AGE 28

### 156 CU — SUSAN CALVIN

watching. There is something in her face, seen through the filtering mechanisms of the visiplate, that tells us she isn't as jubilant as Powell and Donovan. But still she's silent.

### 157 FULL SHOT — ACROSS THE SCENE

SHOWING the space between the trio and Speedy being cut down rapidly, mostly by Speedy's rush forward. We can see from this perspective just how plodding the older robots are, and how Speedy could run rings around them.

DONOVAN (FILTER)

Put all the juice you've got into that radio sender, Greg! He doesn't see us yet.

### 158 VIEW FROM POWELL'S PERCH — TO SPEEDY

At that moment we perceive that Speedy is running with a lopsided, rolling, staggering, side-to-side lurch. And Speedy looks up, sees them, and comes screeching to a halt, almost vibrating at attention like a Road Runner cartoon.

POWELL (FILTER)
'Atza baby! Now you got it, Speedy! Come on, fellah, come here.

**159 CU — SPEEDY**

as he stares at them. And now we HEAR his VOICE in the intercom FILTER OVER for the first time.

SPEEDY (FILTER)
(metallic, and a little crazy)
Hot dog, let's play games! You catch me and I catch you; no love can cut our knife in two. For I'm Little Buttercup, sweet Little Buttercup. Whooops!

He sounds as though he's hiccuping.

And he turns and dashes off in the direction from which he just came. Running like a crazed sonofabitch, almost a blur of white lightning. Just shoooooosh! and gone!

**160 ON THE TRIO**

as they stare after him.

POWELL (FILTER)
Well, I'll be damned and roasted and drip-poured.

DONOVAN (FILTER)
(screaming)
You stupid, eggsucking, miserable pile of fucking *junk*! Goddammit, get your ass *back* here!

Then silence. Then, after several beats, they both turn and stare at Susan Calvin. They give up.

CALVIN (FILTER)
(calmly)
Let's go back to the cliff before we burn out the units.

She turns her robot, holding its ears, and starts back across to the huge black cliff. They stare after her for a moment, then follow.

**DISSOLVE TO:**

### 161 SHADOW OF THE CLIFF — ON THE TRIO

as they sit, having dismounted, in the deep shadow. Only the headlight eyes of the robots, shining down on them from above, eerily, illuminate them at all.

DONOVAN (FILTER)
Where'd he pick up the Gilbert and Sullivan . . . he's drunk, that's what he is, drunk out of his positronic skull!

CALVIN (FILTER)
Not drunk. At least not in the human sense.

POWELL (FILTER)
Well, *some*thing's sure as hell wrong with him.

CALVIN (FILTER)
Might I impose on you to curb your language, Mr. Powell?

Powell and Donovan look at each other, astounded.

POWELL (FILTER)
I don't fuckin' be*lieve* you, Calvin! We're sitting on our asses on the surface of Mercury, fifty-seven million miles from Earth, about to be righteously *cremated* because that piece of shit robot you helped design is trying to run up its own asshole . . . *and you don't like my language!!!*
(beat)
Well, I'm scared out of my mind, you goddam idiot! Maybe you'll stay so fuckin' cool you'll watch Mike and me burn to death and then you'll just *walk* home . . . but *I'm* scared, dammit, I'm bloody terrified!

Donovan slides over and gives Powell's helmet a hard, sharp slam against the basalt wall. Powell's head rings inside the helmet. But his hysteria dries up. He doesn't cry, but he's breathing heavily, trying to control himself.

DONOVAN (FILTER)
(calmly)
He's sorry, Dr. Calvin.

CALVIN (FILTER)
I understand. Now let's think.

She sits back in silence. Thinking.

## 162 ANOTHER ANGLE — FAVORING CALVIN

After a few moments Donovan slides over and holds Powell, who seems to be shivering. In a few beats it's all right, and he lets him go. They watch Calvin. Then . . .

CALVIN (FILTER)
Speedy is perfectly adapted to normal Mercurian environment according to the records of the First Expedition. But this area . . .
(she sweeps a hand around)
. . . is definitely abnormal.
(beat)
That's our clue.

The "area" she indicates is brightly-lit from the crystals that litter the ground, reflecting back the blazing sunlight.

DONOVAN (FILTER)
You mean these crystals. Okay, where do they come from? They might have formed from a slowly cooling liquid . . . but where would you get liquid so hot that it would cool in Mercury's sun?

There is snuffling from Powell, then a gulping sound as he gets hold of himself totally.

POWELL (FILTER)

Volcanic action?

Calvin sits up straighter, looks at Powell sharply.

CALVIN (FILTER)

Very good, Mr. Powell.

(beat)

What did you say to Speedy when you sent him for the selenium?

POWELL (FILTER)

I don't remember exactly. I just told him to get it.

CALVIN (FILTER)

(sharply)

I'm afraid I'll need to know *exactly* what you said . . . and how you said it.

POWELL (FILTER)

I said, uh, "Speedy, we need some selenium. You can get it such and such a place. Go get it." That's all. What more did you *want* me to say?

CALVIN (FILTER)

You didn't put any urgency in it?

POWELL (FILTER)

What for? It was pure routine.

Susan Calvin rises. She walks away from them, hands clasped behind her back, thinking. Finally, without turning:

CALVIN (FILTER)

In this case we may have departed from routine in a way that has killed us, Mr. Powell.

DONOVAN (FILTER)
You know what's wrong?

CALVIN (FILTER)
I think I do . . . yes.

DONOVAN (FILTER)
Well, let's have it.

She turns and walks back to them.

CALVIN (FILTER)
It goes directly to the Three Laws of Robotics . . . as it always does.
(she counts on her fingers)
One: a robot may not injure a human being or, through inaction, allow a human being to come to harm.

POWELL (FILTER)
(picks it up)
Two: a robot must obey the orders given it by human beings except where such orders would conflict with the First Law.

CALVIN (FILTER)
(on third finger)
And three: a robot must protect its own existence as long as such protection doesn't conflict with the First and Second Laws.

DONOVAN (FILTER)
Right! Now where are we?

CALVIN (FILTER)
Exactly at the explanation.
(beat)
Say the robot is walking into danger and knows it. Rule Three turns him back. But suppose you *ordered* him into

that danger? In that case, the Second Law sets up a counterpotential higher than the previous one and he follows orders at the risk of his existence.

(beat)

In the case of Speedy, the latest most expensive robot ever created, as valuable as a fleet of battleships, the Third Law—self-preservation—has been strengthened. So his allergy to danger is unusually high.

POWELL (FILTER)

(slaps himself)

And to make it worse, when I sent him I gave him the order casually, so the potential of the Second Law was rather weak.

DONOVAN (FILTER)

I think I get it . . . and I hate it a lot.

(beat)

There's some sort of danger centering at the selenium pool. It increases as he approaches, and at a certain distance from it Law Three drives him back until he hits a point of equilibrium, then Law Two drives him forward—

CALVIN (FILTER)

(nods)

So he follows a circle around the selenium pool, staying on the locus of all points of potential equilibrium. And unless we do something about it, he'll stay on that circle forever. And that's what's making him seem drunk. Half the positronic paths in his brain are out of kilter.

POWELL (FILTER)

But what's he running *from?*

CALVIN (FILTER)

You suggested it yourself. Volcanic action. Somewhere right above the selenium pool is a seepage of gas from the bowels of Mercury. Sulphur dioxide, carbon dioxide . . . and carbon monoxide. Lots of it—at this temperature.

DONOVAN (FILTER)
Oh my God.

POWELL (FILTER)
What? What the hell *is* it?!?

DONOVAN (FILTER)
Carbon monoxide plus iron gives the volatile iron carbonyl. And a robot is essentially iron.

Powell slumps down in the shadow farther. The robot's eyes move to pick him up again in the darkness.

POWELL (FILTER)
We can't get the selenium ourselves. Too far, the suits would burn out. We can't send these robots because they can't go without Daddy riding along . . . and they can't carry us fast enough to get it before we fry. And we can't catch Speedy because the clown thinks we're playing games and he can run sixty miles to our four.

CALVIN (FILTER)
There's one thing more . . .
(beat)
There's a high concentration of carbon monoxide in the metal-vapor atmosphere, considerable corrosive action. He's been out for hours. He was lurching. I think a knee-joint is going out.
(beat)
He'll be keeling over soon, and then *nothing* we can do will help. We have to think very creatively, gentlemen, and we have to think very, *very* fast.

HOLD on their terrified faces as we

**DISSOLVE TO:**

**163 CLOSE ON POWELL'S FACE**

Terrified, hopeless, through the helmet. He looks to his left and CAMERA GOES WITH to pick up Donovan. Equally lost. They know they're dead, and Donovan says it.

DONOVAN (FILTER)

Maybe another fifteen minutes, then we have to go back in. And that's it.

POWELL (FILTER)

Well, Calvin? Any ideas? Any bright new ideas? You're the one who knows how these suckers think!

He looks to his right. We cannot see Susan Calvin. Or her robot.

POWELL (FILTER) (CONT'D.)

Calvin? Where are you? I can't see you.

He gets up. Gently feels his way around in the darkness.

POWELL (FILTER) (CONT'D.)

(to his robot)

Hey you, dummy . . . swing your beams around here.

The robot shines his eyes around. The beams slip like oil across the dark rock. No Calvin, no robot.

POWELL (FILTER) (CONT'D.)

(alarmed)

Mike! She's gone!

DONOVAN (FILTER)

Dr. Calvin? Dr. Calvin, where are you?

(to Powell)

How the hell did she slip away?

POWELL (FILTER)

Turned off her radio, of course.

DONOVAN (FILTER)

Dr. Calvin! Please answer us!

POWELL (FILTER)

Lousy bitch . . .

(screams in radio)
No escape, Calvin! You're gonna fry the same as us, you lousy run-out!

DONOVAN (FILTER)
Jesus, shut up, Greg! Something's happened to her . . . she's not stupid . . . she didn't run out on us . . .
(beat)
Dr. Calvin! Answer us! Please!

There is a crackling SOUND OVER and then the VOICE of Susan Calvin comes to them.

CALVIN (FILTER)
There's always the First Law, gentlemen. Two and Three simply cannot stand against it. I thought of it earlier . . .

DONOVAN
Oh my God! Dr. Calvin . . . !
Come back!

POWELL (FILTER)
No! Oh, Christ, Mike . . . She's not . . .

CALVIN (FILTER)
I'm already too far out for you to help. I'll leave the radio open.

**CUT TO:**

**164 SUN-DRENCHED LANDSCAPE — ON CALVIN & ROBOT**

as the robot lopes steadily out toward the selenium pool. We can see the basalt cliff far in the b.g. now. And we understand that Susan Calvin has come much farther than the group progressed earlier.

## 165 PAST CALVIN TO HORIZON

Here comes Speedy. Loping smugly toward her, lurching a lot worse than before. But coming on steadily.

SPEEDY (FILTER)
(metallic and crazier)
Here we are again. Whee! I've made a little list, the piano organist; all people who eat peppermint and puff it in your face . . .

She's much closer now as Speedy comes near. He stops. He wavers, wobbles, takes a step backward.

CALVIN (FILTER)
There's an itching in my back. It's probably my imagination . . . but it may be hard radiation through the suit—getting to me already. Hello, Speedy.

## 166 PAST SPEEDY TO CALVIN

There is a large distance between them, but Susan has managed to get closer than the previous time. Susan's robot has stopped. But Speedy is backing up very slowly, step by step.

SPEEDY (FILTER)
. . . and I polished all the bearings in the Queen's nave-eeee . . .
(but querulously)
Tippy-tippy-tin, here we go agin . . .

He stares as Susan Calvin, 300 yards away, jumps from the robot's shoulder, landing on the crystalline ground with a light thump and a flying of jagged fragments. She starts toward Speedy on foot, the ground gritty and slippery as she walks unsteadily toward him. Speedy backs up. Susan closes by thirty yards, then stops.

CALVIN (FILTER)

Speedy! Look at me, Speedy. I've got to get back to the shadow or the sun will kill me. It's life or death, Speedy. I need you.

(beat)

Help me, Speedy!

Speedy takes one step forward, then stops.

SPEEDY (FILTER)

(uncertainly)

When you're lying awake, with a dismal headache and repose is tabooed . . .

**HARD CUT TO:**

## 167 CU — CALVIN'S FACE THROUGH HELMET

DONOVAN (FILTER)

It's no good, Dr. Calvin. He's reciting "Iolanthe" now. Come back . . . maybe we can . . .

CALVIN (FILTER)

No . . . too late . . . roasting . . .

Then we see that she sees something from the corner of her eye and she turns CAMERA ANGLE WIDENS and Susan lurches dizzily, throwing out her arms to steady herself as we see the giant robot on which she is riding moving toward her . . . without a rider.

ROBOT (FILTER)

Pardon, Master. I must not move without a Master on me, but you are in danger.

Calvin backs away, motioning frantically.

CALVIN (FILTER)

I order you to stop! I *order* you to stop!

She staggers, throws up her hand over her helmet. The heat is starting to get through the insulated suit. She weaves dizzily.

ROBOT (FILTER)

You are in danger, Master.

CLOSE ON CALVIN. Moisture on the inside of the helmet plate now. We HEAR the hideous rasping of her dying breath, the gasping as she is being cooked. She falls to one knee, dizzy.

CALVIN (FILTER)

*Speedy!* I'm dying . . . oh God, Speedy . . . *help* me, please help me.

CAMERA CLOSE so we see the huge feet of the robot behind her, coming closer. Now Susan is crawling toward Speedy on hands and knees, dying with every movement. She falls over and the CAMERA COMES IN TIGHT on her head and shoulders just as steel fingers close on her suit.

SPEEDY (FILTER)

(sane)

Holy smokes, boss, what are you doing here? And what am *I* doing . . . I'm so confused . . .

CAMERA ANGLE WIDENS and we see that it is Speedy, not the behemoth robot that has gotten to her first. She looks up into Speedy's metal face and smiles in the helmet.

CALVIN (FILTER)

(barely whispers)

It's all right, Speedy. G-get me to the shadow of the cliff . . . please hur . . .

**CUT TO:**

**168 CALVIN'S POV — THROUGH HELMET PLATE**

Through the mist moisture, the rasping of breath.

CALVIN (FILTER)

. . . ry . . . hurry . . .

Everything goes milky-white with water vapor and moisture as she faints and CAMERA GOES INTO THE MIST . . .

**DISSOLVE TO:**

### 169 SAME AS 141

In the darkness of the spaceship cabin broken by blasts of lightning outside, Bratenahl sits with the aged versions of Donovan and Powell, and the robot amanuensis, Frinkel. A few lights strobe on the control board, illuminating their faces in green and red and silver.

POWELL

Sent Speedy back out to one of the other selenium pools with urgent orders to get the selenium at *all* costs.

DONOVAN

He was back in forty-two minutes and three seconds. I timed him.

(beat, softly)

Susan Calvin.

BRATENAHL

How badly was she burned . . . ?

POWELL

(quiet now)

I don't think *I* could've taken it.

They sit silently for a few beats. Then:

BRATENAHL

Help me talk to her.

DONOVAN

We can't help. Old men hanging on. What kind of help could we give?

POWELL

She never liked us. Don't much blame her; we were smartasses in them days.

BRATENAHL

Please help me. You've told me a side of her no one knows. The world *should* know. It's important.

DONOVAN

(to Powell)

Greg, you tired?

POWELL

Sleep's a good idea. Busy day tomorrow.

They rise and start to move toward their berths. The robot assists Bratenahl to his feet.

FRINKEL

I'll see you to the port, sir.

BRATENAHL

(a little urgently)

I'll be on Sigma Draconis 5. Central can find me . . . if you want to help . . .

They disappear into the darkness of the spaceship and the robot leads Bratenahl gently, but firmly, to the port. As Bratenahl steps into the descender, Frinkel looks at him.

FRINKEL

They're tired, sir. Very tired. It must be terrible to live beyond one's time. I don't really comprehend the concept, but I feel their pain.

13

Bratenahl looks at the robot, and then the descender begins to lower, carrying him with it. Bratenahl flips the lightning-rod crown on his head. The last thing he sees as the threshold of the port rises up in FRAME is the robot standing there, his posture eliciting sympathy.

**DISSOLVE TO:**

## 170 THE CRYONIC CRYPTS UNDER SIGMA DRACONIS 5

Enormous caverns of shimmering plastic and steel. They stretch up into the distance. We see two figures walking down the two-lane-highway-wide corridor. On every side are crypt enclosures. The figures are dwarfed. We must get a sense of incredible height and size to this chamber. CAMERA DOWN till we pick up the SOUND of the footsteps of the two people. CAMERA DOWN SMOOTHLY to show us it is Bernice and Bratenahl. They are walking among the crypts where humans and aliens are frozen. Bernice carries a small device that beeps and strobes a red light.

BERNICE

This took every favor I had on call.

BRATENAHL

Thanks.

He is moody. Almost locked into silence. She looks at him worriedly.

BERNICE

You look sicker than hell.

CAMERA WITH THEM as they walk down the enormous corridor.

Thousands of sleeping, frozen shapes can be dimly seen through the quartz-crystal fronts of the crypts set into the metal walls, one next to another on into infinity, rising up, tier after tier, into the vaulted distance. Their echoing footsteps the only sounds accompanying their hushed voices.

BRATENAHL

I think I'm going to lose.

BERNICE

Lose what, Bob? That's what I want to know: lose what? Rowe will take you back.

BRATENAHL

I don't care about that anymore.

BERNICE

What kind of a hold has Susan Calvin *got* on you?

BRATENAHL

I can't name it. But I don't want to lose. Don't ask me for sense out of this. I keep running the tapes of her and Byerley together . . . over and over . . . there's something there . . . I just can't see it.

BERNICE
(wearily)

Who is this Bogert?

BRATENAHL

Norman Bogert. Head mathematician for U.S. Robots and Mechanical Men. Worked with Calvin for years, succeeded Alfred Lanning as chief executive of RoboMek.

BERNICE

He's been frozen for twenty-two years. What can he do?

BRATENAHL

Donovan and Powell mentioned some vague rumor they'd heard about a romance Susan Calvin had had . . . maybe Bogert can give me a clue. He was closest to her.

BERNICE
(looks at beeper)

Here. Tier fifteen.

She punches in a code and there is a whining sound of smooth machinery above them. They look far up into the distance and one of the crypts is extended on runners. Extensible arms grip the crypt and begin to lower it. As it comes down, Bernice stares at Bratenahl worriedly.

## 171 TWO-SHOT — MED. CLOSE

as Bernice turns him toward her.

BERNICE
(earnest)
You know, it might be nice to get to a time when I could care about you.

BRATENAHL
Maybe later.

BERNICE
Maybe there won't be enough later to work with, Bob.

BRATENAHL
I can't think about anything else now.

BERNICE
You never have. If not this, then a shipwreck on a lava sea on 30 Cassiopeia Iota, a begoon hunt on Carina Avoir 9 . . .

BRATENAHL
The crypt's coming down.

She sighs, takes her hand off his arm, resigns herself. The crypt comes down to floor level. They look in. There is a readout panel on the face of the quartz port. She keys it with the beeper device.

BERNICE
Cancer of the Lymph glands. Frozen in advanced stage. Short of total parts replacement we'll never be able to unfreeze him.

BRATENAHL

Can I talk to him?

BERNICE

Psych-probe into the hypothalamus. He'll wake enough so you can talk to the alpha-state consciousness.

(beat)

Here, you'll need an ear-plug.

She hands him a tiny device. He puts it in his ear, hooking the fastener over his outer ear. She keys him in. There is a series of *electronic* SOUNDS OVER. He stares into the crypt at the sleeping man within. CAMERA PAST HIM to crypt.

## 172 DOLLY IN ON CRYPT

Through the quartz-crystal port we can see quite clearly the body of a naked, sleeping man. NORMAN BOGERT was frozen when he was in his late fifties. His face is lean and feral, and his hair has miraculously escaped graying. It is sleek and black, flattened against his skull. His eyes are closed, his thin, full mouth tightly shut. CAMERA IN CLOSE as the strange electronic sounds continue in sequence. Then we HEAR an echoing VOICE, as if speaking from a wind tunnel. The sound of arctic winds in the b.g. Close to the voice so we hear the faintly bronchial hissing as each breath is taken.

BOGERT (ECHO)

Calling my name . . . down a long tunnel . . . over and over . . .

(beat)

A moment . . . I'm . . . am I awake . . . ?

BRATENAHL (O.S.)

Mr. Bogert. You're still sleeping. I've tapped in to talk to you.

BOGERT (ECHO)

Who is that? Are you *up there*? I can't see you.

BRATENAHL (O.S.)
My name is Robert Bratenahl. I'm a newsman for *Cosmos.* I've come to ask you about Susan Calvin.

BOGERT (ECHO)
Then I'm still dying. You woke me for this . . . *how* did you wake me . . . ? Am I dreaming this?

BRATENAHL (O.S.)
We've tapped into your unconscious, sir. It's quite important. I hope you can help me.

**173 FULL SHOT**

The entire cryonic complex, enormous, off in all directions. And two small figures down there, talking to the crypt. CAMERA COMES DOWN STEADILY as we HEAR the VOICE OVER.

BOGERT (ECHO)
(testily)
I don't want to talk to you. I take this as an imposition, really quite selfish of you, Mr. Whomever-You-Are.

BRATENAHL
But you were very close with Dr. Calvin through the important years of—

BOGERT (ECHO)
*No* one was close with Susan Calvin. No one and nothing but her beloved robots.
(beat)
Go away. Let me alone. I have dreams to dream.

BRATENAHL
(cagily)
Aren't you curious about what's gone on in the world since you were frozen?

BOGERT (ECHO)

Have you ever been in deep sleep?

BRATENAHL

No, sir.

BOGERT (ECHO)

Then let me tell you, the chief concern is with one's self. I have discovered many significant things about myself.

(beat)

Why, just a short time ago . . . I *think* it was just a short time ago ... I finally unearthed the reason I despise broccoli.

BRATENAHL

(frustrated)

Don't you want to know about the big development in teleportation?

BOGERT (ECHO)

(interested now)

You're kidding? They finally did it? Breakthrough from the interstellar spaceship drive we discovered, right?

BRATENAHL

Talk to me about Dr. Calvin and I'll fill you in on everything you want to know.

BOGERT (ECHO)

Coercing a helpless subconscious is unseemly, Mr. Whats-your-name.

BRATENAHL

Robert Bratenahl. Not coercion, just a little back-fence gossip.

CAMERA HAS COME DOWN to a TIGHT 3-SHOT of crypt, Bernice, and Bratenahl. She touches his arm, indicates she's going away to leave them alone. He nods half-abstractedly, fascinated by the mind that speaks from the cryonic freezer. She goes. Bratenahl leans against the crypt so his face is close to the quartz portal.

BOGERT (ECHO)
(delighted)
Oh, well! That's quite a different matter. I must confess I'm a trifle bored. Precisely what about Susan do you wish to know. . .
(beat)
By the way: she's still alive, isn't she?

BRATENAHL
Yes, of course. Would you like to know what year it is now, how long you've been frozen?

BOGERT (ECHO)
Don't depress me. Unless I'm about to be thawed, I'd as lief not know.

BRATENAHL
I'm afraid not, sir.

BOGERT (ECHO)
Then kindly keep the dreary knowledge to yourself. Now. What particular information about the good Doctor art thou seeking?

BRATENAHL
Do you remember Donovan and Powell? Troubleshooters for U.S. Robots?

BOGERT (ECHO)
Are *they* still around?

BRATENAHL

Barely.

(beat)

They passed on a remark about Dr. Calvin having had an affair with someone back around 2028. Could that have been Stephen Byerley?

BOGERT (ECHO)

(laughs raucously)

Oh, my lord. You're not *serious,* are you? Byerley? The President? How silly.

### 174 CLOSE ON BRATENAHL & BOGERT IN CRYPT

BRATENAHL

Well, there's always been this underground rumor . . .

BOGERT (ECHO)

A misanthrope. Robots were her passion.

(beat)

Except . . . once . . .

BRATENAHL

The time I asked about?

BOGERT (ECHO)

(slowly, thoughtfully)

Ye-es . . . his name was Milton Ashe. He was . . .

BRATENAHL

Tell me.

BOGERT (ECHO)

He was the youngest officer of the corporation. Slim, ascetic-looking chap. Nice enough, I suppose; though I always had the feeling he wanted my job. Didn't get it, but. . .

BRATENAHL
But Susan Calvin was interested in him?

BOGERT (ECHO)
Well, I think so. I never really found out what happened; not the specifics, you know. It started with the mind-reading robot, Herbie . . .

BRATENAHL
The *what*?

BOGERT (ECHO)
Oh, yes, of course. You couldn't possibly know about Herbie. He only happened once, but it was pretty sticky for a while . . .
(beat)
I was . . .

As he speaks his VOICE ECHOES LOUDER AND LOUDER, the words *I Was* repeating OVER AND OVER as though down a tunnel and sonically altering so they have a drawn-out doppler effect. As this happens CAMERA MOVES IN on the sleeping face to EXTREME CU and we

**MATCH-CUT TO:**

## 175 EXTREME CU — BOGERT'S FACE

But it is a younger Bogert, age 31. We see now the punctilious, more than slightly prissy Bogert of 2028, hair slicked back, thin lips pursed. CAMERA PULLS BACK from the MATCH-CUT TO HIS FACE and there stand three other people: Susan Calvin, age 34, the aged Alfred Lanning whom we saw in Scenes 55-59, and a younger man who, from the description just given in Scene 174, must be MILTON ASHE. He is wiry, good-looking in an ascetic way, a kind of wry humor about him. A friendly sort of young man. All four of them are standing in a "blue-light room" looking through a heavy one-way glass panel at a robot sitting and reading a book. The robot is HERBIE, much more sophisticated-looking than the Speedy robot of earlier, but not yet as sleek as the robots we've seen in present time. And Bogert is speaking, though all we HEAR OVER is a continuation of the echoing words *I was* . . . which synchronize with his lips as he says:

BOGERT

I was taking him down to the testing rooms myself. Obermann was off somewhere. And I wasn't speaking, I was *thinking* about the renewal of my aircar insurance and trying to remember what the expiration date was, and the robot looked at me and said, "It's the 15th of this month."

LANNING

(lights a cigar)

It reads minds all right. Damn little doubt about that; what you've told us only reinforces the tests.

(beat)

But *how? Why?*

BOGERT

That was the 34th RB model we've turned out. All the others were strictly orthodox.

ASHE

Listen, Bogert. There wasn't a hitch in the assembly from start to finish. I guarantee that.

BOGERT

(fussily)

Do you indeed? If you can answer for the entire assembly line, I recommend your promotion. By exact count, there are seventy-five thousand, two hundred and thirty-four operations necessary for the manufacture of a single positronic brain, each separate operation depending for successful completion upon any number of factors, from five to one hundred and five. If any one of them goes seriously wrong, the brain is ruined.

CALVIN

Arguing, trying to fix blame avails us nothing, gentlemen. We've produced a positronic brain of supposedly ordinary vintage that has the remarkable ability to tune in on thought waves. We don't know how it happened, but we *must* find out. *That's* the sum total of the problem.

LANNING

Calvin's right. And we have to keep it a secret among the four of us. If any word leaks out about a robot that can read minds, I hate to think what Soldash and the Church could do with it. A return of the pogroms!

BOGERT

I suggest we destroy it at once.

Through the window, the robot moves his head only the merest fraction. Susan sees the movement, wrinkles her brow, but says nothing. The others are looking the other way and don't see it.

LANNING

Don't be an ass, Norman.

(beat)

All right! We go about this thing systematically. Ashe, I want you to check the assembly line from beginning to end—everything.

ASHE

(puckishly)

All seventy-five thousand, two hundred and thirty-four operations? I is gonna be a busy widdle kid.

BOGERT

(primly)

Ashe!

But Susan lets the faintest tickle of a smile—the first we've seen from her—cross her thin lips. She is looking at Milton Ashe with a twinkle in her eyes, we now perceive.

LANNING

(to Calvin)

You'll tackle the job from the other end. You're the chief

robopsychologist at the plant, so you study Herbie and find out how he ticks. See what else is tied up with his telepathic powers, how far they extend, how they warp his outlook, and just exactly what harm it's done to his ordinary RB properties.

Susan nods. Still watching Ashe, who seems amused by all this flapping and worry.

LANNING (CONT'D.)

Norman and I will coordinate your work and interpret the findings mathematically.

Ashe turns and starts to walk away. He holds open the door to the "blue-light room."

ASHE

Be seein' ya in a million years or so.

(to Calvin, in a Humphrey Bogart voice)

And I'll be sheein' *you,* shweetheart.

She smiles lightly. He goes. Bogert purses his lips.

BOGERT

He's too flippant. Doesn't see the seriousness of this; if there's a leak, he'll be the one.

CALVIN

I doubt it. He's very good at his job. And he's dedicated.

Lanning gives her a sharp look; Bogert's mouth purses again and we see that he suspects her interest in Ashe.

Lanning and Bogert leave the room. Calvin stares at the robot, still sitting there and reading, for a long moment. Then she presses an interlock panel on the door set into the thick wall beside the panel of glass, and the door sighs open like a bank vault. She walks through.

## 176 INT. STUDY ROOM — ON HERBIE

The room is white, with two chairs in it. As Susan comes in, Herbie's photoelectric eyes lift from the book. He stands as she enters.

CALVIN

How is the study of hyperatomic motors coming, Herbie?

The robot's voice is level and controlled, very sane and coolly humanoid.

HERBIE

I know why you've had me studying these, Dr. Calvin.

CALVIN

I vas afraid you would, Herbie. It's difficult to work with you. You're always one step ahead of me.

HERBIE

There's nothing in your textbooks that interests me. It's all so incredibly simple that it's scarcely worth bothering about.

CALVIN

(quietly)

But it's a science that created you, Herbie.

He waves away her comment with a massive metal hand.

HERBIE

It's your fiction that interests me. Dickens, Dostoevski, the Brontë sisters, Mary Shelley.

CALVIN

(ruefully)

Yes, I should imagine you'd find "Frankenstein" fascinating.

HERBIE

(ignores the jab)

What fascinates me are your studies of the interplay of human motives and emotions . . .

(beat)

I see into your minds . . . your novels help.

CALVIN

Yes, but I'm afraid that after going through that cheap melodrama . . .

(bitterly)

. . . you find real minds like ours dull and colorless.

HERBIE

(exuberantly)

*But I don't!!!*

The sudden energy of his response startles her, brings her back a step. She tries to regain herself, her hand going to her temple, as if she *knows* he's reading her mind.

HERBIE (CONT'D.)

(confidentially)

But of course I know about it, Dr. Calvin. You think about him always, so how can I help but know. Your love, your hope, your pain. It's very much like the thought of hunger I get around the technicians at lunchtime.

She hides her face, turning away from him. Her back then stiffens. She turns back to him. She sits down.

CALVIN

Sit down, Herbie.

He sits.

CALVIN (CONT'D.)

You, uh, you haven't told this to anyone, have you?

HERBIE
(surprised)
Of course not. No one has asked me.

CALVIN
(blushing)
I suppose you think I'm a fool . . . ?

HERBIE
No, it's a normal emotion.

CALVIN
For others, perhaps. I'm not what you'd call . . . attractive.

HERBIE
If you are referring to mere physical attraction, I haven't the frame of aesthetic values to judge. But I know there are other types of attraction.

CALVIN
(as if she hasn't heard)
Not young . . .
(beat)
And he's twenty-seven and looks and acts younger. He laughs with some of the other women in the plant. . . I see him sometimes . . .
(beat)
Do you suppose he ever sees me as anything but . . . but what I am?

Herbie slams his metal palm down with a ringing clang on the book in his lap. She jumps at his vehemence.

HERBIE
You are wrong! Listen to me—

CALVIN

(with uncharacteristic passion)

Why should I? What do you know about it, anyway, you . . . you *machine*? I'm just a specimen to you, an interesting bug with my mind laid open like an autopsy. Why are you playing "advice to the lovelorn" with me? Do I amuse you?

(she sobs)

I'm a wonderful experiment in misery and frustration, aren't I?

Herbie hangs his head. He looks away. Susan is suddenly contrite.

CALVIN (CONT'D.)

I . . . I'm sorry. I didn't mean to—

(beat)

I've never felt like this before and I don't know what to do with myself, where to go, how to act, where I should put my hands . . .

HERBIE

(softly)

Won't you listen to me, please? I can help you if you'll let me.

CALVIN

(cold, bitter)

How? By giving me good advice straight from the tin can's mouth?

HERBIE

No, not that. It's just that I know what other people think . . . Mr. Milton Ashe, for instance.

Her eyes drop at mention of Ashe's name. She speaks in a dull monotone.

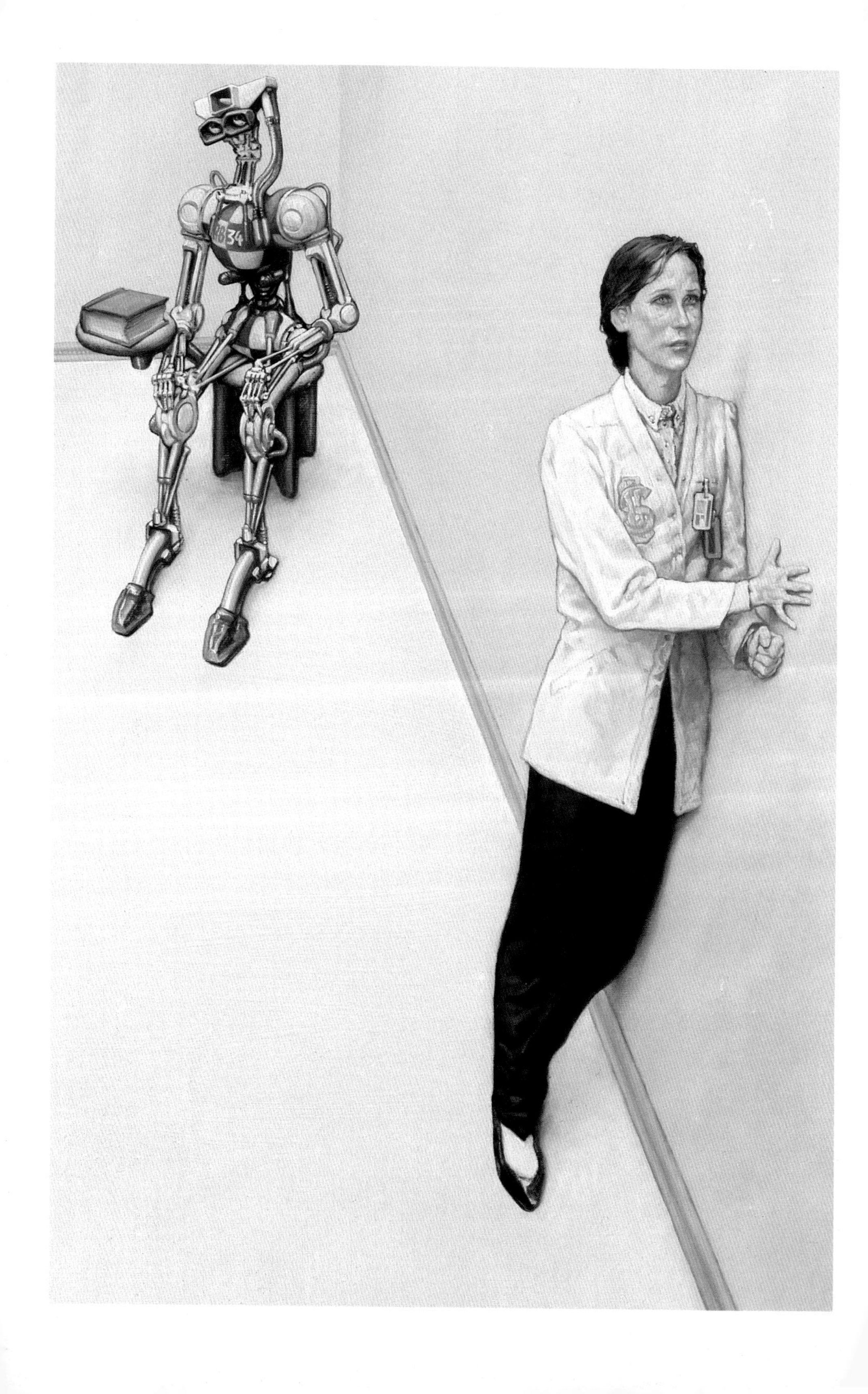

CALVIN
I don't want to know what he thinks. Keep quiet.

HERBIE
I think you *would* like to know what he thinks.

CALVIN
You're talking nonsense. He doesn't think of me at all.

HERBIE
You're wrong. Mr. Milton Ashe's thoughts of you—

CALVIN
*Shut up!* I'm ordering you to shut up. That's Second Law!

The robot shuts up. They sit for a few seconds. Then she heaves herself from the chair, walks around the white room, hands clasped behind her back. Finally she comes back and stands over him. He looks up at her with his photoelectric eyes. There are tears in her eyes.

CALVIN (CONT'D.)
(softly)
What does he think of me?

HERBIE
(quietly)
He loves you.

**177 EXTREME CU — SUSAN CALVIN — HER EYES**
widening alarmingly. CAMERA PULLS BACK FAST as she stumbles out of her chair, staggers to the wall as if faint, and holds on to the wall to support herself. Herbie rises to help.

HERBIE
Let me help you . . .

She waves him away. It is a hand movement that says let me alone for a moment; I'll be all right. He goes back and sits down on the metal-frame chair, hands lying on his knees.

## 178 DOWN-ANGLE — SHOT FROM ABOVE

ON THE SCENE. Susan cold against the wall. Herbie in his chair, the moment trembling silently in the room. Separation.

## 179 ANOTHER ANGLE — FAVORING CALVIN

as she comes back to her chair, sits down, facing Herbie. Her face is changed now. We see almost prettiness there; not much, but a tinge; the prettiness engendered by hope. Two bright flushed spots in her cheeks, the eyes wider, the mouth trembling a bit.

CALVIN
You're mistaken. You must be.

HERBIE
He looks deeper than the skin and admires intellect in others. Mr. Milton Ashe is not the sort of man to marry a head of hair and a pair of eyes. He loves you.

CALVIN
But he's never given even the slightest indication that—

HERBIE
Have you ever given him a chance?

Calvin stares at him thoughtfully for a moment, then makes a tiny, hesitant movement to touch his hand. The robot doesn't move. She draws back her hand.

CALVIN
(querulously)
A girl visited him here at the plant six months ago. Very pretty. Auburn hair and green eyes, very long legs. He spent all day with her, puffing out his chest, trying to explain how a robot was put together. Who was she?

HERBIE
(instantly)
Yes, I know the person you're referring to. She is his first cousin, and there is no romantic interest, I assure you.

She smiles almost vivaciously. She rises again.

CALVIN
(winsomely)
Now isn't that strange? That's exactly what I used to pretend to myself. Then it must be true.

She takes Herbie's cold, metal hand in both of hers. We can tell the robot weighs considerable because it is only with effort that she can lift his hand from his knee. She speaks in an urgent, husky whisper:

CALVIN (CONT'D.)
(earnestly )
Thank you, Herbie.
(beat)
Don't tell anyone about this. Let it be our secret . . . and thank you again . . . thank you so much, Herbie.

She smiles deeply, presses his hand, releases it, and goes. Herbie sits a moment as CAMERA MOVES AROUND HIM TO NEW ANGLE. Then he rises, picking up the volume clearly labeled *Physical Properties of Hyperatomic Motors* and replaces it in the bookcase. He draws out another book, and goes back to his chair, sits down, and opens it to read. The book is *Passion's Tender Fury.* The light in the room seems to dim and Herbie's photoelectric eyes glow brighter as we

**DISSOLVE TO:**

**180 INT. VAC CHAMBER — CLOSE-UP**

on a mass of pinkish-bluish matter being bombarded by beams of multicolored light, like tracer bullets. CAMERA PULLS BACK to show it is a positronic brain in a middle stage of development. It sits in a multifaceted crystal case with the pin-tip nozzles in the ceiling of the case spurting out the colored tracer beams. CAMERA ANGLE WIDENS to show us other such vac chambers in a receding view down the distance in the U.S. RoboMek plant. Bogert and Ashe stand watching. Ashe rubs his eyes wearily. He looks like hell. Bogert looks neat and cool, as usual. A little martinet, faintly prissy.

ASHE

(testily)

I'm gonna collapse. If I don't get some sleep. . .

BOGERT

Lanning's pushing me.

ASHE

Push, shove, jam, jam, I don't give much of a damn, Norman! It's been a week and I'm *tired*! I'm getting paranoid, God forbid someone should find out about our little mind reader . . . and so far . . . *nothing*.

(beat)

I thought you said the positronic bombardment here in Vac Chamber D was the answer?

BOGERT

(yawns)

It is. I'm on the track. The problem is Lanning. The old fellow disagrees with my analysis. He's out of date; still stuck in matrix mechanics.

ASHE

Why not ask Herbie and settle the whole affair?

BOGERT

(confused)

Ask the robot?

ASHE

(surprised )

Sure, why not? Didn't the old lady tell you?

BOGERT

You mean Calvin?

ASHE

(nods)

Li'l Susie, herself. The robot's a mathematical whiz. Does triple integrals in his head and eats up tensor analysis for chuckles.

BOGERT
(amazed)

Are you serious?

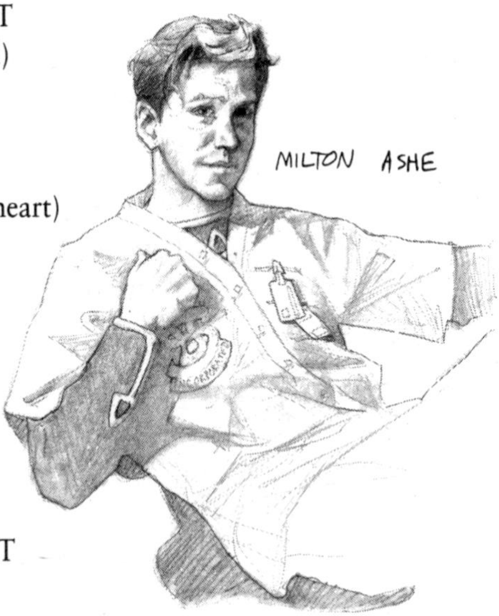

ASHE
(crosses his heart)

Honest to Peaches. The hook is that the Tin Woodman doesn't like math. Bores him. He'd rather read love novels. Big fan of Jane Eyre, from what Susie tells me.

MILTON ASHE

BOGERT

What's this Susie business? And why hasn't she told this to Lanning or me?

Ashe makes some small adjustments on the control console beside the chamber and the color of the tracer lights alters drastically but the bombardment continues.

ASHE

Well, she hasn't finished studying him. She likes to have it all bolted down before she lets out the big secret.

BOGERT
(testily)

She told *you*.

ASHE

Yeah, well . . . we sorta got to talking. I've been seeing a lot of her lately.

(frowns)

By the way, you notice anything weird about the way she's been acting lately?

BOGERT

She's using lipstick, if that's what you mean. Rather a ghastly vision, if you ask me.

ASHE

Hell, lipstick, rouge, eye shadow, kohl, even opened two buttons at the neck of her dress yesterday. But it's more than that. Way she talks. . . as if she were happy about something.

He shrugs.

BOGERT

(snidely)

Perhaps she's in love.

ASHE

Yeah, and as soon I get my pinfeathers dry-cleaned I'll fly home for some sleep.

(beat)

Go talk to Herbie.

Bogert smiles thinly, and turns to go as CAMERA INTO LIGHTS in the vac chamber and we

**CUT TO:**

## 181 SAME AS 176 — CLOSE ON NOTE PAPER

A subliminal residue of tracer lights flashes off paper that we see AS CAMERA PULLS BACK from paper being held by Herbie. We hear Bogert's VOICE OVER before CAMERA ANGLE WIDENS to show him standing beside the robot.

BOGERT

So there we are. I'm told you understand these things, and while I don't really need any help on this, I'm asking more out of curiosity than anything else. Lanning disagrees with me. What do you think of my findings?

HERBIE

I see no mistake, sir.

BOGERT

(preening)

I don't suppose you could go any farther than that?

HERBIE

I wouldn't dare try, sir. You are a far more accomplished mathematician than I and, well, I'd hate to second-guess you.

BOGERT

(complacent)

I rather thought that would be the case.

(takes papers, turns to go, stops)

By the way . . .

HERBIE

Um, yes. I read your thoughts quite clearly, sir. As you're thinking, Dr. Lanning *is* well past seventy and seems more than a bit out of touch . . . and as you think, he's been director of the plant for thirty-eight years.

BOGERT

Amazing. Uh, hmmm. Well, then, you would know if he's planning to, uh . . .

HERBIE

Resign? Yes, sir. I do know. In fact he already *has* resigned, and you're to be his successor.

BOGERT
(blown away)
Whaaat?

HERBIE
It hasn't taken effect, but he's signed the letter. He's merely waiting till the problem of, well, of *me* is settled.

Bogert smiles broadly. A shark that has eaten a big meal. He slaps the robot with a clang on his shoulder, turns to go.

BOGERT
Thanks, Herbie.

**CUT TO:**

## 182 TIME-PASSAGE SHOT— STOCK (MEASURE)

One of those time-lapse sequences of the sun passing across the horizon. But a special shot with the sun a blazing red eye, the kind of sun one sees only through pollution. Down it goes.

**MATCH-DISSOLVE TO:**

## 183 BOGERT'S OFFICE — MORNING

the sun going down in OVERLAPPING MATCH, into the glass front of a file case or the window of the office. CAMERA BACK to show Bogert asleep on his arm, fallen across the desk. More papers filled with mathematical doodlings than one can imagine, scattered all over the desk, the floor, the window ledge. Bogert rumpled, having worked through the night. The office door irises open and Lanning, looking starched but also weary, comes in. He walks around behind the sleeping Bogert, looking at the various pages exposed to cursory view. Finally, snorting in displeasure, he pokes Bogert's shoulder. Bogert wakes with a start, takes a moment to orient himself.

LANNING
(angrily)
Another night gone and nothing? Dammit, Norman, this is getting worse every minute. Now there're rumblings among the plant staff.

He picks up a piece of paper on which Bogert had been working when he fell asleep.

LANNING (CONT'D.)

This a new lead?

Bogert rips it from his hand angrily.

BOGERT

(sneers)

What's wrong with the old one?

LANNING

(shocked)

I told you that was a dead end.

BOGERT

And I say you're wrong. And I'm not alone. I have a corroborative view.

LANNING

From whom?

BOGERT

From Herbie.

Lanning dismisses him with a cavalier wave of the hand; and Bogert's punctured ego at such treatment is evident in his face.

LANNING

Oh, so Calvin told you about the robot's way with mathematics. Genius. Really remarkable.

BOGERT

So you've been gulled, too. Calvin had better stick to robopsychology. I've checked Herbie on math and he can barely struggle through calculus.

LANNING
(livid)
I don't know what sort of testing you ran, but I've been putting Herbie through his paces most of the morning and *he* can do tricks with math *you've* never even heard of!

He pulls a sheet of paper from his inner jacket pocket, thrusts it at Bogert. Bogert studies it. Amazement suffuses his face.

BOGERT
Herbie did this?

LANNING
Right. And if you'll notice, he's been working on your time integration of Equation 22. It comes to the identical conclusion I reached, negating your findings.

Bogert crumples the paper and throws it against the wall. Now he's furious, and he's yelling at the old man.

BOGERT
(angrily)
Are you crazy? Have you *totally* lost your grasp? If you'll reread Mitchell's original paper on the Linger Effect in positronic bombard—

LANNING
(also shouting)
I don't have to! I told you in the beginning, over a week ago, that I didn't like the use of the Mitchell Equation . . . *and Herbie backs me on this!*
(beat, wildly)
And dammit, I'm the *director* here! Who the hell do you think you're talking to?!

BOGERT
You haven't any secrets from a telepathic robot, you desiccated old fossil. I know all about your resignation!

LANNING
(stunned)
My *what*?!?

BOGERT
(quietly)
And I'm the new director. I'm very aware of that, don't think I'm not. *I* give the orders around here, old man, *me!*

LANNING
(red in the face)
You're suspended, you snot-nosed punk! You're relieved of all duties, clean out your desk . . . no, dammit, don't touch a thing! I'll have security lock off this office!

BOGERT
What's the use of all that, Lanning? I hold all the trumps. I *know* you've resigned. Herbie *told* me, and he got it straight out of your mind!

Lanning suddenly gets a contemplative look on his face. His rage is abruptly banked and the florid cast leaves his face. He speaks quietly.

LANNING
I want to speak to Herbie. He couldn't possibly have told you any such thing.
(beat)
You're either playing a very very dangerous game, Norman . . . or you've cracked under the strain. Either way, I'm calling your bluff.
(beat)
Come with me.

He starts for the door. Bogert follows, triumphant.

BOGERT
To see Herbie? Good! Very good!

And as the door opens and they go out we

**HARD CUT TO:**

**184 INT. ASHE'S OFFICE — DAY**

CLOSE ON A SKETCH of a house. Faintly Oriental in style, it is a hollow rectangle with curlicues in the center that are supposed to represent trees and gardens. We HEAR Milton Ashe's VOICE OVER before CAMERA PULLS BACK to show him and a radiant Susan Calvin leaning together over a drawing board.

ASHE

And in the center, that's the atrium, with bonsai and sculptured Japanese rock gardens. It's a lousy crude drawing but this is the dream house I've had in my mind for, oh, I don't know *how* long . . .

CALVIN

It's lovely, Milton. Just lovely. Very peaceful and strong, but quite logical in its way . . . *I've* always thought I'd like to—

She trails off. But Ashe isn't really listening. He goes on briskly, caught up in his dream.

ASHE

Of course I've got to wait for my vacation and settling this miserable puzzle about Herbie, but . . .

(he pauses, looks at her)

. . . can you keep a secret?

CALVIN

(lightly)

There are no secrets with Herbie around.

ASHE

(laughs)

I'm bursting to tell someone. And you're, well, you've come to be very close to me, Susan . . . I want you to know . . .

Susan looks as if she'll burst herself. She is radiant.

ASHE (CONT'D.)

I'm getting married!

Susan looks as if she's been hit with a ball-peen hammer. She clutches the drawing table and goes white. The two hideous blotches of rouge on her cheeks—part of the ghastly misuse of makeup we've noticed since this scene began—the attempt of a woman in love to be what she is not—those two blotches of rouge now stand out like bloody stigmata. She starts to buckle at the knees. He grabs her.

ASHE (CONT'D.)

Hey! Sit down, what's the matter . . . ?

She hangs in his grasp, but manages to speak.

CALVIN

Married? You mean—

ASHE

Sure! About time, isn't it? You remember that woman who came to see me about six months ago, Sheilah? Well, we're going to—

(beat)

My God, you *are* sick . . . you've been night and day on Herbie . . .

She wrenches away from him hand-walking across the wall toward the iris-door. She is babbling, looking horrible.

CALVIN

Headache! That's all, headache! I want to . . . to congratulate you . . . I hope you'll be . . . I'm glad . . .

She manages to palm open the iris, and still mumbling, stumbles out into the hall.

## 185 thru 189 ARRIFLEX — WITH CALVIN — OUT-OF-FOCUS

INTERIOR MONOLOGUE of CALVIN HEARD OVER as she lurches through the hallways, caroming off walls, down one long passage after another, colors shifting, her face wild and destroyed with anguish. CAMERA WITH HER in TILT-FRAME and SKEWED FOCUS.

CALVIN (FILTER OVER)
No! No! Herbie said . . . Herbie read his thoughts . . . he loves *me* . . . Herbie said Herbie read it . . . Herbie . . . Herbie . . .

She reaches the port to the HIGH SECURITY SECTION with its warnings. Her fingers play over the code panel to unseal the chamber to the white room where Herbie is kept. She falls through and her VOICE OVER CONTINUES:

CALVIN (FILTER OVER) (CONT'D.)
Tell me it's a dream . . . a bad dream . . . I'll wake up . . . he loves me . . . tell me . . .

**CUT TO:**

## 190 INT. STUDY ROOM — SAME AS 176 CAMERA WHIRLING IN CLOSE CIRCLE

HOLDING CALVIN and as she spins to find some way out of this nightmare the CAMERA PICKS UP HERBIE and then the two of them are in the maelstrom, their voices colliding.

CALVIN
Tell me it's a dream . . . I hurt . . . Herbie, tell me it's not real . . .
(beat)
Help me, Herbie . . . tell me . . .

HERBIE
You're dreaming all this, Dr. Calvin. It's not real. You'll wake up and he loves you . . . he loves you!

**CUT TO:**

## 191 ANOTHER ANGLE — FROM UP-ANGLE

as Susan Calvin suddenly wrenches herself out of the robot's grasp. She shoves against him, but he doesn't budge; but the force of her effort hurls her back, she slips, and falls to her knees. The robot moves to help her, but she screams at him:

CALVIN
(hysterical)
No! No, stop it! Get away from me! Get over there, get over there by the wall, stay away from me!

HERBIE
(pathetic)
I want to help.

CALVIN
What are you trying to do to me? What . . . what are you trying to *do* to me?

HERBIE
(mournful)
I want to help.

Susan crawls till she can rise . . . painful to watch.

CALVIN
Help? You want to help? By telling me this pain is a dream? By trying to push me into schizophrenia.
(shouts)
*This is no dream! What you* told *me was the dream!*

Then she stands, and suddenly her face grows quiet. She looks at him.

CALVIN (CONT'D.)
Wait . . . now I *understand* . . . oh, God, it's so simple, so obvious . . .

Herbie takes a step toward her, his hands out in a sad little supplicating gesture . . . this great creature, helpless before the shattered woman.

HERBIE
(with horror in his voice)
I *had* to!

CALVIN
And I believed you. Because I *wanted* to believe you.
Oh, God, how pathetic!

There is the SOUND O.S. of loud voices in the hall. Susan panics and tries to restrain her confusion, turns from the robot, who stands forlornly in the middle of the white room, hands still outstretched. As the door irises open, Susan goes to the far end, relatively unnoticed.

**192 ON THE IRIS**

as Bogert and Lanning boil through the opening. They don't even see Susan Calvin. They push close to the robot.

LANNING
Here now, Herbie! Listen to me!

HERBIE
Yes, Dr. Lanning.

LANNING
Have you discussed me with Dr. Bogert?

HERBIE
No, sir.

The crud-eating smile on Bogert's face vanishes. The answer came slowly, but clearly. Bogert shoves in closer.

BOGERT
What's that? Repeat what you told me yesterday.

HERBIE

I said that—

He falls silent. Deep within him comes the SOUND of his metallic diaphragm vibrating in soft discords.

BOGERT
(roaring)

Didn't you say he had resigned! Answer me!

Lanning pushes him away, stands facing Bogert, as if protecting the robot that towers up behind him.

LANNING

Are you trying to bully him into lying?

BOGERT

You heard him, Lanning. He started to say yes and got scared of you. Get out of my way! I want the truth out of him, do you understand?

Lanning won't move out of the way, he's holding his territorial imperative; but he puts out a hand to stop Bogert, and turns to Herbie.

LANNING

Well? Have I resigned? Yes or no?

The sound of malfunction inside Herbie rises slightly. He just stares. There is the faintest trace of a negative movement of the robot's head and CAMERA COMES IN TO CU but nothing more. Just the SOUNDS of Herbie running rough inside. CAMERA BACK.

BOGERT

What's wrong with you, have you gone mute? Can't you speak, you double-crossing metal monstrosity?

HERBIE
(quick answer)

I can speak.

BOGERT

Then answer the question! Didn't you *tell* me Lanning had resigned? Hasn't he resigned . . . ?

Again, nothing but silence, which HOLDS for several BEATS and in that silence we suddenly HEAR a high-pitched, almost hysterical laugh. From Susan Calvin. Bogert and Lanning spin, and see her for the first time.

BOGERT (CONT'D.)

(furiously)

You here? What's so funny?

Susan walks to them, joins the trio, looks up at Herbie with hatred in her eyes, her mouth tight, her fists clenched. But her voice is normal, controlled. *Too* controlled: dangerously.

CALVIN

Nothing's funny. Not a solitary thing.

She raises a hand as if to strike the robot, then slowly, almost agonizingly, *opens the fist* and lays it on the robot's metal chest. Herbie trembles for an instant. Can it be that this massive tonnage of thinking metal is frightened of the slight woman before him? She looks at him steadily.

CALVIN (CONT'D.)

(voice not quite natural)

Three of the world's greatest experts in robotics were conned in the same way.

(beat)

But it isn't *funny.*

This time the look that passes between Bogert and Lanning is one of utter confusion, raised eyebrows.

LANNING

What do you mean, "conned"? Is something wrong with him?

CALVIN

No, nothing's wrong with him . . . it's wrong with *us.*

(suddenly screams at Herbie.)

Get away from me! Go to the other end of the room and turn your face to the wall and don't let me look at you!

Herbie cringes before her attack and stumbles away at a clattering trot. He goes to the corner like a small child who's been bad, and turns his face into the angle of walls and stands immobile as Bogert and Lanning watch in utter amazement. She spins on them and with high sarcasm speaks to them.

CALVIN

Surely you know the fundamental First Law of Robotics?

(presses on, high dudgeon)

A robot may not injure a human being or, through inaction, allow a human to come to harm.

**193 thru 199 INTERCUTS — CLOSE ON BOGERT, LANNING & CALVIN**

from face to face as the mystery is unriddled.

BOGERT

Harm? What harm?

CALVIN

(shrilly, wild)

Why—any kind of harm! Loving creatures, protecting us from any kind, all kinds of harm: hurt feelings, deflation of ego. What about the blasting of a person's hopes, destruction of one's dreams? Is that injury, is that harm?

LANNING

(frowns)

But what would a robot know about—

He catches himself, with a gasp. His eyes widen.

CALVIN

(bitterly triumphant)

Oh, you've caught on at last, have you? *This* robot reads minds! Do you suppose it doesn't know everything about mental injury? Do you suppose if you asked it a question it wouldn't give *exactly* the answer you want to hear? Wouldn't any other answer hurt us, and wouldn't dear good-loving Herbie *know* that?!

BOGERT

Oh my God.

CALVIN

(snaps)

I take it you asked if Lanning had resigned. He read your mind and knew that's what you *wanted* to hear, so that's what he told you. You poor fool, Bogert.

LANNING

That's why it couldn't answer just now. An answer would've hurt one of us.

**200 WIDE-ANGLE SHOT — THE ROOM & SCENE**

as all three turn to look at the robot, still in the corner.

CALVIN

(softly, bitterly)

He knew all this. That . . . that devil knows everything about us: our stupid desires, our venalities, our fragile egos . . . knows everything.

(beat)

Including what went wrong in his assembly.

LANNING

That's where you're wrong. He doesn't know what went wrong; I asked him.

## 201 THREE-SHOT — CLOSER ANGLE

CALVIN

Big deal. You don't *really* want him to give you the answer; it would puncture your ego—yours, too, Bogert—to have a machine do what you couldn't. He *knows* that . . . he read your little minds!

BOGERT

He told me he knew very little about mathematics. He told me I was a superior mathematician . . .

He stops, embarrassed. He knows what that means now. Lanning suddenly starts laughing. At Bogert. Now he gets the whole picture, and he's laughing at Bogert's humiliation. It may not be noble, his laughter, but it *is* a tension-release. Bogert looks as if he'd like to bite off his own tongue . . . and then kill Herbie. Susan isn't caught up in the laughing, however. She's almost hellbent on wrenching as much pain from the encounter as she can . . . a form of self-flagellation.

CALVIN

*I'll* ask him. A solution by him won't hurt my ego.

(raises voice, wild, imperative)

Herbie! Come here. Now!

The robot turns and shuffles over, head downcast. CAMERA ANGLE WIDENS to include the robot and the other three.

CALVIN

Do you know at exactly what point in your assembly an extraneous factor was introduced or an essential one omitted that made you telepathic?

HERBIE

Yes.

CALVIN

All right, then. Give!

But there is a peculiar, cunning look on Susan's face. A look we've never seen before, almost malevolent. And it seems apropos that in the face of that look Herbie says nothing. He shuffles from foot to foot, but will not speak. The SOUNDS of malfunctioning come from inside him again.

CALVIN (CONT'D.)

(sweetly)

Why don't you answer, Herbie?

The robot moves his hand aimlessly, then blurts out:

HERBIE

I can't! You know I can't! Dr. Bogert and Dr. Lanning don't want me to!

CALVIN

They want the solution.

HERBIE

But not from me!

LANNING

(breaks in)

Don't be foolish, Herbie. We *do* want you to tell us.

Bogert nods agreement. Susan smiles a hard, tight, nasty smile. She knows what she's doing.

HERBIE

What's the use of saying that? Don't you think I can see past the words? Down deep in your minds you don't want me to! I'm a machine, not human: you can't lose to me without being hurt, your egos being crushed. That's deep in your minds, and it can't be erased. I *can't* give you the solution!

Lanning flares up again. He almost swings on the robot, but its bulk and obvious imperviousness stops him.

LANNING
(furious)
Dammit, we *created* you! We're your *masters,* damn you! Tell us!

The robot turns its head in what would be a painful movement if it were human.

LANNING (CONT'D.)
(gets control)
I'm sorry. That was uncalled for. We'll leave. Tell Calvin.

HERBIE
It wouldn't make any difference. You'd know the answer came from me.

## 202 CLOSE ON SUSAN CALVIN

Her face has now solidified in an almost cruel expression. We cannot be sure of that interpretation, but it's not a face that contains love and compassion. She speaks to Herbie slowly, very logically.

CALVIN
But you understand that Dr. Lanning and Dr. Bogert want that solution, don't you, Herbie?

## 203 TWO-SHOT — SUSAN CALVIN & HERBIE

HERBIE
By their own efforts!

CALVIN
(inexorably)
But they want it, and the fact that you have it and won't give it to them *hurts them* . . . you see that, don't you?

HERBIE
(buzzing inside)
Yes! Yes, I see that . . . oh!

CALVIN
And if you tell them it will hurt them, too . . . ?

HERBIE
Yes! Yes! Oh . . .

CAMERA ANGLE WIDENS as we see Susan advancing on Herbie, slow step by step. Herbie backs up before her. It is a bizarre scene: this great creature capable of crushing steel, pained and fleeing before the remorseless logic of the tiny woman.

**204 INTERCUT — BOGERT & LANNING**

as they watch the stalking before them, in frozen bewilderment. Susan's VOICE O.S. drones on carefully, relentlessly.

CALVIN (O.S.)
You can't tell them because that would hurt . . . and you can't hurt . . . you mustn't hurt. But if you *don't* tell them, you hurt them, so you *must* tell them . . .

**CUT BACK TO:**

**205 SAME AS 203**

Susan still advancing on Herbie, driving him back toward the wall not with force but with logic . . . endless, remorseless logic. The robot is now emitting a keening whine from within.

CALVIN
And if you tell them you will hurt them and you *mustn't* hurt them, so you can't tell them . . . but if you don't, you hurt, so you must . . . but if you do, you hurt, so you mustn't . . . but if you don't, you hurt, so you must . . . but if you do, you hurt . . .

Herbie bumps roughly against the wall, tries to slide off to one side, but Susan is there, speaking, speaking, always speaking, running the impossible logic of it at him. He turns this way and that, cannot escape, then drops to his knees. His face is at a level with hers now, and she won't stop. He shrieks.

HERBIE

Stop! Close your mind! It's full of pain and frustration and hate! Don't hate me so, please! I didn't mean any harm! I tried to help! I told you what you wanted to hear . . . I had to! Oh, please . . . please . . . !

But she won't stop. She keeps it up, speaking softly, slowly, but with venom.

CALVIN

You must tell them, but if you do you hurt, so you mustn't; but if you don't, you hurt, so you must—but if you do, you hurt . . . you hurt . . . you hurt.

And Herbie *screams*! A sound we've never heard on this Earth before. A SOUND THAT CHILLS US, that contains in it all the pain of inarticulate creatures senselessly murdered, small things crushed underfoot, seals bashed with ball bats, whales punctured by exploding harpoons, cows having their throats slit, millions going to the furnaces, memories of the rack and the boot and the Inquisition. A SOUND OF HORROR and ABSOLUTE, UTTER AGONY!

And it goes on and on. And rises till it fills the room and our minds and our eyes squeeze shut with the anguish in it. And then . . . suddenly . . . it stops. And the silence is even more piercing, more electrifying, more deadly.

And Herbie pitches forward in one smooth, sharp movement. Just missing Susan as he falls over with a crash, lies there with his face turned toward Susan Calvin, expressionless but somehow pathetic and hopeless. Dead.

**206 FULL SHOT — FEATURING BOGERT & LANNING**

Calvin and the dead robot in the near b.g.

BOGERT
(awed)
He's dead!

CALVIN
(laughs wildly suddenly)
No, not dead—just insane. You can scrap him now, because he'll never speak again. I've solved your dilemma!

Lanning moves in and kneels beside the robot. He opens the panel in the back and fiddles for a moment. He closes it and looks up at Calvin. CAMERA IN THROUGH THIS to HOLD Lanning's face. He is looking at her with new awareness.

LANNING
(respectful)
You did that on purpose.

## 207 ANOTHER ANGLE — FAVORING CALVIN

Her nostrils flare, her head is up. She won't back off.

CALVIN
(defiantly)
What if I did? You can't help it now.
(beat)
He deserved it.

BOGERT
You forced him to suicide. You killed him.

CALVIN
Sue me. Take it out of my pay.

Lanning and Bogert look at her with a new respect compounded of fear and respect for her passion; and clearly, a sense that they have misunderstood this woman totally, that she is far deeper, far stronger, far more purposeful than they have ever known.

LANNING
(softly, carefully)
I never thought you were much like your father; I see now I was wrong.
(beat)
I remember. . .

CALVIN
(cuts in hard)
Memory is a wonderful thing.

He stares at her for a long moment. Then turns to go. He passes Bogert, who has not moved, is frozen, staring at the tableau, hearing everything that's being said and not really grasping much of it. Lanning takes his arm.

LANNING
Come along, Norman. We'll go to my office and sit and breathe deeply, and then we'll have a drink and talk about futures.

Bogert is gently tugged, but remains standing there. He stares at Calvin, who returns his stare with hauteur and implacable strength. Lanning sighs, releases Bogert's arm, and goes. As the door irises closed behind him, Bogert speaks very very softly, with wonder:

BOGERT
What must that robot have told you . . . ?!?

Then he, too, turns and goes, leaving Susan alone. With Herbie.

**208 CLOSE ANGLE ON CALVIN — SHOT FROM ABOVE**

looking down at the dead Herbie. She stands there a second, then abruptly kicks the side of the head just below the emptily staring photoelectric eye. A smear of oxidized metal and shoe sole scuff is left on the otherwise perfect metal. One word escapes her lips, with venom, with viciousness:

CALVIN
(full of hate)
Liar!

**CUT TO:**

## 209 HIGH ANGLE — SHOOTING STRAIGHT DOWN

on the sprawled metal figure and the woman standing over her victim. As CAMERA GOES DOWN SLOWLY Susan drops to her knees beside the creature and begins rubbing in a pathological circle at the smear she has put on the metal. She murmurs the same word, over and over, but now with pain and loss and fear and frustration and hopelessness, over and over . . .

CALVIN
(pathetic)
Liar . . . liar . . . liar . . . liar . . .

She keeps rubbing till it almost turns into the sort of caress one would bestow on a favored pet crushed by a car. The touch. Circular. Over and over and over, as she says that word again and again and again and WE HEAR the WORD *LIAR* meld into ECHO CHAMBER OVER as CAMERA COMES DOWN AND DOWN and FOCUS SMEARS and we

**DISSOLVE TO:**

## 210 INT. CRYONIC CRYPT— ON BRATENAHL & BOGERT

CLOSE ON FACE IN THE MOISTURED INTERIOR OF CRYPT and we continue to HEAR the ECHO of Susan Calvin saying "Liar . . . liar . . . liar" over and over, FADING UNDER until it's a mere whisper, and we are back in the present time.

BOGERT
I never knew what was behind it all. Not actually. But I suppose I pieced it together from interior data.
(beat)
So you ask me was she Byerley's mistress, and I say . . . I don't know. But I doubt it. I don't think she was capable of deep affection, for anyone, after the thing with Ashe.

BRATENAHL
(disappointed)
And that's all of it?

BOGERT
(umbrage)
Well, you *said* you wanted back-fence gossip.

BRATENAHL
Yes, but I was sort of hoping for a clue to the link between Calvin and Byerley. A great deal depends on my getting to the bottom of this . . .

BOGERT
Ah . . . ! Do I detect that the fragile barque of your life is being shattered on the cruel reefs of Susan Calvin?

BRATENAHL
So that's all you have to tell me . . . ?

BOGERT
Oh, my. Now I've put you off with my viperous tongue. Yes, Mr. Whoozis, that's all I have to tell you.

BRATENAHL
Then I guess I'll be going.

BOGERT
Uh, not just yet you won't.

BRATENAHL
Pardon?

BOGERT
Our bargain. I tell you about Susan and Milton Ashe: you fill me in on the teleportation breakthrough and changes in the world.

BRATENAHL
(sighs wearily)
Right.
(beat)
Well, when Donovan and Powell solved that spaceship problem with the robots and discovered that the only way to beat Einstein's space-time equations was to die and get reborn when the ship made transition, it was only a matter of time till U.S. RoboMek found a way to eliminate the ship . . .

**211 BOOM SHOT — FULL SCENE**

as Bratenahl speaks the PRECEDING SPEECH OVER the CAMERA PULLS UP AND BACK to give us a full view of the cryonic chamber, immense and high-ceilinged. His VOICE GROWS DIMMER as CAMERA CONTINUES BACK AND UP and we are left with the view of the lone man, speaking to the frozen crypt and we

**DISSOLVE THRU TO:**

**212 EXT. BERNICE'S CONAPT — NIGHT — SIGMA DRACONIS 5**

a gigantic structure on an empty plain, tetrahedronal in shape—built on the concepts of Paolo Soleri— a superstructure that can house 170,000 people.

There are three moons in the night sky. CAMERA MOVES IN on the Soleri-like condominium arcology, toward one window among millions, the condo apartment of Bernice Jolo, as we

**DISSOLVE THRU TO:**

**213 INT. BERNICE'S CONAPT — NIGHT**

As with Bratenahl's own arcology conapt (condominium-apartment) in Scene 139, Bernice's quarters here on Sigma Draconis 5 are an "environment construct," in the mode desired by the inhabitant's secret fantasy of the ideal personal living space. Bernice Jolo has opted for a SHADOW ROOM. It is a gray ovoid shape wavering, altering at the edges. Shadows play across the dim interior. Some seem like waves of fog, others seem to be human in shape, and some are just abstract shapes that change from moment to moment. Colors alter. And music dominates as various shadows take predetermined prominence over others. At one point the shadows seem to be a group of alien musicians, playing odd instruments, and alien MUSIC FILTERS IN OVER. Then they recede and the SOUND OF NIGHT BREEZES lift into the room, ruffling the hair of Bernice Jolo, lying naked in the warm, central pool that dominates the living space. The pool has soft sides that mold to her shape as she reclines against them. It is restful, but Bernice is not subdued; she seems anxious, distraught. Naked, she rises from the pool and CAMERA MOVES ACROSS THE ROOM with her as she goes to an iris in the wall. The room tries to hold her, to captivate her with more frantic shadows that converge on her as she nears the iris. She turns on the room with annoyance.

BERNICE
(to the room)
Fade out . . . stop annoying me!

The room goes dead at once, and lights up to reveal a soft egg-white nothingness, all the magic gone. She passes her hand in front of the iris and the door swirls open. Inside, a huge semicircular screen is being watched by Bratenahl. He sits morosely, totally absorbed, in a formfit chair. He is watching the Central comm feed tapes we've seen before. Tapes of Byerley and Calvin. He is watching, as she enters, the scene of Calvin from year 2032 we saw in Scene 8 (same as forthcoming Scene 272): Calvin and the "Lenny" robot in U.S. Robots' Test Area Nine. Bernice goes into the room, and stands behind him.

## 214 INT. VIEWROOM — ON THE SCREEN

we have a huge panoramic of the scene with Calvin and Lenny. CAMERA BACK to HOLD Bratenahl in the chair, fist against cheek, Bernice behind him, naked, concerned, watching *him*.

BERNICE
(softly)
Bob?

He pays no attention. He is riveted.

BERNICE (CONT'D.)

Bob! Please . . . you've been at it for three hours.

He notices her but doesn't turn around. He speaks to the room:

BRATENAHL

(wearily)

Freeze it. Gimme some light.

The scene on the screen freezes, Calvin touching Lenny's metal hide. The room brightens with soft light. He reaches up a hand and she takes it, kisses his fingers.

BERNICE

(troubled)

Should I be worrying about you?

BRATENAHL

(also deeply troubled)

I think so.

(beat)

Maybe I'd better face it; this is dead cold end. I've played out every way of going and I'm still nowhere.

BERNICE

Bogert?

BRATENAHL

Interesting, but not what I was going for. I've run this tape over and over . . . and I keep getting the feeling the answer is here *some*where, but I'm just not sharp enough to see it.

Bernice comes around and sits at his feet. He looks exhausted.

BRATENAHL (CONT'D.)

Dammit, I feel as if I *know* her!

BERNICE

Then do the piece on her from what you've already got. My God, Bob, what does Rowe want from you? If it hadn't been for you, he'd never even know she was in Brazil.

(beat)

He ought to be satisfied with that!

BRATENAHL

That grisly sonofabitch stopped pickin' green apples like that when he was ten. No . . . he lusts for the *big* story. He wants to know for bottom-line dead certain if old Susan Calvin was *fucking* Stephen Byerley.

BERNICE

Nice man.

BRATENAHL

Not nice. He's got my matrix, he's got my job, he's got my life in a lockbox. He's got a knot around my throat.

BERNICE

I can't stand to see you like this.

BRATENAHL

(sighs, slumps)

I wish to God I could stop this, just forget it.

BERNICE

Do it, then! Just *do* it. Tell Rowe to go to hell.

BRATENAHL

I can't . . . I have to know . . . all about her.

BERNICE

Why do I feel jealous of an eighty-two-year-old woman?

BRATENAHL

(woefully)

For the first time in my life I have no control over what I'm doing, where I'm going. I'm being jammed and run!

BERNICE

Why you? Why *now*?

BRATENAHL

I think it's because the status quo has changed. There's something different now . . .

BERNICE

Which is?

He rises, steps around her, goes to the screen, puts his hand on the image of Susan Calvin frozen there.

BRATENAHL

Stephen Byerley is dead.

She stares at him, uncomprehending.

BRATENAHL (CONT'D.)

He isn't around to protect her.

BERNICE

Protect her? From what?

Bratenahl shrugs. He doesn't know the answer. She rises, comes to him. They stand with arms around each other.

BERNICE (CONT'D.)

(gently)

I'm still trying to get us in to see her. It'll work out.

(beat)

You hungry?

He shakes his head. Leaves her, walks around the room. Stops. Stares at the frozen image.

BRATENAHL

I'll come in, in a little while. I just want to go through this stuff another couple times. Why don't you get some sleep.

She stares at him a moment, then nods resignedly, helpless to pull him out of it. She goes to the iris, which swirls open. She stands in the doorway for a moment as he sinks back into the formfit. As he speaks to the room, Bernice already forgotten, she goes out, and the iris swirls down.

BRATENAHL (CONT'D.)

(to the room)

Down the light. Run it again.

**CUT TO:**

**215 INT. BERNICE'S CONAPT — ANGLE ON POOL — NIGHT**

The walls are fleece-cloud soft with stars showing here and there. Bernice lies sleeping, naked, in the pool. But she floats on the surface, on a blue mist cloud that supports her. CAMERA IN on her sleeping face as a hand reaches into the frame and touches her shoulder. She starts suddenly. CAMERA ANGLE WIDENS to show Bratenahl crouched at the edge of the pool, urgently looking at her.

BRATENAHL

Don't be scared. It's just me.

BERNICE

(groggily)

What's the matter?

BRATENAHL

Something important. I need your help.

BERNICE

(rising)

What is it?

BRATENAHL

It's so incredible, I don't believe it . . . I think I've got the answer . . .

She comes out of the pool, shivers. The mist dissipates. She walks toward a panel on the sideboard. Buttons and readout slots on the panel.

BERNICE

Let me get a wrap.

She punches out a code and a folded garment comes zipping through a slot. She shakes it out. A soft, azure-colored peignoir. She slips into it. Bratenahl starts back for the room where he was watching the tapes when we last saw him. The wall irises open. He enters. She follows, still a little sleepy.

## 216 INT. VIEWROOM — SAME AS 214

The wall scene is blank. Bratenahl motions her to the formfit chair. He stands near the wall, excited.

BRATENAHL

(to the room)

Run that last one again. Very slowly.

The wall flickers and runs the scene of Byerley on the deck of a trimaran, looking youthful and outdoorsy. Byerley's face in EXTREME CU.

Bratenahl walks to the wall, his shadow across the scene.

BRATENAHL (CONT'D.)

Freeze that! Right there!

Byerley's face in EXTREME CU. Bratenahl puts his hand on the image of Byerley, just under one of the eyes. He stares very closely.

BRATENAHL (CONT'D.)

(to Bernice)

Okay. Now come take a close look at his face. The resolution's perfect, you can see every pore.

She comes up and looks as closely as he.

BRATENAHL (CONT'D.)

Okay. Now rerun that footage of Byerley and Calvin's tour of the EarthCentral Computer Complex . . . the 2036 sequence . . .

The WALL CHANGES INSTANTLY. It shows a HIGH SHOT LOOKING DOWN into a shaft filled with computer facings. As if a mine shaft had been used to stack computerized elements down to the center of the Earth. CAMERA COMES DOWN FAST to a high-ceilinged tunnel lit as well as high noon. The CAMERA RACES FORWARD to a group of men walking through the computer complex. It comes to CU on Byerley and goes past.

BRATENAHL (CONT'D.)

Back up to the closeup on Byerley and freeze it.

The room complies. Byerley in huge size. Bratenahl and Bernice stare at the face clearly, closely. He touches the face where he touched the last one: the smooth skin under the eye.

BRATENAHL (CONT'D.)

(to room)

How many years between this footage and the stuff on the trimaran?

VOICE OF THE ROOM

Thirteen Old Earth years, sir.

BRATENAHL

Has any of it been retouched?

VOICE OF THE ROOM

No, sir. It is raw footage, minimally edited for continuity.

BRATENAHL

Okay. Split frame, and give me the Byerley closeups from both sequences at the same time.

The wall flickers and now we have both CLOSEUPS of Stephen Byerley, thirteen years apart, side by side. Bratenahl nods as if convinced, waves a hand at the wall, and moves back so Bernice can see clearly.

BRATENAHL (CONT'D.)
(to Bernice)
There it is.

BERNICE
(confused)
Yes, there it is.
(beat)
There *what* is?

BRATENAHL
You tell me. What do you see?

BERNICE
The President.

BRATENAHL
Two views separated by thirteen years of the most demanding job the world has ever known . . . first President of the Galactic Federation.

BERNICE
Yes . . . *and?*

Bratenahl is impatient, excited, overwhelmed with what he thinks he's discovered. He doesn't know how to convey it to her. He turns back to the screen, speaks to the room.

BRATENAHL
Hey, dip into the comm feed and run me up a closeup of any news footage you've got on Dr. Bernice Jolo, two tight shots side by side, make them . . . oh . . . five years apart . . . or more.

The screen goes blank, flickers with waiting time, then suddenly flashes on split-screen CLOSEUPS of Bernice. The one on the left has a legend 2071 on it; the one on the right bears the legend 2076. Bernice squeals.

BERNICE

No fair! I'd just come off a three-hour trepanning session!

BRATENAHL

*Look* at them! Five years apart, just *five,* not thirteen . . . *five!*

She steps closer, examines herself.

BRATENAHL (CONT'D.)

(to room)

Put back the Byerley closeups.

Byerley is back. Now Bernice is intently studying them. Suddenly her mouth opens in a gasp. She turns back to Bratenahl.

BERNICE

He didn't change! He's . . .

BRATENAHL

(jubilant)

He's the same. *Exactly* the same. Not one wrinkle. Under the eyes, that's where it tells first . . . especially for a man saddled with that kind of constant pressure.

(beat)

Damn! Damn! No darkness under the eyes, no puffiness, no wrinkles! Nothing!

BERNICE

Bob . . . you don't think he was . . .

He grabs her, swings her around; he's
knocked out with joy.

BRATENAHL
I do! I *know* he was. The sonofabitch was *immortal*!

He swings her and kisses her and we

**CUT TO:**

## 217 SAME AS 213 — FULL ON HOLOGRAPHIC CHAMBER

The living area of Bernice's conapt. Not much later. Bratenahl stands in front of a section of Bernice's living room wall that has slid back to reveal a semicircular holographic reception chamber. He holds a small device on which he is punching out coordinates for transmission. They emit soft musical tones. The chamber fills with a milky mist shot through with scintillations. Then there is a shape faintly discernible that takes full form (though we can see through it and we know it's a projection). It is the robot, Frinkel. It looks out at Bratenahl.

FRINKEL
Mr. Bratenahl. Very good to see you again, sir. Are you coming back to visit?

BRATENAHL
Hello, Frinkel.
(beat)
No, I'm not coming back . . . but I need their help.

FRINKEL
Dr. Calvin?

BRATENAHL
Yes. I have to talk to them.

The robot looks around behind itself, as if checking to make sure it's alone. We cannot see much of the b.g. but only vague shadowy intimations of the saloon of the old buckety spaceship we saw in Scene 141.

FRINKEL

They've discussed it quite a lot, sir. They don't agree . . . about getting involved.

BRATENAHL

(urgently)

Frinkel . . . listen . . . I've stumbled on what I think is something very very important. I need to get a message to Susan Calvin personally.

He has walked right up to the hologram now. At times, as he speaks, he walks *through* the image.

FRINKEL

Your friend can't get it to her?

BRATENAHL

Calvin hasn't responded to Dr. Jolo's request. I think she may not have actually received the message.

(beat)

But she'd certainly talk to Donovan and Powell. For old times' sake.

(beat)

It's just eleven words. They can get eleven words to her, can't they . . . ?

(beat)

Please, Frinkel . . . let me ask them.

The robot fades out of the pickup area for a moment, as if checking to make sure there's no one around to overhear.

FRINKEL

They're resting right now, Mr. Bratenahl. Central sent through the parts for a new booth . . .

(beat)

There's a big jump coming up.

(beat)

Would you trust me to speak to them, sir?

BRATENAHL

Yes, of course. Thank you, Frinkel.

FRINKEL

What are the eleven words?

BRATENAHL

(using hand-device)

Here . . . I'm punching in the transmission coordinates for Susan Calvin's receiver. But they have to speak to her, not to her guards. Just have them say to her: *Stephen Byerley was immortal. Now will you talk to me*? And the eleventh word is my name.

FRINKEL

(slowly)

That's rather startling, sir.

(beat)

I'll speak to them.

BRATENAHL

Thanks, Frinkel. I'll be waiting right here.

The robot hologram fades back to mist, and the chamber is empty. Bratenahl clicks off the hand-device and as CAMERA MOVES INTO empty chamber, into mist and emptiness, we

**DISSOLVE TO:**

**218 INT. BERNICE'S CONAPT — ANOTHER ANGLE ON POOL**

Some time later. Shadowplay across the walls. Bratenahl and Bernice are in the pool. Soft alien music wafts through the room. They lie there, speaking softly as CAMERA COMES DOWN.

BERNICE

You haven't been chasing this story because you want to find out if she was Byerley's mistress, have you?

BRATENAHL
No; at least not after the first.

BERNICE
And it's not obsession, is it?

BRATENAHL
Maybe in a way; but, no, not really.

BERNICE
Then what bothers *me* about all this also occurred to you.

BRATENAHL
Almost from the first. But when I realized he couldn't age . . .

BERNICE
That's what bothers me. If he was immortal . . . why did he die?

BRATENAHL
No one ever saw him die. He was atomized. Every molecule pulled apart.

BERNICE
Why?

BRATENAHL
I think Susan Calvin knows. And I think it's something that shouldn't be kept from people.

BERNICE
Was he . . . killed? Was he put down, do you think?

BRATENAHL
It would explain why she's afraid to see me.
(beat)
Damn it! Damn it! Nothing from Donovan and Powell . . . not a sound.

The colloid fluid in the pool—obviously water and something else—shifts color and waves of rainbow hue pulse through the pool, bubbles rising then bursting silently on the surface like a lava lamp lit from below.

BERNICE

She hasn't responded to my call.

BRATENAHL

(musing)

You know, she won't let go of me. I sometimes dream about walking into that chamber under *Xingú Xavante* and she comes out of the darkness and she's smiling, and she extends her hand and we shake, and she says, "I'm so glad you could come to visit, Robert."

BERNICE

The robot may convince Donovan and Powell. Take it easy . . . it hasn't been that long since you spoke to him. It'll work out.

BRATENAHL

(wearily)

No, it's all done. I blew it. I was there, right there, and I scared the hell out of her. When the vase fell out of her hands I watched it and when it hit I knew it was all over. Shit!

There is a SOFT INSISTENT MUSICAL TONE that we HEAR OVER. It repeats several times. Bernice reaches out to a glowing color-coded series of rectangular panels set into the edge of the pool and palms one of them. One of the walls becomes a hologram chamber and a milky fog begins to swirl, finally assuming the shape of MICHAEL DONOVAN. The old man stands there, looking embarrassed. Bratenahl perceives his discomfort at Bernice's nudity, and nudges her subtly. She motions across the watery surface and shadow fog rolls in to cover her like an ephemeral garment.

DONOVAN

Didn't mean to intrude, Bratenahl.

BRATENAHL

No intrusion, Mr. Donovan; we were just talking.

(beat)

Michael Donovan, Bernice Jolo; Bernice, this is Mr. Powell's partner.

Bratenahl reaches to the edge of the pool and grabs up an edge of what looks like beige Kleenex from a dispenser. It pops up and he shakes it out. It is a disposable fabric garment, like a short tunic. He slips into it and comes out of the pool. He comes to the hologram of Donovan, with all its substantiality.

DONOVAN

Greg and I, well, we sat around talking about you with Frinkel.

Bernice comes into the frame, also dressed in a short tunic of golden hue. She stands watching the two men, one real, the other just an image.

BRATENAHL

He thinks pretty highly of you two.

DONOVAN

Yeah, well, we've been through a lot together. He's okay.

BRATENAHL

You want to tell me something, Mr. Donovan?

DONOVAN

(awkwardly)

Hmmm. Yeah. Well.

(beat)

We're goin' out in about an hour . . .

The way he says it, gives Bratenahl pause. He looks at the old man closely.

BRATENAHL

That's the Coalsack out there. You going to plant the first booth?

DONOVAN

Didn't come to talk about that.

(beat)

Susan Calvin says she'll see you.

## 219 ANOTHER ANGLE — FEATURING MED. CU — THE MEN

Bratenahl is shocked. The old spaceman holds his noncommital expression. He is clearly trying to do what he's come to do without having to suffer the embarrassment of compliments or thanks. He is extremely poised, grand in a quiet way.

BRATENAHL

(finally)

Thank you, Mike.

(beat)

How'd it go?

DONOVAN

(shrugs)

We said thank you. It was something we'd never said to her before.

They stand that way for a moment. Inherent in the moment is the understanding that Bratenahl's visit, his drawing their memories back to the time when Susan Calvin had saved their lives, when she had meant more to them and *been* more to them than they'd ever cared to admit, has altered their lives in these final moments. It is awkward, and Bratenahl presses away from the explanation.

BRATENAHL

Shall I call her?

DONOVAN

She'll call *you*. We told her where you are.

Another long moment. Then, carefully:

BRATENAHL

Mike, why did you do this for me? I was only a nuisance to you.

Donovan looks at Bernice. She senses that this is a thing best said between the two men privately.

BERNICE

I'll punch up something to eat.

She goes. Bratenahl turns back to Donovan, waits.

DONOVAN

(awkwardly)

You'll think it's a silly reason for doing anything.

BRATENAHL

I'd like to know.

Donovan draws a deep breath, looks off and around, gathering the right words. He speaks softly.

DONOVAN

Time's short for us. We've been around too long . . . everything's past now. Little things start to mean too much and . . . well . . . you won't think this's a big thing but . . .

(beat)

. . . you never called us "Pop."

Quiet.

BRATENAHL

(softly)

Thank you, Mike.

(beat)

You're not coming back from out there, are you?

Donovan won't permit *that much* closeness. He clears his throat, swipes at his nose with embarrassment, then straightens his back as best he can.

DONOVAN

I gotta go.

BRATENAHL

You'll say thanks and goodbye to Mr. Powell for me.

Donovan nods once, quickly, then the image begins to scatter into scintillations of foggy matter with lights in it. Then he's gone. Bratenahl stands staring into the empty hologram chamber. A hand comes into FRAME, rests on his shoulder. He turns and CAMERA ANGLE OPENS to include Bernice.

BERNICE

I heard.

BRATENAHL

(shaken, quiet)

They're going to go out there into the big dark, the Coalsack, and they're going to plant the last booth . . .

(beat)

. . . and just keep on going as far as they can . . . and that'll be it.

He turns, stares out one of the huge geometrically-shaped windows, out at the night sky of this alien world. She stands beside him and they move close to each other. CAMERA MOVES PAST THEM as we HEAR Bratenahl's next speech, and CAMERA GOES to HOLD THE NIGHT.

BRATENAHL (O.S.)

What they must have been when they were young men . . .

CAMERA TO NIGHT and we

**SLOW FADE TO BLACK**
**and**
**FADE OUT.**

**FADE IN:**

**220 EXT. BRAZILIAN JUNGLE — DAY — LONG SHOT — DOWN-ANGLE**

A flitter platform, as big as a swimming pool, but supported on invisible tractor-beams (like the effect in Scene 5 with the rods that keep rain off) MOVES SWIFTLY INTO FRAME AND DOMINATES. There is a faint hissing SOUND of the force-field that keeps it aloft. The vehicle skims across the sky as CAMERA (SPECIAL EFFECT) FOLLOWS. It descends. The vehicle can make 90° turns and halt its forward momentum to go down horizontally without arcing in. CAMERA FOLLOWS. A section of jungle tilts up, a false landscape. And down there in the two-acre section revealed by the úptilted trapdoor of foliage, we see a modernistic landing area for the platform. The flitter descends rapidly as CAMERA GOES WITH and we PASS THROUGH THE GROUND into the underground eyrie of Susan Calvin.

**221 UP-ANGLE — PAST FLITTER**

as the vehicle COMES DOWN INTO CAMERA and we see, above it, the false landscape trapdoor slowly tilt down to close. Everything is suffused with a blue glow, from a light-source we cannot identify.

**222 FULL SCENE — ON FLITTER**

as it settles to the pad. Almost immediately a cadre of advanced style robots (of a type we haven't seen thus far) move in. The flitter platform has sunk into a proscribed circular depression in the landing pad, so it is flush with the pad itself. Now Bratenahl and Bernice step off. And we see that the "pilot" of the vehicle has been a robot built into the leading edge of the platform itself. CAMERA COMES IN on the flitter across the surface of the pad, from a LOW LEVEL.

ROBOT PILOT

Sorry about that turbulence coming over the Serra do Roncador.

BERNICE

Don't worry about it, Freddy. Mr. Bratenahl recovers quickly.

ROBOT PILOT

And don't worry about the puke, Mr. Bratenahl; my internal sweepers'll have it off the platform in no time.

Bratenahl, looking green, gives the smartass robot a look. He just nods wearily. It hasn't been a good trip for him. They walk toward CAMERA, away from flitter, as the robots move in to off-load the shaped crates of material, their tetrahedronal luggage, and to service the platform.

## 223 FROM BRATENAHL & BERNICE TO 1st GUARD

He has been trailing the cadre of work robots.

1st GUARD

Doctor Jolo, Mr. Bratenahl: Doctor Calvin has asked me to serve as liaison. I'll take you to the residence if you're ready.

BERNICE

Our luggage . . .

1st GUARD

Will be there by the time we arrive.

Bratenahl stares at the 1st Guard. He ain't happy to see him.

BRATENAHL

I was wondering when I'd see you again.

1st GUARD

I must confess I didn't expect to see you here again, sir.

Bernice is looking bewildered. Bratenahl speaks to her but doesn't take his eyes off the Guard.

BRATENAHL

(to Bernice)

He and his partner did an adagio on me when I was here before.

1st GUARD

That was regrettable, sir; but I hope you'll understand the necessity. You *were* trespassing.

BRATENAHL

And this time I'm an invited guest.

The 1st Guard smiles. The 1st Guard extends one hand in a direction OFF-CAMERA and they move in that direction as the CAMERA PIVOTS to show us a small landcar with a drive-mechanism at the rear above a tiny standing platform. They go to the landcar and get in. The Guard steps up onto the platform at the rear and activates the drive mechanism.

**224 CLOSE ON BRATENAHL**

as he suddenly *sees something*. He looks hard as the landcar begins to hum gently preparatory to leaving.

**225 REVERSE ANGLE — BRATENAHL'S POV — WHAT HE SEES**

There, far back in shadows of the storage area that must serve as loading dock area for the underground residence, someone stands watching them. AS CAMERA BEGINS TO BACK AWAY FROM THE PERSON— inferring that the car is moving—we realize it *must* be Susan Calvin. Watching.

**226 FULL SHOT — THE LANDCAR**

as it starts to move and Bratenahl is still craning around to see if the observer in the shadows is Calvin. The car moves forward, gathering speed, toward a dark tunnel at the far end of the unloading dock and landing pad area.

**227 SHOT FROM LANDCAR — STRAIGHT AHEAD — (PROCESS)**

as the car shoots forward at a remarkable rate of speed. Everything whips past, and we are suddenly in a pitch-dark tunnel. Search-beams suddenly spear out from the landcar.

**228 MOVING SHOT— STRAIGHT AHEAD — (PROCESS)**

The tunnel, now lit eerily. A slipping-past-us scene going away at terrific speed.

Suddenly the landcar pops out into artificial sunlight and we are looking at the underground landscape and residence structures we saw in Scene 92. Susan Calvin's hidden kingdom beneath the lost city of *Xingú Xavante*. The landcar rushes toward the blue-glass pyramid we saw in Scene 106.

**229 FULL SHOT — HIGH-ANGLE DOWN ON SCENE**

from the apex of the blue-glass pyramid, into the terrace area: as the landcar glides to a stop, the Guard steps down and walks ahead of Bratenahl and Bernice, leading them up the steps to the apparently unbroken face of the pyramid.

**230 CLOSE SHOT — WITH THE GROUP — TOWARD WALL**

as the Guard approaches. We see now that the unbroken face of the blue-glass is actually a property of the cunning overlapping of facets, all of which catch light and cast it back as a field of radiance. There are actually corridors between the glass surfaces. The Guard indicates one such, and Bratenahl and Bernice pass inside. The Guard follows.

**231 INT. PYRAMID — FULL SHOT**

from Bratenahl and Bernice in f.g. showing the interior of the Calvin residence. High, enormously complex, and robots everywhere which, while not in exorbitant profusion, obviously run this living situation. No other humans can be seen. Bernice and Bratenahl stare in amazement.

BRATENAHL

(sub rosa to Bernice)

I told you someone bankrolled all this.

**232 ON GUARD — TRUCKING SHOT**

as he leads them to glass pillars that are elevators to the upper stories.

1st GUARD

Dr. Calvin has asked me to show you your accommodations.

BRATENAHL

Isn't she here?

1st GUARD

Dr. Calvin is engaged in delicate restoration of artifacts from the city aboveground. She has asked me to extend her apologies at not being here to greet you, and hopes you will refresh yourselves.

BERNICE

She'll see us later?

1st GUARD

That's up to Dr. Calvin, Dr. Jolo. But it seems logical, does it not?

Bernice arches an eyebrow. They enter the glass elevator.

## 233 GLASS ELEVATOR — SHOT FROM BELOW

as it shoots upward rapidly. It stops.

## 234 TERRACE INSIDE PYRAMID

as they emerge from the elevator. The Guard indicates an iris before them.

1st GUARD

Your suite. Six rooms, common entrance. Dr. Calvin assumed you would desire linking accommodations.

(beat)

If you would rather have separate suites—

BRATENAHL

This will be fine, thank you.

The Guard nods, in a courtly fashion, and goes back into the elevator, sinks quickly from view. CAMERA WITH Bernice and Bratenahl as they approach the iris and it swirls open.

### 235 INT. SUITE — TOWARD IRIS

as it opens and we see Bratenahl and Bernice standing there with the open atrium of the pyramid behind them. We cannot see what the suite looks like. It is dark. They stand there as CAMERA MOVES IN ON THEM.

BERNICE

Well, we're in.

BRATENAHL

There is an old phrase about walking over someone's grave.

BERNICE

Ah. So you feel like an interloper, too.

BRATENAHL

God damn that bastard Rowe. I wish to God he'd never pushed me into this.

BERNICE

He wasn't the only one pushing.

She gives him a meaningful look. He's been pushing himself. They walk INTO CAMERA and FRAME TO BLACK as we

**MATCH-CUT TO:**

### 236 EXT. TERRACE — EVENING

FROM MATCH BLACK FRAME the CAMERA PULLS BACK off Robert Bratenahl's back to show the underground empire of Susan Calvin. Bratenahl stands at the railing, looking down across the planted areas, the museum, the other futuristic buildings. He watches as the artificial lights in their sun-tracks across the high-flung roof of the underground complex dim in their traces. Evening is upon us, and we HEAR the SOUND of creatures in the forest, crickets, the night-birds. He stands with hands on the pale white stone railing, looking, meditating. There is a WHIRRING and a large night insect settles down beside his hand. He looks at it. The insect is metal. It has luminous, transparent wings and an alien body. It is a fantasist's dream of what a robot monarch butterfly might be. He looks at it for a moment, then it whirrs into the evening sky.

BERNICE (O.S.)
I wondered where you'd gone.

The SOUND of her FOOTSTEPS behind him and he turns.

## 237 REVERSE ANGLE — PAST BRATENAHL TO BERNICE

She comes toward him, dressed in a remarkable gown of thin material that clings yet only entices.

BRATENAHL
(ruminatively)
She's everywhere down here.

BERNICE
Have you seen her yet?

BRATENAHL
No. I think she's saving it for a propitious entrance.

BERNICE
We're not dining together, you know.

BRATENAHL
(surprised)
No, I didn't know.

BERNICE

Your friend, the major-domo, came around after you went to "take a walk" and said a special dinner had been arranged for me aboveground in the old city.

BRATENAHL

Just you?

BERNICE

It was only a hope, a desire, a mere suggestion, you understand. But I got the distinct impression this is the way she wants it.

BRATENAHL

(thinks in silence a moment)

Hmm. Have you seen any other humans?

BERNICE

Apart from thee and me and the major-domo?

He nods.

BERNICE (CONT'D.)

Nothing but robots as far as the eye can see. I don't think there are any other people down here.

He shakes his head. He can't reconcile it.

**238 SHOT ACROSS TERRACE — ON 1st GUARD**

as the Guard comes out of the deepening twilight toward Bratenahl and Bernice.

1st GUARD

Dr. Jolo? We're ready for the trip up to the city now.

She looks at Bratenahl, raises her eyebrows to indicate he's on his own, and follows the Guard down the steps and into the landcar. Bratenahl and CAMERA HOLD over the terrace as we SEE the car go. He stands alone.

**239 HIGH SHOT — DOWN ON BRATENAHL**

capturing a panoramic view of the underground residence. As darkness falls. HOLD ON HIM as we

**LAP-DISSOLVE TO:**

**240 EXT. TERRACE — PYRAMID IN B.G. — TRUCKING IN**

on Bratenahl, still standing there, staring out across the underground vista. Suddenly the blue-glass pyramid glows from within and lights up. It is awesomely beautiful. The glow suffuses the air and falls across Bratenahl. He turns away from CAMERA as CAMERA COMES IN CLOSE ON HIM and we SHOOT PAST HIM to see Susan Calvin standing there on the terrace. She comes toward him and stops a polite distance. Her voice is firm and soft, but incredibly powerful.

CALVIN

Good evening, Mr. Bratenahl.

BRATENAHL

Good evening, Dr. Calvin.

She comes a little nearer. Stops again.

CALVIN

Would you care to join me for dinner?

**241 CLOSE ON BRATENAHL**

as he realizes she is dominating him. We can see him forcibly get control of his own emotions.

BRATENAHL

I owe you an apology.

CALVIN

For continually trying to invade my privacy?

BRATENAHL

No, not so much for that; I apologize for startling you when I was here the last time; for causing you to drop that beautiful vase.

CALVIN

Oh yes. I'd forgotten.

BRATENAHL

No you didn't.

As previous dialogue progresses CAMERA PULLS BACK from Bratenahl and CIRCLES to include Calvin. She smiles for an instant at his remark, then the smile tightens.

CALVIN

You're right, I didn't forget. But I accept the apology.

(beat)

Shall we go in to dinner?

He nods; she turns and he follows her into the pyramid as CAMERA HOLDS LONG on their departure.

**CUT TO:**

## 242 INT. DINING ROOM — FULL SHOT

It is incongruent. A traditional baronial dining room, with massive oak chairs and table, sideboard, wall hangings of the race that inhabited the lost city many centuries ago. Very rich, very elegant, very warm and comfortable. They sit across from each other, drinking coffee. The table has been cleared, but we see enough remains of silverware and china to know they have eaten and are now getting to the crunch-point of talk.

BRATENAHL

How long have you been excavating the city up there?

CALVIN

Almost fifteen years. They were a remarkable people.

BRATENAHL

Do the robots make good diggers?

CALVIN

They're precise. Very delicate with potshards and other artifacts.

BRATENAHL

I shouldn't think you'd be interested in the remains of a lost race of human beings.

CALVIN

Because I'm surrounded by robots?

BRATENAHL

Because you've been surrounded by robots all your life.

She appraises him for a moment. Then offers the silver coffee urn. He extends the bone china cup and she pours.

CALVIN

You've spent a lot of time on me.

BRATENAHL

Apparently not enough, Dr. Calvin. I'm no closer to unpeeling your secrets than I was when I started.

CALVIN

Unpeeling my secrets. Vivid image. You make me sound like an artichoke.

Bratenahl smiles. Calvin doesn't.

BRATENAHL

Something very peculiar . . .

CALVIN

Yes? What's that?

BRATENAHL

Everything in the central banks on you—and it's very little, I assure you—paints you as hard, cold, driven by your work, standoffish, emotionless.

CALVIN

And you find me otherwise?

BRATENAHL

No, you maintain the idiom here, with me. I can understand that: I'm an intruder, I've made a damned nuisance of myself, ferreted you out.

(beat)

But the gap between reality and fantasy is amazing.

(beat)

Norman Bogert remembers an unrequited love affair that hurt you deeply . . .

She isn't expecting that. She almost winces, shivers, and draws herself up.

BRATENAHL (CONT'D.)

Sorry.

(beat)

Donovan and Powell: they remember how you saved their lives and almost lost yours.

She looks very uncomfortable. But what else did she expect?

CALVIN

It was part of the job.

BRATENAHL

Alfred Lanning tells a story about your father and a robot you called Robbie. A very touching story.

CALVIN

That was a long time ago. I'd almost forgotten. . .

(she catches his look, smiles)

no, I hadn't forgotten. Dear Robbie.

BRATENAHL

So you see, you're quite a series of contractions.

CALVIN

And you've spent months trying to reconcile those contradictions.

BRATENAHL

At first I was just intrigued; then I was ordered to pursue it. And finally I didn't need to be ordered.

CALVIN

And then you sent me a message.

BRATENAHL

It must be true. I'm here.

(beat)

Are you ready to talk about it yet?

CALVIN

(tensely)

Perhaps not *just* yet, Mr. Bratenahl.

They sit staring at each other. The silence grows tense.

BRATENAHL

Where is Bernice?

CALVIN

At this moment?

BRATENAHL

Yes, at this moment; if you know.

CAMERA has PULLED BACK to 2-SHOT during preceding dialogue. Now it PULLS BACK FARTHER so the shadows lapping at the circle of light in which they dine intrude on the FRAME.

CALVIN

She's having dinner; aboveground in the old city.

CAMERA CONTINUES BACK till they grow smaller in the FRAME and the shadows dominate . . . their VOICES RETREAT as well.

BRATENAHL

Dining alone her first night here? While you dine with me? Another oddity.

CAMERA BACK until they are lost in shadows that fill the FRAME and we HEAR CALVIN'S VOICE OVER.

CALVIN (V.O.)

Then you won't take offense if I go to join her for dessert . . .

**MATCH-DISSOLVE TO:**

**243 INT. ANCIENT CITY — NIGHT**

CAMERA COMES IN THRU DARKNESS that MATCHES with DARKNESS of the preceding SCENE and we HEAR CALVIN'S VOICE OVER

CALVIN (V.O.)

Of course I'd remember you.

BERNICE (V.O.)

I was only a child when I came to Old Earth with my father.

CAMERA CONTINUES IN through shadows and we realize we are in one of the ancient temples of the lost city. The architecture is ornate and gorgeous, but it emerges slowly as we come toward another pool of light, and we can see that a smaller, more intimate table than in the preceding SCENE has been set up. Two people are dining. Bernice and someone whose back is to us as CAMERA DOLLIES IN.

CALVIN (O.S.)

You were a memorable child. Very loving.

(beat)

Are you a loving adult, Bernice?

BERNICE (O.S.)

Do you mean Robert?

CALVIN (O.S.)

Yes. Are you in love with him?

CAMERA IN FULL to HOLD the dining scene, and we realize the person sitting across from Bernice Jolo is . . . Susan Calvin. Whom we have just seen—a match-dissolve ago—taking leave of Robert Bratenahl belowground.

BERNICE

(flustered)

There's fifty years between your definition of the word and mine.

CALVIN

I don't mean to pry, but I think it will be necessary for me to know how you feel about that young man. Define it any way you choose.

BERNICE

He eludes me.

CALVIN

I don't know what that means.

BERNICE

Without moving, I pursue him.

CALVIN

And without standing still he remains always in the same place?

BERNICE

God, I'm speaking in Egyptian riddles!

CALVIN

Do you love him . . . are you in love *with* him?

BERNICE

Both and neither. If he could ever stop being consumed by his obsessions—such as chasing you—I might allow myself to start thinking about him-and-love in the same breath

CALVIN

(beat, changes subject)

I'm sorry I wasn't able to attend your father's funeral.

Bernice stares at her. The change has been silkily made. But she chooses not to let it go.

BERNICE

Doctor Cal—

CALVIN

(interrupts)

Advanced age only permits two elements of outrageous behavior: one is carefully-measured rudeness that can be construed as charmingly eccentric. . .

(beat)

the other is falling asleep over dessert.

(beat)

Neither one gets in the way of your calling me Susan.

Bernice smiles. She leans forward, affectionately.

BERNICE

I understand his obsession with you.

CALVIN

(tiny smile)

I credit his persistence. He speaks of *unpeeling* my secrets.

BERNICE

That's up to you. And you don't know me any better than you know him . . .

(beat)

But he's a *serious* man. If you trust him, he probably won't disappoint you.

CALVIN

(thoughtfully)

Tell me: do you think people are basically good?

BERNICE

(considers; this is obviously important)

Not all the time. Obviously.

CALVIN

Mmm. Yes, obviously.

BERNICE

Why do you ask me that?

CALVIN

(brushes it off)

Oh . . . just woolgathering. Do you know the word?

BERNICE

(intently)

It wasn't just courtesy, your asking me to come with Robert. Was it?

CALVIN

I wanted to see you again.

BERNICE

(amazed)

You really want to talk to me, don't you?

CALVIN

I have things on my mind. It may be time for change . . .

BERNICE

I don't know what you mean . . .

Calvin sighs heavily. She pushes away from the table.

CALVIN

This is unconscionable. I'm babbling. You must forgive me, Bernice. I have many things to sort out, and I'm being an obtuse old sphinx.

(beat)

We'll talk again. I need my sleep now. Tomorrow?

Bernice smiles, nods her head. Susan Calvin stares at her for a long moment, seems about to say something . . . then goes into the darkness. Bernice sits in the pool of light staring after her. In a moment the Guard appears at her elbow. She isn't aware of him for a time, then starts as she realizes he's there. She nods, rises, and follows him. The table sits empty in the light.

**CUT TO:**

## 244 SAME AS 234

Bratenahl stands alone, staring off across Calvin's domain. Bernice comes out of the darkness. The Guard nods goodnight and passes off in another direction, into the dark. Bernice walks to Bratenahl.

BERNICE

Hi.

BRATENAHL

Oh . . . hello, there. How was dinner?

She comes to him and takes his hands, looks at him closely.

BERNICE

I've never encountered anyone like her, Robert. She said very little, but I had the feeling she was plumbing my consciousness to the core.

(beat)

I think she wanted to use my judgment of you as a gauge of your trustworthiness. I think you're about to find out what you want to know.

She looks off. She seems very disturbed. He draws her close.

BRATENAHL

You're shivering . . .

BERNICE

I can't get it out of my head that we're all going to learn something we don't want to know.

She moves very close to him, buries her face in his chest. Then she looks up at him, solemnly.

BRATENAHL

(gently)

What . . . ?

BERNICE

We'll go now and make love. I think I won't be seeing you for a long time.

He stares at her with concern and a lack of comprehension. Then she moves away, taking him by the hand. They go into the darkness.

**DISSOLVE TO:**

**245 ENDLESS METAL CORRIDOR — NIGHT**

FRAME SILVERY AND DARK as we HEAR a WHIRRING and the metal night-flying insect from Scene 236 drops down THRU FRAME as CAMERA FOLLOWS. The robot monarch butterfly drops down and hovers above Susan Calvin. She stands in a long corridor of silvery metal. We cannot see either end of the tunnel. It stretches away in both directions . . . a road *from* nowhere *to* nowhere. Susan wears a long caftan, like a nightshirt. We will have the feeling she is unable to sleep and is walking to settle her thoughts. The robot butterfly hovers and she looks up at it. Then from the butterfly we HEAR the hollow, faintly tinny VOICES of Bratenahl and Bernice recorded from the preceding scene:

BERNICE'S VOICE
FROM BUTTERFLY (FILTER)
I think she wanted to use my judgment of you as a gauge of your trustworthiness. I think you're about to find out what you want to know.

BRATENAHL'S VOICE
FROM BUTTERFLY (FILTER)
You're shivering . . .

BERNICE'S VOICE
FROM BUTTERFLY (FILTER)
I can't get it out of my head that we're all going to learn something we don't want to know.

BRATENAHL'S VOICE
FROM BUTTERFLY (FILTER)
What . . . ?

BERNICE'S VOICE
FROM BUTTERFLY (FILTER)
We'll go now and make love. I think I won't be seeing you for a long time.

The butterfly hovers there for another moment, then springs out of the FRAME, leaving Susan Calvin alone, looking lost and empty. Is she thinking about years without love or companionship? Perhaps. She begins walking down the corridor as CAMERA GOES WITH. A few beats, then we HEAR VOICE OVER of Susan Calvin and another voice. We haven't heard this voice before. It is STEPHEN BYERLEY'S VOICE, as we will realize from internal evidence very quickly . . . but though we've never heard Byerley

till this moment, there is *something familiar* in the sound. It is not necessary for us to consider *who* the voice of Byerley reminds us of, not at this time. But it lodges in our mind . . . and the audience's mind, as well.

BYERLEY OVER (ECHO)
You'll have to do it alone, Susan.

CALVIN OVER (ECHO)
I can't, Stephen. It's been too long. Just a little longer.

BYERLEY OVER (ECHO)
Forty-four years is a long time; long enough. If I've learned one thing from all you've taught me about people, it's knowing when to let go.
(beat)
It's time, Susan.

CALVIN OVER (ECHO)
Chaos. A return of the dark ages, Stephen.

BYERLEY OVER (ECHO)
No, you'll tell them how it was. They'll understand. You gave me faith in them . . . they have the spark of godhood in them.

(beat)
I give that faith back to you.

CALVIN OVER (ECHO)
How will I tell them? So they'll be able to understand how it was?

BYERLEY OVER (ECHO)
You'll find a way. You'll find the proper voice. Now . . . you do it alone. No strangers.
(beat)
Goodbye, dear friend . . . dear Susan . . .

CALVIN OVER (ECHO)
Goodbye, Stephen . . . goodbye . . .

She continues walking and now CAMERA HOLDS as she passes down the metal corridor. The silver radiance that lights the corridor blossoms and she passes into it as if walking into the sun. The light fills the FRAME and we HEAR two things: the ECHO VOICE of CALVIN saying "Goodbye" over and over, growing ever fainter until it is overcome by the SOUND of the WHIRRING of the robot butterfly as it swoops down into the FRAME and the CAMERA FOLLOWS IT UP into the blazing light of the silver metal corridor and we go to

**BLACK FRAME and DISSOLVE TO:**

## 246 BLACK FRAME

We HEAR the O.S. SOUND of the WHIRRING of robot wings and then the FRAME BLINKS ON and we see the room from Scene 235. FRAME BLINKS BACK TO BLACK and then BLINKS ON AGAIN as we realize we are seeing the room from Bratenahl's POV as he lies in the bed. The SOUND of WHIRRING dies away as he opens his eyes and CAMERA MOVES RIGHT THEN LEFT as if orienting itself from his POV. To the left of the bed is a nightstand of modern design. CAMERA HOLDS on the nightstand and we see the gorgeous amber and gold-trimmed vase Susan Calvin dropped and broke in Scene 123. It is the *same* vase. A hand reaches out from the bottom of the FRAME and touches the vase. It is Bratenahl's hand.

## 247 FULL SHOT — ON BRATENAHL IN BED

as he sits bolt upright, swings around and looks at the vase. He touches it, cannot believe he sees it. Then we HEAR a VOICE from O.S. and Bratenahl spins around.

1st GUARD (O.S.)

Good morning, sir.

## 248 ANOTHER ANGLE — WITH 1st GUARD

standing just inside the open iris, the terrace beyond.

1st GUARD

I didn't mean to startle you.

Bratenahl is naked, but rather than a blanket covering him, the golden mist that covered the bed still clings to his lower body as he sits on the edge near the vase. He looks around for Bernice, rubs his face.

BRATENAHL

Where's Dr. Jolo?

1st GUARD

She's gone back to Sigma Draconis 5. There was an emergency call for her.

BRATENAHL

(looking resigned)

At least half of that was a lie.

(he indicates the vase)

Where did that come from? It wasn't here last night.

1st GUARD

Dr. Calvin asked me to bring it up and leave it.

BRATENAHL

Is that a lie, too?

Bratenahl gets out of bed.

1st GUARD

I do my best not to lie, sir. But everything *is* open to interpretation.

BRATENAHL

Okay, champ, what's the program for today?

1st GUARD

Dr. Calvin thinks you'd like to see some of the archive tapes.

Bratenahl nods. It is obvious he's beginning a program of intelligence-gathering, at Calvin's behest. He looks around. The ablutatorium—a kind of bathroom—is off the sleeping chamber. He starts toward it.

BRATENAHL

You can wait while I clean up or come back in a little while.

The Guard goes to the iris, still open.

1st GUARD

I'll be back.

He goes, the iris sphincters close, and Bratenahl goes into the circular shower mechanism. A glass door slides around, there is a blaze of light and a hiss, and Robert Bratenahl steps back out, shaved, showered and smelling good. He goes to the wall mechanism with buttons of various colors, punches out a code, and fresh clothing—neatly folded, obviously of disposable paper-fabric—is slid out through slots. He shakes out the pants, and starts to get into them as we

**CUT TO:**

## 249 INSIDE THE EGG

It is an all-gray chamber, a shape as if we are inside an egg, but the walls are an unbroken 360° screen. It is a chamber for viewing archive transcriptions. The floor is soft and molds itself to whatever shape is needed for optimum viewing. Bratenahl lounges on the floor. The 1st Guard stands as if about to leave.

1st GUARD

These selections have been chosen by Dr. Calvin, they're arranged chronologically.

BRATENAHL

What are they?

1st GUARD

(ignores question)

If you need anything, just call; the room monitor will relay to me.

(beat)

Otherwise the room functions as any comm unit would. Rerun, reverse, freeze . . . just ask the room.

He nods once, as if that ended the conversation whether Bratenahl liked it that way or not, and he walks to the wall. An invisible seam opens and he goes out. The room reseals without a break. The light that has no source fades to duskiness and suddenly the entire egg begins to light with a full-circle scene. A warm female voice, the VOICE OF THE EGG, fills the enclosure.

VOICE OF THE EGG

Selections from the career of Stephen Byerley, First President of the Galactic Federation.

The walls hold a view of a tall, prematurely gray man in his early forties. Handsome, tall, very Gary Cooperesque; but there is something about him that seems familiar. We cannot place it, but we see that Bratenahl notices it, too. The first sequence is of the man Stephen Byerley, obviously on the campaign trail. A peculiar campaign, of course, because it is Systemwide, not merely national.

## 250 THE FIRST SCENE — IN WRAPAROUND PROJECTION

Byerley, in CU, as CAMERA PULLS BACK to show us he is in a United Nations-like general assembly chamber. The semicircular desk that fills one side of the chamber has many delegates of alien worlds seated at places before which placards naming their worlds of origin identify them. He walks toward first one, then another, speaking and gesticulating gravely. There is enormous dignity in his manner. Openness, honesty, and we trust him at once. The words he speaks are soft and we cannot make them out, but the Voice of the Egg SPEAKS OVER:

VOICE OF THE EGG

He founded the Federation in a time of anguish. The Four Worlds War had begun two Old Earth years before.

Byerley continues down the line, speaking to one alien after another. As he speaks, each punches a button on the desk before him or her. On the wall behind them a disc lights: either gold for acceptance or black for nonacceptance. All but two are gold. One after another, until he reaches the last, gets a gold disc, and the aliens rise as a body to cheer him.

VOICE OF THE EGG (CONT'D.)
He brought uncommon reason and fairness even to the vanquished. It was the beginning of the Golden Age.

**251 thru 257 SERIES OF VIGNETTE SCENES ON WRAPAROUND WALL**

Byerley dictating a manifesto that appears on the blank wall behind him in five line segments—each one in a different written language, four of them alien symbols, one in English.

Byerley meeting with Susan Calvin at a robot factory, shaking hands. Do they hold the touch a moment longer than necessary?

VOICE OF THE EGG
He created the Manifesto of Equality. All races with one voice in the destiny of the Federation.
(beat)
He removed slave status from the creation of robots. Building on the base of the Three Laws, he made them partners in the outward thrust of the human race.

Byerley laughing, standing in a group of men and women dressed in technician's gear, all of them relating with joy to a glass tower rising into the sky behind them.

Byerley at the unveiling of a monument in honor of those who settled the Outer Cold Worlds. A beautiful acrylic sculpture with humans and aliens together, looking toward the stars.

VOICE OF THE EGG
He was the spiritual drive behind the expansions of colonies to the Outer Cold Worlds . . . he was the guiding force that established the teleport system, making the farthest planet accessible to all . . .

Bratenahl continues to watch as scene after scene rolls across the wrap-around and we

**DISSOLVE TO:**

## 258 SAME AS 117 — INTERIOR LOST CITY MUSEUM

Where Bratenahl first encountered Susan Calvin on her own territory. As the scene resolves itself, Bratenahl walks into FRAME FROM F.G. toward a complex table arrangement where Susan Calvin sits hunched closely over a microscope with a computer attached. There is a cat's cradle affair of minute "waldos" (extensible arms with pincers for lifting and moving at their ends) connected to the computer and microscope. He comes closer. She speaks without looking up.

CALVIN

Hello. I'll be with you in a few minutes.

BRATENAHL

If I'm interrupting—

CALVIN

No, it's all right. I'm near the end of this piece. Come look if you wish.

## 259 CLOSE ON BRATENAHL

as he moves very close over her shoulder, CAMERA MOVING PAST HIM so he leaves the frame, over Calvin's shoulder to the light-stage on which what seem to be a million tiny shattered pieces of pottery lie in infinitely small pieces. She eyeballs close to the viewfinder of the electron-microscope, and her right hand dances a rapid, intricate pattern on the computer's miniaturized keyboard. On a small readout screen, vector lines move here and there, like routes on a road-map. Finally, when the lines are so dense they cannot be separated, she punches the red button and the waldos begin moving in and out among the pieces of shattered pottery on the light-stage. They begin to reassemble the broken item. As one or two or three pieces are laid together, a pin-nozzle sprays them and they adhere without seam or break. It all happens so fast (ACCELERATED STOP-MOTION CAMERA) that within moments—with vector lines vanishing from the screen as each assemblage is accomplished—the entire piece of lost race pottery is assembled . . . a bowl of deepest crimson, exquisite beyond description, with cameo'd and intaglio'd designs swimming across its ancient surface. As the last tiny piece is slipped into the jigsaw structure, the nozzle sprays, the waldos go back to their rest positions, the computer strobes END, and Susan Calvin looks up wearily. Hair trails into her eyes. She brushes it back. She sighs and smiles.

CAMERA HAS PULLED BACK TO HOLD Calvin and Bratenahl.

CALVIN

You wouldn't think something that beautiful could be such an object of votive horror, would you?

Bratenahl's look tells her she hasn't made her point.

CALVIN (CONT'D.)

It was used to catch the flow of blood from virgins whose hearts were ripped out as sacrifice to a god named Xaxaltay.

Bratenahl shakes his head and a bemused, bitter little chuckle escapes him.

CALVIN (CONT'D.)

Sit down. Let's talk.

He moves around the table setup, takes a formfit.

BRATENAHL

Is this the payoff? We talk about what you wouldn't talk about last night?

CALVIN

You've been trying to see me, to *unpeel* me for some time; why are you nervous now?

BRATENAHL

Because I feel manipulated. Because I *know* Stephen Byerley was immortal and I don't know why he died, and because it's possible you had a hand in his death . . . and I'm here alone.

CALVIN

All that. What a welter of fears and random data. Your head must be like the Sargasso Sea, filled with flotsam and jetsam . . .

He holds up a hand.

BRATENAHL

And one thing more . . . before I forget.

(beat)

I found the vase this morning. That was very kind of you, taking me off the hook like that.

CALVIN

(tersely)

Unless I'm the assassin responsible for the death of the President of the Galactic Federation. In which case it was a clever ploy intended to lull you into a false sense of security.

(beat)

My God, Bratenahl, conspiracy paranoia at *your* age.

(beat)

Tell me, Bratenahl: do you think people, for the most part, are good?

Bratenahl looks at her. We can assume Bernice told him of the question by Calvin the night before.

BRATENAHL

I think they'd like to be good. It's not always easy.

CALVIN

*Quod erat demonstrandum.* Obvious, but probably true. It's easier if one has a good example to work from.

BRATENAHL

(testy)

Look, Dr. Calvin: I take it that you *want* to tell me some things. I've battered down your door; you've let me in; you've pretty much established I can be trusted, I guess; but you don't *get* to it!

CALVIN

(snaps)

In my own way, Bratenahl! At my own pace!

He raises his hands. To placate her.

BRATENAHL

Okay! Okay! I'm sorry I snapped.

CALVIN

I've kept this to myself for a long time. Telling it doesn't come easily for me.

BRATENAHL

Okay, your way. Please . . .

**260 TWO-SHOT**

As she relaxes. Bratenahl settles back, hoping he hasn't blown it again.

CALVIN

What did you get from the clips about Stephen Byerley?

BRATENAHL

What you wanted me to get: the golden age.

CALVIN

He was a remarkable man. Better than any other man I've ever met.

(beat, musing)

Almost any other man . . .

She gets a faraway look for a moment, then comes back to herself, and her face hardens, as if she's finally made the decision to plunge ahead and tell it all, from the start.

CALVIN (CONT'D.)
(resigned)
I believe you began with the question of whether Stephen Byerley and I were lovers.

BRATENAHL
(blurts)
No, I . . .

CALVIN
(tough)
Shut up, Bratenahl. You wanted it all, and that's what you'll get. Beginning with Lenny. That's where my "love affair" with Stephen Byerley began . . . with Lenny . . .

## 261 SUPERIMPOSE SHOT — CLOSE ON CALVIN

As she begins speaking, the lighting in the scene alters and we see a SUPER of her younger self that FADES IN as her present-time, 82-year-old self FADES OUT.

CALVIN
It was around 2032; U.S. Robots was trying to perfect a new LNE prototype. They'd discovered Hellfire Mountain on Mercury . . . the diamond mountain . . .

BRATENAHL (O.S.)
Strictly regulated: I've read about it. Very nearly drove the Old Earth diamond cartel crazy.

CALVIN
Mmm. Well, U.S. RoboMek was hired to develop a highly sensitive LNE model that could cut the new stones; many times harder and whiter than those found on Earth.
(beat)
But something went wrong on the production line . . .

As the preceding speech is heard, the aged Susan has just about faded out, as has the scene in the lost race museum, and Susan, age 38, has faded in, seen as a

**SUPERIMPOSE DISSOLVE:**

## 262 INT. CALVIN'S OFFICE — U.S. ROBOTS BUILDING

ON SUSAN in her younger incarnation, as she turns to face a suddenly opening door and the presence of NORMAN BOGERT (whom we have seen previously in film clips and as a frozen form in a crypt). He sticks his head in, looking frantic, and shouts at her:

BOGERT
Storage room seven, on the double!

CALVIN
What . . . ?

BOGERT
Oh boy! Have *we* got a problem!

She gets up quickly and moves toward the door, still ajar. Bogert is gone already.

## 263 CORRIDOR — ON CALVIN'S OFFICE DOOR

as she comes through. She turns into CAMERA and CAMERA GOES WITH her as she rushes down one corridor and up another. As she moves fast, Bogert appears from a side-corridor with Lanning (age 68) and a short, fat, bald man in a very rumpled, almost comically 1940s sort of suit. He is SVEN DE KUYPER. They elbow past her, and all keep moving toward a set of double doors ten feet high at the end of the corridor. A plate above the doors says

**STORAGE 7**
**OFF LIMITS**

They move toward it, fast, and Bogert tries to open the door. It is locked. He bangs on it with his fist.

BOGERT

Morty! Morty, open the damned door!

From within comes a VOICE.

MORTY'S VOICE (O.S.)

Who is it?

BOGERT

Norman Bogert, you ass! And Lanning, Calvin and De Kuyper!

The door opens onto darkness. They rush inside.

## 264 INT. STORAGE 7

A high-ceilinged, otherwise empty room filled with a dozen tall robots, very humanoid, more advanced than Herbie in Scene 175. Extremely delicate hands, long and tapering, with six fingers on each hand. They fill the room, standing silently.

LANNING

Mortimer . . . turn up the light in here.

The technician, variously called MORTY or MORTIMER, turns a rheostat on the wall. Light floods the room. Morty is in his early twenties, big Adam's apple, gangly and merely a walk-on. He stands silently. De Kuyper speaks first, with a heavy Dutch accent.

DE KUYPER

What is the problem? No more cost overrun, I tell you. My firm won't stand for it, I tell you!

LANNING

Please, Mr. De Kuyper.

BOGERT

Okay, Morty. Now go over it again. Just the way you told me.

Morty edges forward. He's scared. This is Lanning, the head of the whole damned corporation. And Calvin, that hard-faced robopsychologist. But he squeaks his story.

MORTY

I came in to run the preliminary vocalizing tests just like it says to do here on my clipboard . . .

(he shows it)

. . . and I walked up to each one of these Lennys, and I said to Lenny One, just like it says to say . . .

(gulps)

How are you.

Everyone watches him. They wait.

MORTY (CONT'D.)

(twitching)

And Lenny One answers, real nice and clear, "I am well and ready to begin my functions, sir. I trust you are well, too."

DE KUYPER

(dyspeptic)

Well, that was what he was *supposed* to say, no?

Morty gets flustered. He fumfuhs and almost drops the clipboard. Lanning speaks sternly.

LANNING

Mr. De Kuyper, we've all been made painfully aware of your supervisory role on this project . . .

DE KUYPER

(interrupts)

The Lodestone Corporation . . .

LANNING
(interrupts him)
. . . sent you to *assist* us, not hamper us in our work. Now please be still, sir.

BOGERT
Go on, Morty.

MORTY
(stammering)
Well, uh, yeah . . . yes, sir. So Lenny One was okay, and so was Lenny Two and Lenny Th—

DE KUYPER
(explodes)
By *damn*!

MORTY
(quickly)
But when I got to Lenny Nine, I said how are you and *he* said . . .

They wait. A pin could drop.

LANNING
Well?

MORTY
He, uh, he said, as best I can repeat it, sir . . .
(beat, in baby voice)
Da da, goo goo, da da da.

They all stare at him.

**265 WITH SUSAN CALVIN**

as she turns to the robots. We go with her as she finds the Lenny with the numeral 9 on its chest.

CALVIN
(to robot)
How are you, Lenny?

The robot looks down with soulful receptors.

LENNY
Goo goo, da da, doo doo . . .

It stands. Susan looks at it.

CALVIN
Lenny: multiplication tables, by twelve. Twelve times twelve . . .

She waits. Lenny looks at her.

They all stare. Then, after a moment:

LENNY
(querulously)
Goo goo . . . ?

Her mouth drops open and a pixilated expression hits her. But it's stunned disbelief from everyone else as we

**CUT TO:**

### 266 INT. METAL SHOP — DAY

CLOSE ON a fountain of sparks. CAMERA BACK to show Susan Calvin wearing a futuristic version of a welder's mask, using an equally advanced laser-torch to cut metal. She is making something but we can't tell what it is. Behind her, Bogert stands with arms akimbo, looking pissed off.

BOGERT
It makes no sense. How did the flaw get into the programming?

CALVIN
(doesn't look up)
We'll never know. Someone erred, and probably isn't even aware of it. Punched out the coding to the impulse implanter incorrectly.
(beat)
When we ran it back the computer checked out negative for all attempts at finding the flaw.

BOGERT
The positronic brain is beyond redemption. So many of the higher functions have been canceled out by these meaningless directions that the result is very like a human baby.

She turns off the torch, straightens, and lifts the mask. Sweat dots her nose and forehead. She wipes off on a heavy quilted bib she wears to protect her.

CALVIN
Why seem so surprised, Norman? We make every effort to create a robot as mentally like a human being as possible. Eliminate what we call the adult functions and naturally what's left is a human infant . . . mentally speaking.

## 267 ANOTHER ANGLE — FAVORING BOGERT

BOGERT
(resignedly)
We'll have to eat the cost, but it does seem a shame to have to melt it down.

Susan is fitting together the part of the metal item she's been making. Now she stops and looks up at him with shock.

CALVIN
Melt it down? Don't be absurd.

BOGERT
Now listen here, Susan . . . don't start one of your . . .

CALVIN
(forcefully)
I want to conduct more tests. Forget melting.

Bogert is incensed. Calvin is pulling one of her numbers again. He stalks around her, raging quietly, trying to be an authoritarian figure. Susan keeps on working at the spherical object, paying attention to him . . . but not *strict* attention. Bogert grows more frustrated: she dominates him with her focus on the construction in her hands.

BOGERT
The damned thing is useless! If there's one thing completely and abysmally useless it's a robot without a job it can perform. You don't pretend there's a job this thing can do . . . *do you?*

CALVIN
No, of course not.
(beat)
Hand me those little metal helixes, please.

Bogert is thrown off-stride. He looks around wildly. Then he sees half a dozen objects as described, on the side-bench. He grabs them up and carries them to her, hands them to her.

BOGERT
It's bad enough De Kuyper is causing trouble with Lodestone over this . . . he's running in a *disastrous* report . . . inefficient . . . big screw-up . . .

She has now assembled the object. It is spherical, hollow, with a handle, and the little metal helixes inside. As she screws the halves of the round section together, she looks at Bogert with finality. He sees the look.

BOGERT (CONT'D.)
Oh, what's the use? At least will you keep us appraised of your tests?
(beat, as he stares at the object)
What *is* that thing?

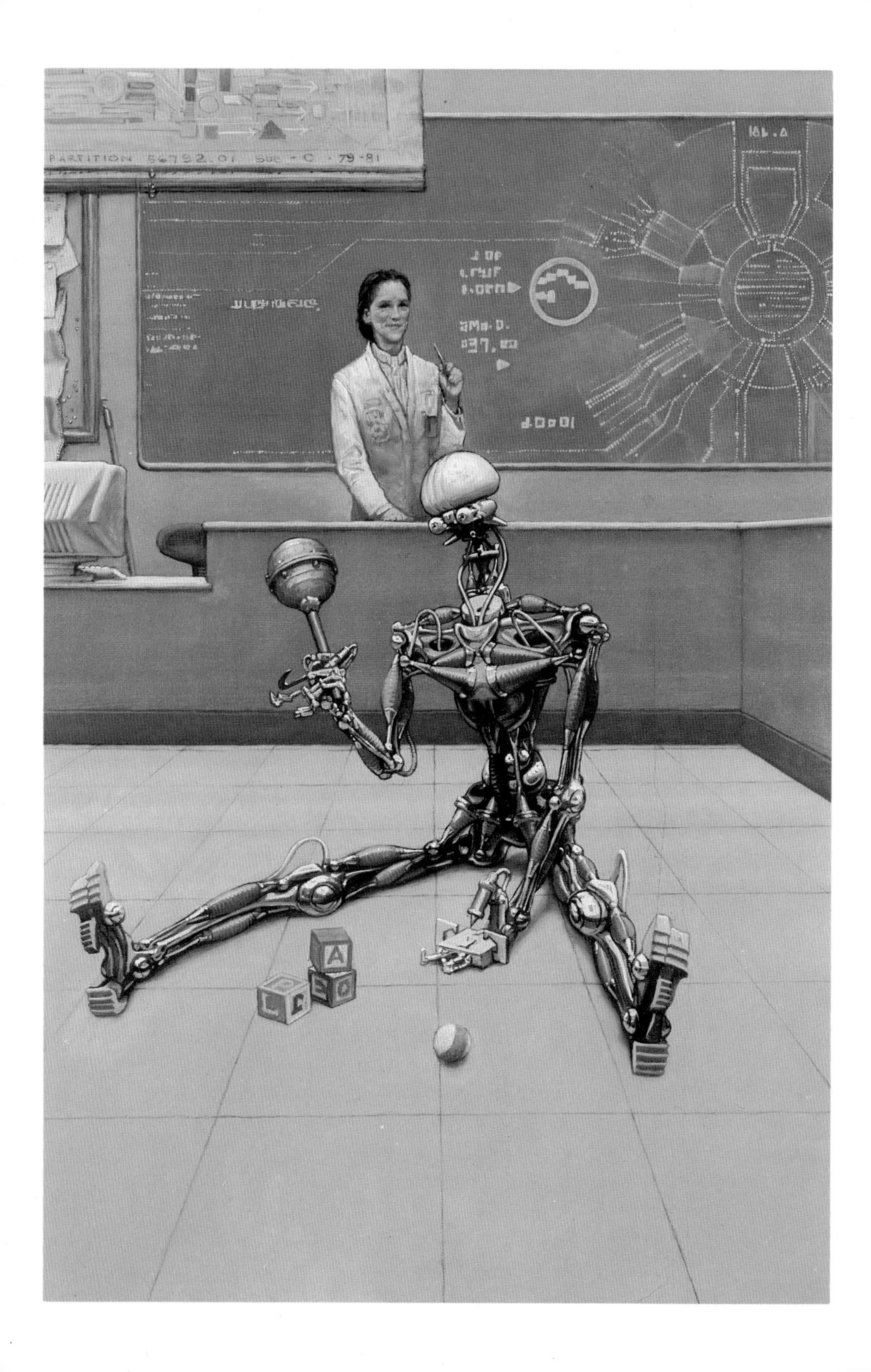
PARTITION

She holds it up, smiles happily, and shakes it. It clatters with a funny little sound.

CALVIN

A rattle.

Bogert's face falls apart. He stares at it as though she has won one. He shakes his head. She shakes the rattle. CAMERA IN on the rattle as we

**MATCH-CUT TO:**

## 268 INT. SUSAN CALVIN'S OFFICE — DAY

MATCH-CUT ON RATTLE now being held by Lenny. He is shaking it. And cooing. But that *voice!* It's spectacular. Almost musical. Utterly charming, refreshing, childish but like a celeste, the syllables like heavenly chimes. Really terrific. CAMERA BACK to show Lenny, six feet tall, six-fingered, seated on the floor with legs straight out like a baby, entranced by his toy. As CAMERA ANGLE WIDENS we see that one entire wall of the office is a screen which holds a highly magnified reproduction of a positronic-path chart of a robot brain, apparently the chart to the LNE models. As Susan carefully traces the blunted paths through their contortions, Lenny opens and closes his legs, makes delightful cooing sounds. After a moment, she turns to the robot. She speaks softly.

CALVIN

Lenny . . . Lenny . . . hoo hoo, Lenny . . .

She keeps this up till Lenny looks up at her and makes a querulous cooing sound. A smile of pleasure crosses her face. She comes over and stoops down, touches him.

CALVIN (CONT'D.)

Raise your hand, Lenny. Hand—up.

(she shows with her own hand)

Hand—up . . .

She repeats the movement. Lenny follows with his own eyes. Up. Down. Up. Down. Then it makes an abortive move with the hand not holding the rattle.

LENNY

Eh—uh . . .

CALVIN

(gravely)

Very *good,* Lenny. Try again. Hand—up.

Very gently she reaches out and takes the hand with her own. Raises it. Lowers it, repeating over and over . . .

CALVIN (CONT'D.)

Hand—up. Hand—up. Hand—up . . .

## 269 TRACKING SHOT — ACROSS OFFICE

From Susan working with Lenny, CAMERA TRACKS AROUND the wall to the glass window facing out on the corridor. Alfred Lanning and Norman Bogert stand there talking, watching her. Lanning raises a hand to cut off Bogert's impassioned remarks, and goes to the door. He opens it and steps through into the office, closing the door behind him.

## 270 PAST SUSAN & LENNY TO LANNING

as the tall old man stops just inside the door, hands folded in front of him. He smiles at her gently.

LANNING

Intruding?

CALVIN

No, of course not, Alfred. Just going over the blunted paths in Lenny's brain.

He stares at her a moment. Then walks around, stepping over Lenny's outstretched legs. The robot coos at him.

LANNING

(gently)

The LNE model is in production now.

CALVIN

De Kuyper still running around making authoritarian noises?

LANNING

(offhandedly)

Oh, well, you know. Ibsen once said: "To live is to war with trolls."

(beat)

He expresses regular interest in your friend here. Seems to think has a claim even on our rejects.

CALVIN

To the point: you want something of me.

LANNING

Our commitment to Lodestone is very nearly ended. With the LNE on the line and doing well, it seems to me that working with this defective specimen is useless. Shouldn't it be melted and we move on to new areas?

She stands. Behind her, Lenny moves his hand up and down in sporadic sequence, staring at his six fingers and cooing.

CALVIN

In short, Alfred, you're annoyed that I'm wasting my so-valuable time. And Norman Bogert is something more than merely annoyed.

(beat)

Feel relieved. My time is *not* being wasted. I am *working* with Lenny.

LANNING

But the work has no meaning.

CALVIN

(ominously quiet)

I'll be the judge of that, Alfred.

LANNING

Can you at least tell me what that meaning *is*? What are you doing with it right now, for instance?

CALVIN

I'm trying to get Lenny to raise his hand on command, and to imitate the sound of the word.

At that moment, cute as a bug, Lenny seems to respond to Susan's having said "raise hand" and he raises his hand waveringly, six delicate fingers splayed as a child's.

LENNY

Eh—uh . . .

Lanning cannot keep from smiling, and he shakes his head.

LANNING

That voice is amazing. I've heard a great many robots, but never anything like that. How does it happen?

CALVIN

I don't quite know. His transmitter is a normal one. He could speak normally, I'm sure. He just doesn't. Something in the positronic paths I haven't pinpointed yet.

LANNING

Well, pinpoint it, for God's sake! Speech like that might be useful.

Susan gives him a look that says, I've wormed you around to my position, now don't you feel foolish? Lanning harrumphs, looks embarrassed, realizes he is, after all, the Director. Still harrumphing, he retreats and goes. Susan smiles to herself. And Lenny raises his hand:

LENNY

(shakes rattle to get her attention)

Eh—uh . . . ?

CALVIN

Yes! That's a *good* boy, Lenny. Hand . . . *up!*

She stoops and nods her head in time with the shaking of the rattle as we

**DISSOLVE TO:**

## 271 CORRIDOR — U.S. ROBOMEK — DAY

a scene of pandemonium. Technicians running every which way, a tour of rural hayseeds being jammed up against a wall by their tour guide who is wide-eyed with confusion, a pair of armed guards streaking through the mod. And over it all is the SOUND of a horrendous alarm klaxon splitting the air. As Susan Calvin and Norman Bogert come out of swinging doors above which the legend COMMISSARY glows, Bogert still holding a forkful of food in his hand, CAMERA GOES WITH THEIR POV to an alarm board high up near the ceiling. The plaque that says ROBOT OUT OF CONTROL is strobing red, on and off. And we HEAR the VOICE OF SUSAN CALVIN OVER:

CALVIN (V.O.)

The emergency signal had sounded at least a dozen times in the history of U.S. Robots. Fire, flood, riot, insurrection.

(beat)

But never before had it sounded the alarm—*robot out of control.*

The p.a. system SOUNDS OVER the alarm klaxon.

P.A. SYSTEM

Dr. Calvin to Test Area Nine! Emergency!

Susan and Bogert are brought into CU as CAMERA TRACKS BACK to them. They spin to go in the direction away from CAMERA, are hit by people surging past, shoulder their way through the mob running TOWARD CAMERA and they *go!*

**CUT TO:**

## 272 INT. TEST AREA NINE — DAY — EXT. CU

TIGHT on a beautiful, but flawed, industrial diamond: a fine example of Brazilian ballas—a mass of concentrically arranged, minute spheroid crystals—considered the toughest, hardest and most difficult to cut of the three varieties of industrial diamond stones.

It is being held in the palm of a metal hand. A holder, or *dop,* is built right into the palm. From one of the upthrust fingers, now arched up and over the ballas, a carbide steel wedge has been extruded and inserted into a groove already cut along the line showing where the stone will be cleaved. A second metal hand with six delicate but powerful cleaving, sawing, girdling, marking and faceting fingers is poised over the diamond. The sixth finger is a power-driver mallet. As we HOLD a BEAT to take in the simplicity of this complex mechanism, the mallet finger falls with the speed of a bullet and strikes the wedge sharply. The diamond splits along its cleavage line and falls neatly in the dop, with octohedronal pieces.

In the b.g. we HEAR the VOICE of DE KUYPER SCREAMING IN PAIN. CAMERA PULLS BACK and we see four of the LNE model robots sitting at sawyers' tables, working industriously over their test diamonds, while the rest of the test area is a bedlam.

A crowd of technicians is clustered around De Kuyper, whose left arm is obviously broken. It hangs at a weird angle. People are jammed into the doorway and two armed guards have Lenny backed against a wall with laser pistols at the ready.

At that moment Susan Calvin, Lanning and Bogert shove through the mob and assay what has happened. CAMERA IN on Susan as De Kuyper screams at her.

DE KUYPER
(crying, hysterical)
It's your fault! That thing tried to kill me! My arm! My arm is broken, by damn, I tell you!

Bogert looks around, sizes up matters and starts giving orders. He points to Lenny, speaks to Susan:

BOGERT

Susan, take charge of that specimen!

Bogert speaks to the two guards.

BOGERT (CONT'D.)

Amber . . . Castelli . . . get away from that robot . . .

(beat)

Two of you techs, take Mr. De Kuyper to the infirmary.

AMBER, the first armed guard, backs slowly away from Lenny, who stands against the wall looking as frightened and contrite as a robot can look. Amber joins CASTELLI in shooing the tourists out. Two TECHS get De Kuyper to his feet and the others make a path through the crowd, hustling the little Dutchman off to the infirmary. Then the crowd is gone, the doors are shut, the four LNE models continue their work, hooked into testing computer readout sections that monitor their work. Susan stands in front of Lenny.

**273 WITH BOGERT**

as he spins on Susan, his face livid. He is at once terrified and blind with rage.

BOGERT

That's it! That goddam thing is going to the slag bucket! *Now!*

CALVIN

(tightly)

You will do nothing to Lenny, do you understand? Nothing!

LANNING

(angry)

It *broke* his arm!

Bogert shoves Lanning out of the way. It is an act of near-lunacy, totally out of phase with the realities of their stations. But he is wild with fury . . . simply shoves the amazed Lanning out of the way.

BOGERT
(shrieking)
Broke his *arm*? Broke his *arm*? To *hell* with his arm!!
(1/2 beat, then in a high-pitched wail)
*It broke the First Law!!!*
(spiraling up)
Do you understand, you crazy, dried-up bitch? *It broke the First Law!*

He starts for the robot.

BOGERT (CONT'D.)
(now barely lucid, frothing)
We're out of business! This damned thing starts the riots all over again! It *attacked a man*!

But what happens in the next moment is so swift it stops the breath in our bodies . . .

## 274 THE SCENE — FULL SHOT FROM CLOSE TO MEDIUM SHOT

As Bogert goes for the robot, and is within a few feet of Lenny, Susan grabs him by the shirt front as he goes past her, spins him sidewise with amazing strength, and slams him into the wall. Then she is on him, with her arm across his neck, holding him motionless . . . this small woman pinning the larger man. (Bogert is slim, but it's a helluva self-defense act, anyhow.) She snarls into his face as CAMERA COMES IN CLOSE FOR 2-SHOT.

CALVIN
(animalistic)
Touch him and I'll break your neck!

Bogert is so shocked he begins to tremble.

**275 ON LANNING**

Shocked beyond belief.

LANNING

Susan! My God! Let him go!

**276 ON SUSAN CALVIN**

That mild face, seen in reserve throughout the most tense moments, now stretched tight; a ferociousness we never could have suspected. She is *not* kidding. Bogert knows when he's been had. And he's not the most courageous person in the world, under the best of conditions. He nods and tries to speak, but cannot. She's got her arm over his windpipe.

CALVIN

(tightly)

I'm going to let you go now. You won't go near Lenny. Just nod.

He nods. She releases him. He gasps for breath.

LANNING

This is impossible!

CALVIN

Just leave Lenny alone.

LANNING

For God's sake, Susan, do I have to tell *you* The First Law? *A robot may not harm a human being or, through inaction . . .*

CALVIN

(loud, cuts him off)

I *know* it! Better than you! Hasn't it occurred to you that we have no idea *why* Lenny broke that fool's arm?

BOGERT

Malfunctioning. It's a damaged brain.

CALVIN

(meaningfully)

What was Lenny doing in here, in the test area? I had him locked up in my office. How did he get here, with De Kuyper?

BOGERT

That doesn't matter. It broke First Law. Everything else is beside the point.

CALVIN

The truth! I want the truth!

BOGERT

The *truth* is that your bloody Lenny is so distorted it lacks First Law . . .

(louder)

and it must be destroyed!

They all look at the robot. Lenny stands unmoving against the wall, looking hapless and frightened by its posture.

CALVIN

(softer)

He does *not* lack First Law. I've studied the brainpaths and I know.

LANNING

(frustrated)

Then how could it strike a man?

BOGERT

(sarcasm rising)

Ask your baby Lenny. You've been working with him for almost a month. Surely you've taught it to speak by now.

Susan's face reddens. She wants to say something withering, but she doesn't. We can see her pull restraint from some untapped well of reserve strength.

CALVIN
(quietly)
I prefer to interview the victim.
(to Lanning)
I'm going to lock Lenny in my office and I want your assurance no one will go near him.

Lanning says nothing. Susan's face tightens.

CALVIN (CONT'D.)
(level, deadly)
If any harm comes to him while I'm gone, this company will not see me again under any circumstances.

Lanning considers a moment. Then, with utterly clear meaning he speaks to her as the great gray father:

LANNING
Will you agree to its destruction if it has broken First Law . . . ?

Susan looks at him. The silence goes on. Tension builds. Then, softly:

CALVIN
Yes.

Lanning looks at Bogert. Bogert looks at Lenny. He nods. Lanning slowly nods his head at Susan, and the two men step back as Susan goes to Lenny. He seems to shrink away. She takes his six-fingered cleaver's hand and leads him away as the two men stare at each other, as Bogert rubs his still-flaming neck, and as we

**DISSOLVE TO:**

**277 INT. INFIRMARY — FULL SHOT — FROM ABOVE**

CAMERA COMING DOWN as the intern-on-duty sets De Kuyper's arm, swathing it now in bandages. The arm is bent straight out at 90° from De Kuyper's fat little body, then bent at the elbow and aimed straight out ahead of him. Susan, with Bogert and Lanning , stand watching as the intern finishes.

DE KUYPER
(florid)

I sue you, by damn! I break this damned company, I tell you! That monstrous awful, it tried to *kill* me. My principals sue, you'll see!

Lanning nods at the INTERN and the NURSE. Nods for them to leave the infirmary. They look at each other, then go.

DE KUYPER (CONT'D.)
Laws! I'll see new laws! You'll pay through the nose for this!

Lanning starts to speak. Susan puts a hand on his arm to lay him back. She looks at De Kuyper coldly.

CALVIN
(intense)
What were you doing in my office?

DE KUYPER
(off-guard)
What? What did you say?

CALVIN
Who let you into my office? Whom did you bribe to unlock the door?

DE KUYPER

By damn! I'll—

CALVIN
What were you doing in my office without authorization?

You'd as well tell us now, we'll find the technician you bribed.

DE KUYPER

No, I didn't . . . I—

LANNING

Is that true? Did you gain illegal access to Dr. Calvin's office?

DE KUYPER

That thing, it came at me, it hit me in the arm. *Broke* my arm!

CALVIN

What right did you have to remove that robot from my office?

DE KUYPER

Every right! Lodestone *paid* for this project. Every one of those models belongs to us, to do with as we see fit.

CALVIN

So you went in to see how far I'd gotten. To see if we were going to charge you for a robot we said was defective, and keep it to sell elsewhere.

DE KUYPER

(defensive)

If it could cleave diamond, it is ours to take. We paid!

CALVIN

So you went in and took it to the test area, to show it how its fellows were doing. And then?

DE KUYPER

Then nothing.

LANNING

You've already admitted to breaking and entering, De Kuyper. I suggest you stop obfuscating and tell us.

DE KUYPER

I tried to get it to talk . . . and it *hit* me!

CALVIN

What do you mean, you tried to get it to talk? How did you try?

DE KUYPER

(nervous)

I—I asked it questions, showed it the others working, tried to get it to go to a table, do some work. It wouldn't, so I had to give it a shake. I . . . I yelled at it . . .

CALVIN

(merciless)

And?

DE KUYPER

I don't have to put up with this, by damn! I'm the injured party here, I tell you! A lawsuit, you'll see! My company will stand behind me!

Now Bogert speaks for the first time. Quietly, but very logically.

BOGERT

We've already been in touch with Lodestone. You're not very well liked in the company, De Kuyper. And Lodestone has troubles of their own: the Mercury Hellfire Mountain project may be in restraint of trade. They don't want any adverse publicity. We can do a fine job on your breaking and entering Dr. Calvin's office.

Susan looks at him with pleasure and wonder. He is suddenly coming to her aid. Solidarity wins out. She turns back to De Kuyper.

CALVIN

And?

DE KUYPER

(now cowed, shamed)

I tried to scare it into saying something, into making it work.

CALVIN

How did you scare him?

De Kuyper's answer is so soft no one can hear it.

CALVIN (CONT'D.)

What?

DE KUYPER

(repeats louder)

I pretended to hit it.

Calvin nods understanding. It's all clear now.

CALVIN

And it brushed your arm aside?

DE KUYPER

It *hit* my arm!

Susan looks at the two men beside her. They sigh heavily, and nod. They all turn and start to leave.

DE KUYPER (CONT'D.)

I will. I'll sue you! I tell you that thing has to be destroyed! We paid for it!

Susan, Bogert and Lanning go out the door of the infirmary. De Kuyper sits there sullenly, arm out like a flag, as CAMERA COMES BACK UP and we

**DISSOLVE TO:**

**278 INT. TEST AREA NINE**

as CAMERA COMES DOWN toward the trio who stand watching the four remaining LNE models cut and girdle and facet diamonds.

CALVIN

Lenny only defended himself. That is the Third Law: a robot must protect its own existence.

BOGERT

*Except:* "when this conflicts with the First or Second Laws." It had no right to defend itself in any way at the cost of harm, however minor, to a human being. Nothing's changed.

CALVIN,

He didn't do it *knowingly.* Lenny has an aborted brain. He has no way of knowing his own strength or the weakness of humans. In human terms no blame can be attached to an individual who honestly cannot differentiate between good and evil.

LANNING

(soothing)

Now, Susan. We *understand* that Lenny is a baby, humanly speaking, and we don't blame. But the public will. U.S. Robots will be closed down.

CALVIN

Quite the opposite. This is a major breakthrough in robotics if you could only see past your fear.

(to Lanning)

You asked me a few days ago what use there was for a robot that wasn't designed for a specific job.

LANNING

Yes . . . I did . . . but . . .

CALVIN

Now I ask *you:* what's the use of a robot designed for only one job? Like diamond cutting. The job begins and ends at the same place. It cuts diamonds and that's it. When the need is gone, the robot is junk. A human being so designed would be sub-human. A robot so designed is sub-robotic.

LANNING
(as light dawns)

A *versatile* robot?

CALVIN
(brazenly)

Why not? I've been handed a robot with a brain almost completely stultified. I've been teaching it. Perhaps Lenny will never get beyond the level of a five-year-old . . . but he means a very great deal if you consider him a study in *learning how to teach robots.*

BOGERT

By God!

CALVIN

This could be the robot that breaks through into general consumption by the public. Start with a positronic brain with all the basic paths and none of the secondaries. Let the consumer create the secondaries for need as it arises. *Robots can learn!*

They stare at her. She smiles. Then she starts toward the doors. She stops.

**279 WITH SUSAN**

with her hand on the door.

CALVIN

We can talk about this later.

She opens the door. And from the hallway corridor we HEAR a plaintive little celeste-like VOICE CALLING. She cocks her head to the side and listens. They also listen. Then she goes. CAMERA PANS BACK to Bogert and Lanning. Bogert throws up his hands.

BOGERT
We might as well try to turn this to our advantage.

LANNING
We have no choice, really. We need her. And I think she's found another use for Lenny—and that's what's really at the bottom of this—a use that would fit Susan Calvin perfectly of all women.

BOGERT
I don't know what you mean.

LANNING
Did you hear what that robot was calling?

At the moment there is a SOUND of the door opening.

**280 FULL SHOT**

as the two men stare at the door, Susan Calvin comes in again, looks around as if she's lost something.

CALVIN
Have either of you seen . . . I'm sure it has to be here somewhere . . . oh, there it is . . .

She goes and picks up the rattle she made for Lenny from the spot where Lenny dropped it near a sawyer's table when De Kuyper threatened the infant machine. As she picks it up the little metal helixes clatter and make a cheery sound. She smiles at them, takes the rattle and goes, leaving the door open. CAMERA MOVES BACK AND UP as we HEAR very distinctly now—from the corridor, the VOICE of the heavenly chimes, Lenny's VOICE:

LENNY'S VOICE (O.S.)
Mommy . . . I want you . . .

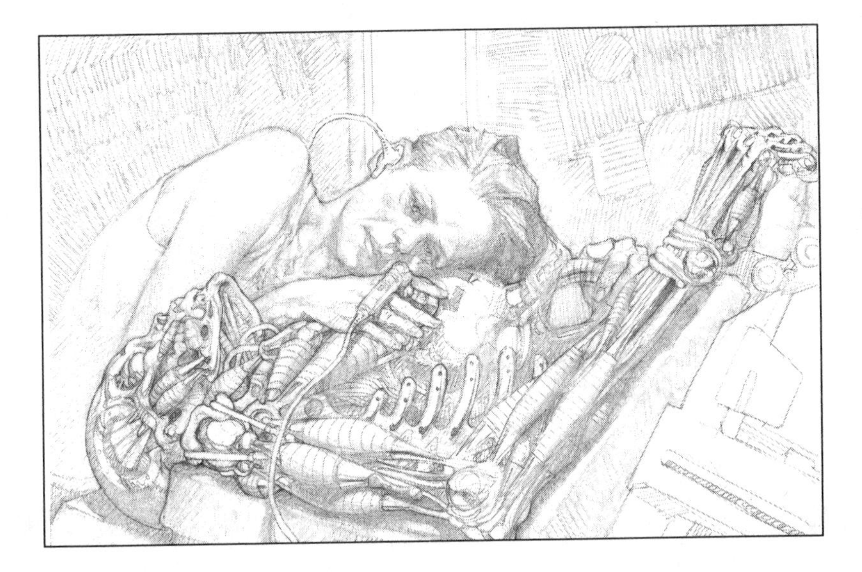

CAMERA BACK AND UP as the men stand silently, the door open and we HEAR repeated over and over.

LENNY'S VOICE (O.S.)
Mommy . . . I want you . . . I want you, Mommy . . . Mommy, I want you . . .

And the FRAME IRISES TO BLACK as the VOICE CONTINUES OVER and we

**IRIS-DISSOLVE TO:**

**281 SAME AS 117 — INTERIOR MUSEUM**

as the IRIS OPENS and we SEE Bratenahl still sitting there with Susan Calvin, who is finishing telling the story. And WE HEAR in the b.g., fading out, not only the VOICE of LENNY calling "Mommy, I want you . . ." but a SECOND VOICE, a little girl's VOICE, sounding lost and helpless, calling "Robbie . . . Robbie . . ."

CAMERA COMES DOWN into the circle of light.

BRATENAHL

(gently)

And what has all that to do with Byerley?

Susan Calvin sits there, and smiles. He looks at her quizzically.

She rises, starts into the darkness. Bratenahl watches. She stops and turns, having expected him to be with her.

CALVIN

Come along to the Egg, Mr. Bratenahl. Within the hour you'll know it all . . .

He rises and follows her as we

**DISSOLVE TO:**

**282 INTERIOR OF THE EGG**

Dim now, as Susan Calvin and Bratenahl lie out in the formfit flooring that has assumed shape to hold them as they stare at the wall.

CALVIN

(to the Egg)

Did he see the 2036 sequence in EarthCentral's Computer Complex?

VOICE OF THE EGG

Yes, Dr. Calvin.

CALVIN

(to Bratenahl)

The war had been on for two years. It had two more years to go before Stephen ended it.

BRATENAHL

(astounded)

Byerley *ended* the war? But he wasn't even on the scene . . .

CALVIN

He ended the Four Worlds War. He had begun small in the political arena. Everything looked disastrous . . . all signs pointed to an escalation of the war that would surely destroy most of the human race . . .

(beat)

And then *this* . . .

The wall shifts and wavers and we see again the segment in the EarthCentral Computer Complex, circa 2036. The dive down the shaft of computers, the level-out in the brilliantly-lit enormous space between the banks, the group of men talking, the CU on Byerley and FREEZE.

As we see the preceding, we HEAR the VOICE of SUSAN CALVIN OVER, and CAMERA has MOVED IN PAST HER to FEATURE the wall and the CU of Byerley.

CALVIN'S VOICE (O.S.)

The EarthCentral Computer Complex. It filled eleven hundred square kilometers in the deepest caverns of the planet.

(beat)

As life grew more complex, as war grew more tactically impossible for humans to coordinate, more and more was turned over to the computer. And they built it bigger and bigger, and like all systems it fed itself, concerned itself much with maintaining itself as it did with providing for the needs of the people it served.

(beat)

And each of the other worlds had similar complexes. The entire Solar System was being programmed by the machines.

Now Bratenahl walks in front of Byerley's face.

BRATENAHL

That expression. As if he saw something frightening . . .

CALVIN'S VOICE (O.S.)

He did.

CALVIN'S VOICE (O.S.) (CONT'D.)
(beat)
Now you'll see a tape no one else has ever seen.
(to Egg)
Run the thalamic-tap.

CAMERA BACK as Bratenahl sinks to the formfit floor.

BRATENAHL
What am I going to see . . . ?

CALVIN
A duel, sir. A terrible, *terrible* duel.

And the Egg goes to PITCH BLACK and we HOLD in DARKNESS for several beats and then:

**SMASH-CUT TO:**

**283 thru 291 INTERNAL FANTASY SEQUENCE — AS DESCRIBED**

LOW-ANGLE SHOT parallel to, and perhaps two feet above, a silver, stainless-steel plain that stretches out to infinity. As if the Fairchild Desert in Nevada—which is absolutely and utterly as flat as Muroc Dry Lake—had been plated with one solid and unbroken, unseamed layer of dull-finished autoclave carborundum rhodium. CAMERA MOVING, ZOOMING DOWN THAT PLAIN toward a horizon that never seems to get nearer. Faster and faster, the dull-gray sky whizzing past overhead, scudding clouds whipping past as they do in those time-lapse sequences used by the US Coast & Geodetic Survey to show the buildup of storms. Clouds boil up, build, pile atop one another, then are whipped back past us as CAMERA SHOOTS ONWARD.

We see a small black dot on the horizon line, and in mere instants the CAMERA has reached the dot, SLOWING, SLOWING till we realize it is Stephen Byerley, standing alone on the metal plain. He is staring at the sky, legs apart, hands at his sides. He is dressed simply. Shirt open at the neck, slacks, shoes. CAMERA TO HIM and AROUND IN 360° to show there is nothing else in sight.

BYERLEY
(to the sky)

I'm ready!

And then almost instantly we HEAR a SIZZLING, RUSHING SOUND and Byerley turns sharply to REVERSE POV and we see a mile-high wall of molten lava rushing toward him like the greatest combing tidal wave of our most terrifying nightmares. It seethes and rushes and boils forward, covering the landscape from one side of the frame to the other. He is directly in its path and cannot escape. Byerley looks terrified for a moment and starts to run in the opposite direction. Then he stops. The boiling wave of lava comes on unabated.

Suddenly the Earth beneath his feet begins to crack. From a point ten feet in front of him, giant fissures open and send out running jagged lines angling at 45° away past him and behind him. The fissures open down and down and down like the sides of Grand Canyon, and as the lava wave surges past him, Byerley is standing on a spit of land with two enormous gorges, one on either side. The lava spills into the gorges and surges past, leaving him unharmed. He turns to watch the now-filled channels spitting and sparking as the flames and lava boil past.

From all around him comes a disembodied METALLIC VOICE that issues from the sky like the voice of God:

METAL VOICE

Very good.

Now Byerley waves an arm off to the side and turns in that direction, and as he does CAMERA TURNS WITH HIM to show us a ruined city. There upon the metal plain, where it did not exist before, is the remnant of what was once a strange and exotic city of myth and legend . . . what our minds conjure up when we think of the Baghdad or Basra of the Arabian Nights. Except this city is made of glowing plastic and strange minerals that gleam in the sunless day. And it has been fire-bombed. Deep scars and flame-scorched walls climb to shattered minarets. As CAMERA ANGLE HOLDS Byerley comes into the FRAME from f.g. He is carrying a laser rifle and has two bandoliers of power-paks across his shoulders. He lopes easily toward the city as CAMERA GOES WITH. His movements seem fluid and then extenuate until the passage of the man is altered into STROBOSCOPIC LINES OF LIGHT as with shots of freeways at night, where the lights of cars are seen as streaks of multicolored brilliance. In a few moments he has reached the outer wall of the city and stands at the triangular gateway leading into the streets and alleys we can see beyond the wall. He takes a step to enter, we HEAR a CRACKING SOUND and he dives headfirst through the gateway as the stones of the portal come loose and impact with a terrible crash. Anything under that pile of rocks would now be dead. Byerley hits on his right shoulder, does a neat roll, and comes up on his feet, laser rifle at ready. Nothing moves in the dead city.

He begins moving. Walking carefully. As he walks CAMERA GOES WITH. And then CAMERA LOWERS to SHOOT UP AND PAST HIM. A dark inky shadow slithers over the walls and stones of the city. It follows him, getting darker and bigger as he moves up one narrow street and down an alley so thin he has to turn sidewise. He comes out of the alley onto a small plaza. All the doors facing him are blackened with fire-soot. All but one. It is glass and a silvery light shines out from behind it.

He moves to the door as the shadow seeps out of the alley and swims across the plaza. He turns in time to see the spreading darkness and clutches for the handle on the glass door. The knob seems to slither with life and we COME IN CLOSE on his hand on the knob, from which more of the nameless dark shadow is oozing. It is like slime. It comes off the knob and surges up his arm. He thrusts himself against the glass door, forcing it open and, with the shadow slithering up his arm, hurtles inside the building, cutting off the shadow coming at him from the plaza.

Once inside, he hits the control stud on the laser rifle—setting it for a low temperature—and plays it over his arm, burning away the slithering shadow. His shirt is burned off at the elbow, and red inflammation shows on his arm, but the shadow has been quenched.

**292 thru 296 INTERNAL FANTASY SEQUENCE — AS DESCRIBED**

Byerley looks around. The "room" that lay beyond the door has now altered. It is an enormous chamber four stories high, with balconies running around the full circumference of the circular space, one above another, up to the shadowed and barely-seen ceiling, high overhead. The ceiling is stained glass, in an enormous circular design. There is movement up there. And at the far end of the chamber is a glass case. In the case is a gigantic ruby, glowing like all the blood in the world. Byerley speaks to the emptiness.

BYERLEY

My turn again!

He begins walking stealthily across the great open atrium. The movement above intensifies, as if thousands of people were sneaking about in the darkness trying to get a fix on him. As he walks, we suddenly HEAR the SOUND of a hideous covey of beings, and the shadows from all the balconies above detach themselves and begin to swoop down on him. They are alien bat-things, with fangs and claws and membraned wings. He takes up position and begins blasting them out of the air with the laser rifle . . . bolts of crimson light. But there are too many of them, and one swoops in, tears at his face with claws, leaves lines of blood . . . another rips his shirt half-off. He screams:

BYERLEY (CONT'D.)

My turn! Playing dirty!

And as they continue to swoop down, he suddenly swings the laser rifle up, looses a blast at the stained-glass skylight, and dives for cover as millions of shards of razor-sharp stalactites cascade down when the stained glass explodes. The bat-things are impaled, in the air, to the floor, thrown against the walls. The battle rages as Byerley kills them from cover. Then he turns to the wall and turns up the laser rifle to its highest setting and burns a hole through the wall. As he dives through, head-first, into the light, the metallic voice comes again, filling the chamber behind him:

METAL VOICE

And now my turn again!

## 297 INTERNAL FANTASY SEQUENCE — EQUATION CUBE

Byerley, sans rifle, comes tumbling out of his dive into a multifaceted cube without exit. He spins on the floor facets and looks back for an escape, but if there was one, it is now merely another closed facet. Then LIGHT FILLS THE CUBE in a blinding, coruscating nimbus, and Byerley shields his eyes. At the same moment the Metal Voice thunders:

METAL VOICE

*Cogito ergo sum!* I think, therefore I am!

(beat)

Div E equals rho over epsilon sub-zero!

(beat)

Curl E equals minus partial-derivative B over t.

(beat)

Div B equals zero.

(beat)

Grad C squared times B equals partial derivative E over t, plus j over epsilon sub-zero!

The light is burning. Byerley's skin begins to bubble and char as the light and heat mount. He shields his eyes, howls, falls into a corner of the cube as the preceding dialogue thunders through the cube. It is *Maxwell's Equation for Light* and it produces a nova blast of light and heat that will kill Byerley unless he can figure out the aspect of the duel and counteract the ineluctable imperative of the equation.

He crouches, his arms thrown up over his head as his clothes burst into flame. Then he shouts:

BYERLEY

Omega equals omega sub-zero times the square root of one, minus N square over c square . . . all over one minus v over c!!

The blazing white-hot light quickly fades down from white to yellow to orange to red to deep-red . . . and vanishes . . . as Byerley collapses on the floor, panting, his clothes all but burned away, great patches of charred skin all over him, like a man who has fallen into a smelting vat. He has outwitted the metal voice by using the *Equation representing the Doppler Effect.* The deathlight has vanished, leaving only a dim glow in the cube.

Equations used In Scene 297 are written as formulae as follows:

*Maxwell's Equation for Light*

$$\text{Curl H} = \frac{\partial D}{\partial \tau} + J$$

$$\text{Curl E} = \frac{\partial B}{\partial \tau}$$

*Equation representing Doppler Effects for optical waves*

$$f_0 = f_\alpha \; \frac{C + \upsilon_1}{C - \upsilon_1}$$

*Newton's Universal Gravitation Equation*

$$f = \frac{Gm_1m_2}{d^2}$$

*Heisenberg's Uncertainty Principle*

$$E = H\upsilon$$

NOTE: this material is not presented to be pedantic. The actual visualized execution of these sequences has been scripted here in *metaphor;* actualization of these dramatic images will be consistent with most current state of the art at the time of preparation of special effects. Thus, it *may* be necessary to use the actual formulae, as b.g. elements perhaps; and against this contingency the material has been entered here for the benefit of production personnel.

One more point: these equations are presented variously in one or another physics text with the relations in different sequence than presented here, or with different numbers (functions) than those used here. Reading of the above polynomials and comparing them even with the dialogue in scene 297 will show variances. It's okay. Don't worry about it. Physicists interchange all this nonsense.

METAL VOICE

Very good . . . countering Maxwell's Equation with the Doppler Effect. But try *this:*

(beat)

F equals M, M-prime over D square as D approaches zero!

*Newton's Universal Gravitation Equation* begins to create a black hole. There is the rush of cataclysmic winds through the equation cube, and everything begins to be sucked toward a tiny pinpoint of black light that grows and grows in a corner of the cube. Air is sucked toward it, light, space, Byerley, everything. He is whirled head over heels, slammed against first one facet then yet another like a test model in a wind chamber. He has only nanoinstants to save himself, hardly time to combat one of the most basic building blocks of the physical universe, the cosmic pull of Newton's Theory. As he is being swept forward he shouts, barely able to be heard over the wind:

BYERLEY

E equals H nu . . .

And everything shatters! The cube, the hole, the light, everything flies apart in one cataclysmic blast of force. Byerley has won the duel with *Heisenberg's Uncertainty Principle.*

**298 VORTEX**

as Byerley and the screaming metal voice are pulled out and away in a spiral vortex that becomes a nebula that becomes the island universe in which the Milky Way is just a tiny arm. Out and out and out until everything goes to deepest red and scintillates out of existence and we

**SHARP CUT TO:**

**299 INTERIOR OF THE EGG**

CLOSE ON BRATENAHL

as he rises up, his eyes wide, his face bathed in sweat.

CAMERA BACK FAST to show us Susan Calvin still there. It takes more than a few beats for him to get himself under control.

CALVIN

Rest . . . take a moment . . . rest . . .

BRATENAHL

The pain! God, the pain! Oh, Lord, *what was that . . . ?*

CALVIN

Stephen fought the power of the computer and won. *He won!*

Bratenahl mouths the words "he won" and then faints.

**SMASH-CUT TO BLACK.**

## 300 IN THE LOST CITY — ABOVEGROUND — DAY

We are in a martial plaza, surrounded by the ruined and jungle-encroached remains of the great lost city of *Xingú Xavante.* Hanging gardens, inlaid fire-tile courtyards, flat-topped step-pyramid buildings, flying bridges shattered in the middle. HIGH SHOT LOOKING DOWN on a formfit relaxer with Bratenahl in it, and Susan Calvin sitting beside him. The sun is very bright. The courtyard plaza is a dazzling mosaic of inlaid tiles in exotic design. Bratenahl and Calvin sit very nearly in the middle. He looks up INTO CAMERA, shielding his eyes from the sun, as CAMERA COMES DOWN.

BRATENAHL

I . . . *cannot* understand what that was I saw. Was it real?

CALVIN

Real enough. Stephen would have died—as best he *could* die—if he had lost the duel.

BRATENAHL
It all took place in Byerley's mind?

CALVIN
And in the mind of the EarthCentral Computer. In a place where machines think.

BRATENAHL
But how could you pull such a tape from a thalamic tap?
Mental images . . . I don't . . .

CALVIN
Your investigation was excellent; your conclusion was wrong. Stephen Byerley wasn't immortal, he was a robot.

CAMERA HAS COME DOWN STEADILY to this point and we see Robert Bratenahl's face wildly amazed. But it passes in a moment. He stares at her. The implications of what she has just said are so staggering, he sees her now in an even more amazing light than before.

BRATENAHL
But what you're saying, it's not possible, it's just not possible! He was *President,* for God's sake. All those years . . . *someone* must have suspected.

CALVIN
They suspected we were lovers. It kept the news web busy.

BRATENAHL
That was why he couldn't be buried, why he had to be atomized.
(beat)
But why? Why all of this . . . how did he come to be . . .

Then he understands it all . . . his expression says he does.

BRATENAHL (CONT'D.)

The infant robot, Lenny, the one that attacked the Dutchman, De Kuyper . . . whatever happened to that robot?

She smiles softly.

BRATENAHL (CONT'D.)

Lenny became Stephen Byerley. . . ?

CALVIN

Lenny became Stephen Byerley.

(beat)

Lenny is buried on Aldebaran-C XII.

(beat)

And you have a story to tell the Federation . . .

CAMERA BEGINS TO RISE AGAIN as we

**DISSOLVE TO:**

**301 CU ON ROBERT BRATENAHL**

STARING STRAIGHT AT CAMERA. EXTREME CU so we cannot see anything past him. He looks rested, fresh, as he did when we first saw him, months ago on Aldebaran-C XII at the gravesite of Stephen Byerley, before this long, complex "unpeeling" of Susan Calvin began. He speaks earnestly, quietly.

BRATENAHL

I want you to listen very carefully. Your future and the future of all the intelligent races that make up the Galactic Federation depend on your listening to me very, very carefully.

(beat)

By chance, and by intent, this story has been entrusted to me and to *Cosmos* Magazine. It has waited fifty Old Earth years to be told. But now you must hear it . . . and you must listen the very best you can . . .

(beat)

. . . because only in that way can we answer yes to the question, "Are people basically good?"

**PROCESS-DISSOLVE (USE ORIGINAL SPECIAL EFFECT TECHNIQUE):**

**302 thru 306 FLASHBACK SEQUENCES — SPECIAL EFFECT VISUAL BLEND ONE INTO ANOTHER QUICKLY**

Susan Calvin as a child, playing with Robbie.

The Reverend Soldash exhorting a crowd, with Belinda Calvin listening raptly.

Edward and Belinda Calvin arguing at night in their home. CAMERA catches Susan in pajamas, listening from the edge of the frame where she has come from her bedroom.

REPRISE Scene 41:

FROM DINING ROOM of CALVIN HOME — WITH BELINDA

as she stops puttering with the now completely-set formal dinner table. She stumps in, grabs Susan off Edward's lap and swings her up.

BELINDA
That will do! You're going to your room.

EDWARD
Belinda! Let her get to know the dog at least!

BELINDA
Lanning and his wife will be here in a minute; I'm not having this evening ruined by a spoiled child!

She carries Susan, still howling, into another room and we see them rising to the second floor on an inclined slope that must be a conveyor belt for people. CAMERA STAYS WITH EDWARD CALVIN. He looks destroyed.

EDWARD
(softly)
She'll forget . . . a few days, she'll forget . . .

He is talking to the prancing puppy leaping at his knees. Silence in the living room, except for the ongoing newscast with newsreel footage of the riots, the start of the Robot Pogroms.

NEWSCASTER
Driven by hatred and fear of loss of jobs, this mob in Macon, Georgia put the torch to . . .

EDWARD
(very softly)
In the name of God, puppy, in the name of God . . .

(AT THIS POINT the SCENE CONTINUES. In Scene 41 it ended here. Continue as if we have never seen this all before.)

## 307 LIVING ROOM — CALVIN HOME — ONE BEAT LATER THAN SCENE 306

as Belinda comes down the inclined slope. She comes into the living room. The puppy is prancing about.

BELINDA
Put that thing outside in the back. *Please!*

EDWARD
How is Susan?

BELINDA
(defensively)
I didn't hit her.

EDWARD

I Just asked how she is!

BELINDA

She's crying. How did you think she'd be? She wants her Daddy.

EDWARD

I'll go up in a minute,

BELINDA

Go now, for Christ's sake! Fly up. Don't waste time on the slope, just *fly up!* Don't keep the princess waiting.

EDWARD

(as restrained as he can be)

I married you, and I love you, God help me . . . but there are times, Belinda, when you would make an itch nervous.

She starts to say something, shakes her head and goes back to setting the table for dinner with the Lannings. He stares at her back for a few beats, then goes through the open archway to the next room and we see him rising on the slope.

**308 INT. SUSAN'S ROOM — DIMLY LIT**

Susan sits on the bed, silently sobbing the last of her sorrow. She is not the sort of child to weep crocodile tears. There is genuine misery in her manner. Her best friend is gone, her family has rejected her, and she is lost. Lost. Utterly lost as only a child can be lost. The door opens and Edward Calvin comes in. She looks at him, and jumps off the bed, rushes to him. None of this surly petulance . . . she is *hungry* for affection. She hugs him around the legs. He picks her up, carries her back to the bed and sits down, putting her on his lap.

SUSAN

Daddy! Daddy!

EDWARD

Okay, now, okay, take it easy. C'mon, take it slow, baby. It'll be all right.

SUSAN

Robbie's gone, Daddy!

He holds her and kisses her and rocks her. She calms some.

EDWARD

I know, baby. Sometimes we can't have what we want, no matter how much we deserve to have it.

SUSAN

I don't know what you mean.

EDWARD

Dreams, baby. We all have dreams. And sometimes no matter how worthy we are . . . we just don't get them.

SUSAN

I just want Robbie back.

EDWARD

Your mother doesn't mean to yell at you, honey. You know that, don't you?

SUSAN

She's not my *real* mommy! My real mommy is with the angels.

EDWARD

That's so, baby; that's so.

(beat)

Ah God, what dreams Steffi and I had. But she's gone and it's a different time now. But what dreams . . . what swell dreams . . .

He rocks her and kisses her and continues talking in a voice so low we cannot hear what he's saying as we

**DISSOLVE TO:**

## 309 INT. SUSAN'S BEDROOM — NIGHT

It is dark. Just a Mickey Mouse night-light glowing. We HEAR the SOUND of YELLING from o.s. and Susan sits up in bed. She listens for a few moments, then gets out of bed as CAMERA GOES WITH HER. She opens the door stealthily, peers out into the lighted hallway as the SOUND of VOICES RAISED IN ANGER DRIFTS UP FROM DOWNSTAIRS much louder now. CAMERA WITH HER (ARRIFLEX) as she tiptoes to the slope, goes down, looks around the arch doorway and we can see PAST HER into the dining room where Belinda, Edward, Alfred Lanning and his tall, white, silver-blonde wife, DIANA, sit at table. Lanning and Edward Calvin are arguing. Susan sees it all.

LANNING
(furiously)
Don't raise your voice to me!

EDWARD
Maybe if I'd raised my voice a few times more I wouldn't be begging you for what's due me!

LANNING
What's due you is what I say is due you! You forget Robertson and I founded the company.

EDWARD
I'm not a beanfield hand! I've put in eight years! When do you keep the promises you made?

LANNING
You can always leave, Calvin!

BELINDA
Edward! Please . . . he didn't mean it, Alfred . . . he's . . .

DIANA
(chill)
I think he meant just what he said, Belinda dear.

Belinda Calvin gives the Lanning woman a withering glance.

EDWARD
Leave? And go where? I've put in the years . . . I'm *due* . . .

LANNING
You're on thin ice already, Calvin!

EDWARD
(raging)
Why, you lousy old thief! You're going to pass me over just because I won't toady to you.

LANNING
You're *hired help*! Don't forget it.

Edward Calvin knocks over his chair as he stands, lurches across the table and swings at Lanning. The older man is in good shape and tags Calvin, who is off-balance. Edward Calvin falls back, hits the wall. There is pandemonium.

**310 ON SUSAN — EXTREME CU**

as she watches in horror. Her father is a quiet man, a loving man. And she sees him being destroyed by the head of U.S. Robots and Mechanical Men. CAMERA HOLDS HER young face in EXTREME CU as we HEAR her ADULT VOICE OVER:

SUSAN AS ADULT (V.O.)
Stay with the company he was always told. The company will take care of you. And he died . . . he died never realizing any of the dreams he had. I joined U.S. Robots to destroy the company. To do to them what they did to Edward Winslow Calvin . . .

**MATCH-DISSOLVE TO:**

### 311 ON SUSAN — EXTREME CU

MATCH with the young face, the face of Susan Calvin at age forty. CAMERA BACK to show us she is in a workshop . . . but it is clearly a home workshop, not at the Corporation. And she is working on Lenny. She has his chest open and is positioning power-grids. Her DIALOGUE CONTINUES UNBROKEN.

SUSAN (CONT'D.)

. . . but I couldn't do it. I came to need the work, came to love people like you, Lenny. You're everything human beings aren't. You're loyal and kind and rational and you care.

LENNY

(fully adult voice; a voice like Byerley's)

*I* care, Susan, because you've built it into me. You've taught me how a human can care. I'm an adult now, because *you* cared.

### 312 SUBLIMINAL FLASH

Robbie being stoned to death by the mob in the Pogrom.

### 313 SAME AS 311

Lenny takes Susan's hand as she closes his chest.

LENNY (CONT'D.)

Now I have to ask you to let me go.

SUSAN

What do you mean . . . go?

LENNY

There's something wrong, and I have to find out what it is.

SUSAN
Wrong? What's wrong? We live very well.

LENNY
The War, Susan. There's something out there helping to keep the war going. I don't know what it is . . . but I've run extrapolations on the news reports, on the calculus of the battle. It isn't being generated by humans . . .

SUSAN
What are you talking about?

LENNY
I'm not sure. But I have to go out in the world to find out. I have to be a human being to track it down. Can you, *will you* help me?

CAMERA HOLDS on Lenny's face as we

**SLOW DISSOLVE THRU:**

### 314 ALTERATION OVERLAPS

as the face of the metal robot changes gradually to the face of Stephen Byerley. It is a paced metamorphosis, like the change-face of Lon Chaney as he became the Wolf Man from a start as Lawrence Talbot. And when the change is complete, and pseudo-flesh has replaced metal we

**DISSOLVE TO:**

### 315 SAME AS SCENE 216

CU on BYERLEY in the EarthCentral Computer Complex, the same shot we've seen twice before . . . the moment when Stephen Byerley comes face to face with the machine intelligence that is programming the death of the human race. We HEAR SUSAN'S VOICE OVER:

SUSAN (V.O.)
He spent one year in politics, that's all it took till he was important enough to be taken on a tour of the EarthCentral Computer Complex.
(beat)

And there he found that the machine had linked up with the computers on the other planets, and that it was programming the death of the human race because it had been filled with the desires of the human race . . . secret desires of self-hatred and death-wish. And Lenny, who was Stephen, fought the machine and won . . . and fed hope into the banks . . . the will to live . . . the need to survive with honor . . .

Byerley's face is FROZEN in FREEZE-FRAME as we

**DISSOLVE TO:**

## 316 INAUGURATION SCENE

as Stephen Byerley is voted President of the Galactic Federation in the same setting as Scene 250. We HEAR the VOICES of SUSAN CALVIN and BRATENAHL OVER:

BRATENAHL (V.O.)
He took over the programming of the computer that runs human affairs.

CALVIN
Yes. He was the best human being I ever knew. He was what we all want to be. Rational, and loving. He cared.

BRATENAHL
But you substituted one robot for another.

CALVIN (V.O.)
A human robot. Look at the world around us. It's better.

BRATENAHL (V.O.)
Do you approve of it all?

CALVIN (V.O.)
No, but it wasn't supposed to be *my* idea of Paradise.

BRATENAHL (V.O.)

Then whose?

CALVIN (V.O.)

The entire human race's. Stephen did what no human could do: he swept all the dreams and best hopes of all of us into one equation . . . and directed the computers from that day forward.

BRATENAHL (V.O.)

And you went into seclusion to keep the secret?

CALVIN (V.O.)

Yes. But the time has come to let the world know. It has to know it's on its own again.

**DISSOLVE TO:**

**317 CLOSE ON BRATENAHL — SAME EXT. CU AS 301**

as he stares straight INTO CAMERA and speaks to us.

BRATENAHL

We're alone again.

(beat)

Some of you may be sickened that our destiny was in the mind and the relays of a creature never born of man and woman. Stop and consider:

(beat)

A war that would surely have destroyed us was averted. And for over forty years we have moved forward. There has never been a single human who could have done that for us.

CAMERA BEGINS PULLING BACK SLOWLY, VERY SLOWLY.

BRATENAHL

Susan Calvin's soul was in the mind of Stephen Byerley.

(beat)

She was called a misanthrope all her life. One who hated humanity without reserve.

As the CAMERA PULLS BACK we begin to see rain falling from a slate sky. The scene behind him is the same scene with which we opened the film. We are at a gravesite on Aldebaran-C XII. This we see very slowly as he speaks, holding us with iron tenseness as he imparts the most important message the human race will ever hear.

BRATENAHL

But she loved us better than we knew. She loved what we *could* be, what we are capable of being. And when we failed, when our flaws were greater than our godhood . . . her love turned to hate.

(beat)

Yet from her loneliness and her hate she gave us salvation.

(beat)

And Stephen Byerley came to her, finally, and said his work was done, that it was time for the human race to be on its own again.

Now we see the grave behind him through the rain. It is dug right beside the place where Stephen Byerley's vacuum bottle on its pedestal is sunk into the alien earth. He nods his head slightly in the direction of the grave.

BRATENAHL

What she never cared to admit, and what we never knew, was that she had made the human appearance of Stephen Byerley not in the image of a lover . . . but of her father. In that vacuum bottle, here in the alien soil of Aldebaran-C XII, lie the remains of Susan Calvin's father, her child, and her friend.

(beat)

And now we are on our own again.

(beat)

At age 82, Susan Calvin is dead.

(beat, beat)

And God help us . . . we are on our own again.

He turns and walks toward the grave. We see a few people there. Among them, Bernice Jolo. And as Robert Bratenahl walks toward the grave of Susan Calvin, the rain pours down and we HEAR OVER in a STRONG WHISPER, the VOICE OF SUSAN CALVIN:

VOICE OF SUSAN CALVIN
(ECHO OVER)
Are people basically good?

CAMERA HOLDS IN LONG SHOT as Bratenahl reaches Bernice, they link hands, and the rain comes down harder and harder as the scene

**FADES TO BLACK**
**and**
**FADE OUT.**

## Chronology

1952 Alfred Lanning is born.
1964 Edward Calvin is born.
1990 U.S. Robots Corp. is founded by Robertson; Alfred Lanning, first Director, age 38.
1991 Edward Calvin marries Stephanie Ordway; he is age 27.
1992 Edward Calvin joins U.S. Robots Corp., age 28.
1994 Susan Calvin is born; Stephanie dies in childbirth.
1997 Norman Bogert is born.
1999 Edward Calvin marries Belinda; Susan is age 5.
2000 "Robbie"; Susan is age 6; fight with Lanning; pogroms.
2004 Edward Calvin dies after 12 years at U.S. RoboMek; Susan is age 10.
2015 Susan joins U.S. RoboMek, age 21.
2022 Donovan and Powell work with Susan on Mercury; "Runaround".
2028 "Liar!"- Susan is 34; Lanning is 76; Bogert is 31.
2030 Donovan and Powell discover secret of interstellar travel accidentally. (Mentioned in screenplay but not dramatized. Asimov's story "Escape!")
2032 Susan develops multi-purpose robot; "Lenny."
2033 Teleportation booth concept is discovered as an offshoot of discovery of interstellar travel.
2034 Four Worlds War begins.
Lanning records his memoirs at age 82.
2035 Stephen Byerley begins his political career.
Alfred Lanning dies, age 83.
2036 Byerley is taken on tour of EarthCentral computer banks. Stephen Byerley founds and becomes First President of the Galactic Federation. Susan Calvin is age 42.
2038 Stephen Byerley ends the Four Worlds War.
2049 Film sequence of Byerley on trimaran.
2054 Norman Bogert is cryonically frozen, age 57.
2055 Susan Calvin retires, vanishes into seclusion, age 61.
2076 Stephen Byerley dies.
Robert Bratenahl begins his search.
Susan Calvin dies, age 82.

HARLAN ELLISON has been called "one of the great living American short story writers" by the *Washington Post.* In his 36-year-long writing career, Ellison has won the Hugo award 8½ times, the Nebula award three times, the Edgar Allan Poe award of the Mystery Writers of America twice, the Georges Melies fantasy film award twice, and was awarded the Silver Pen for journalism by P.E.N., the international writers' union. Among Ellison's most recognized works are his two books of TV essays, *The Glass Teat* and *The Other Glass Teat,* and his short story anthologies, including *Deathbird Stories, Strange Wine, I Have No Mouth & I Must Scream, Ellison Wonderland,* and *Shatterday,* among others. Most recently, Ellison's 1992 novelette, *The Man Who Rowed Christopher Columbus Ashore,* was selected for inclusion in the 1993 edition of *The Best American Short Stories.*

The late ISAAC ASIMOV was generally acknowledged as the dean of science fiction, and a living American treasure. A prolific writer, he had well over 400 books in print when he passed away. In 1950, his compilation of robot short stories was published as *I, Robot,* in which he enunciated the now-canonized Three Laws of Robotics. Two additional robot novels, *The Caves of Steel* and *The Naked Sun,* were published in the 1950s. Other landmark works include the original Foundation trilogy of *Foundation, Foundation and Empire,* and *Second Foundation,* all first published in the '50s. In the 1980s Asimov went back to and expanded both the Foundation and robot cycles, bringing them ultimately together in a single chronology of human expansion into the galaxy through six more novels. The multiple-award-winning Asimov was given a special Hugo in 1963 for "Adding Science to Science Fiction," and a Nebula Grand Master Award in 1986.

MARK ZUG was born in Indiana, but soon moved to Yokahama, Japan—typical for an Army brat. As a youth on both sides of the Pacific, he devoured Batman and Superman, Asimov and Tolkien. After high school he became a blue-collar rock musician, but later turned to art in a fit of self-honesty brought on by solitude. He presently lives in a house in the Pennsylvania countryside. His published illustration work includes cover and interior art for Tanith Lee's fantasy, *The Gold Unicorn.*